A Fortune to India

Also by Tony Foot:

A Dorset Footprint
The Fortunes at War

A Fortune to India

Tony Foot

CHAPLIN BOOKS

www.chaplinbooks.co.uk

Printed in the UK by Imprint Digital

Chaplin Books
5 Carlton Way
Gosport PO12 1LN
Tel: 023 9252 9020
www.chaplinbooks.co.uk

To Sue for her patience and support

The Indian Mutiny
Jack Finch's Map
1851 ~ 1859

Sikar
Jaipur
Alwar Hills
Delhi
Meerut
Agra
ROHILKHAND
Khamaspur
Jhansi
Banda
Calpee
Fatehpur
Allahabad
R. Yamuna
BUNDELKHAND
Khajuran
R. Betwa
Benares
R. Ganges
Sitapur
Lucknow
Gonda
R. Ghaghara
Jumna-ki-Serai
OUDH
Grand Trunk Road
Calcutta
Barrackpore
Bay of Bengal
Arabian Sea
Bombay

Chapter One

The August midday sun was hot: my face was already burning and rivulets of sweat were trickling freely down my back. I had very mixed feelings regarding the task I was about to carry out and the heat made me wish I had never embarked on it at all.

Nevertheless, I jumped down from the brougham, waved away the driver I had hired in Winchester and marched boldly towards the large wrought-iron gates that stood black and unyielding in the summer sun. The padlocked gates were twice my height and each had a coat of arms picked out in gold. To the left was a smaller gate hinged to a brick pillar. From either side of the gates a wall taller than a man stretched as far as the eye could see.

A figure appeared, buttoning his waistcoat as he emerged from the gatekeeper's lodge. I judged him to be an ex-navy man from the rolling gait that brought him towards me. I would discover many years later that he had indeed been a sailor and had taken part in the battle of Navarino Bay in October of '27 when a combined British, French and Russian naval force had almost totally destroyed the Egyptian and Turkish fleets. Something to do with Greek independence, I recalled. I would also later reflect that this was all very strange: first of all the French are our enemies and the Russians are friends, then, in the Crimea, the French and Turks were on our side against the Russians. How confusing! This moved me to conclude that the governments who decide there needs to be a war should be the ones to fight it, instead of sending soldiers to be killed.

Behind the man at the gate I could see small faces at a window of the rather drab grey lodge. From nearby, perhaps from the fenced enclosure behind this sombre-looking dwelling – I took it to be a garden – came the urgent barking of a dog. A very large animal, I imagined it to be, from the deep and menacing tone that assailed my ears.

The gateman looked at me with suspicion at first while his eyes took time to focus, though all such creatures seem to resent those whose appearance interrupts their midday nap and requires them instead to attend the gates. I gazed back at him, ready to announce myself.

He unlocked the gate and bade me advance.

"They are expecting you," he said, bowing slightly and pointing towards a large house some distance away.

His words, together with those I had read in the letter that had set me on my present quest, were still ringing in my head as I set off at rifleman's pace down the tree-lined drive towards Broughton House. I walked on, my shiny, highly polished boots crunching on the gravel that ran like a sandy-orange river between neatly tended grassy banks on either side. I reached a point where the drive curved to the left and then went on to describe a semi-circle that brought it to the foot of a grand stone staircase. There, carriages would stop to allow society visitors to alight and to go on up and into the house. The drive then continued to complete the other half of the circle and bring it back to where I now stood. The drive then carried on its way back down to the gates and out to the open highway to Salisbury, Southampton or Winchester.

I stood there for a minute or two looking across at the ornamental garden and fountains that filled the space contained in that circle. I regarded with some envy the cool, splashing water disgorging from the mouths of some nymphs that might – on a less important and sombre occasion – tempt me to refresh my freely perspiring face.

What to do now, though? Go to the left until I came to the kitchens and the servants' entrance, or walk confidently up the steps?

That hesitation was allowing me too much time to think. I was beginning to feel just like I did when facing the enemy: that eyes were watching me. Though thankfully, no bullets would be smashing into me as I stood before Broughton House. In the Crimea not too many months ago, that had been more than a strong possibility.

Straightening up and brushing real or imagined dust from my very best uniform with its large gold crowns on the sleeves and with medals from my recent service glinting in the summer sun, I moved purposefully towards the staircase leading to a heavy-looking pair of doors. I gripped a large acorn-shaped bell-push and leant on it. I could hear nothing, no response. I pushed it again. I smiled to myself, recalling that when faced with such a grand house in the very recent campaign, my usual method of entry had been to kick it down, then charge in with rifle and sword, along with a score of riflemen behind me.

A butler suddenly appeared, making a great show of opening one of the doors. He had that look which all butlers have in my very limited experience, the sort of facial expression that indicated that one or the other of us, probably me, had stepped in something unpleasant.

"Sergeant-Major Finch, sir, you are expected. Please follow me," he said, in the melancholic tone that also seemed to be the preserve of that class of servant.

What did puzzle me, though, was how exactly everybody seemed to be expecting me. It had only been on this very day, on a whim, that I had decided to come to this house and fulfil an obligation that I felt I owed the writer of that letter.

The butler led me across the entrance hall, my boots echoing on the wooden floor, then up a highly polished flight of stairs.

As we climbed, rows of eyes seemed to stare back at me from the portraits on the walls, several centuries of Broughton ancestors imprisoned for all time in their gilt frames.

We stopped at a plain cream-coloured door. My guide knocked surprisingly delicately for such a burly-framed man. He opened the door, bowed gravely and ushered me in, closing the door behind me.

I stood there, uncertain what to do next. My soldier's natural habitat is the hills and forests of Her Majesty's enemies and not the withdrawing room of the rich and titled.

Towards the other end of the room was a figure I knew slightly. Lady Eleanor was clad in a blue dress worn slightly off the shoulders, the neckline dipped to reveal two milk-white mounds. My acquaintance with her was not through any social intercourse. She was of this house, after all, while I was from the wrong end of a local village. I knew her to be a little older than me. My earlier awareness of her was seeing her arrive at Durford Hall when I was about fourteen and she about seventeen. She had looked just as breathtaking as she did now, in a sparkling white dress, her dark hair piled high on her head and glittering with precious stones. She had been accompanied by James Fortune of the Rifle Brigade, a Lieutenant as he had been then. As they went into the Hall for the evening's entertainment, my duties were to help the Hall's grooms escort coachmen and their now-empty carriages to the stables. I had – as one of the footmen was pleased to point out – been doubly blessed, in the first place by being able to look on my elders and betters, and in the second by being paid a few pennies for the privilege. What more could a poor country boy ask?

Now here was I standing in very different circumstances in the presence of this beauty.

To Lady Eleanor's left was a silver-framed photograph of James Fortune in his Captain's uniform and on the wall behind, a painting of the same man. I knew him much better than Lady Eleanor because not only had I served with him, I had dragged him – badly wounded – back to our lines overlooking Sevastopol. Then I noticed next to the photograph of James was a book, quarter-bound in blue leather with its title picked out in gold leaf: 'Jane Eyre' by Currer Bell. I had seen a review of this book in a newspaper discarded by one of our officers. It had been written by a woman, but in order to get it published she had not used her own name, Charlotte Bronte. The book had raised many hackles in the way it had questioned how women were supposed to behave in the middle of our nineteenth century, a modern age that had fuelled the Great Exhibition but which was backward-looking in its treatment of women. Not that women, in my experience as a humble village boy and latterly a soldier, were the only people treated unequally. Judging by her reading, Lady Eleanor might prove to be a modern, forward-looking woman.

I was both pleased and a little surprised to find her alone, unchaperoned, in the room. On the other hand, most of the women of my acquaintance during the last few years were hardly the sort to require the addition of such a companion.

"Please sit here," she said, motioning me to a large chair opposite her own. "We have been expecting you but were not quite sure exactly when. How are you, Sergeant-Major Finch? Oh, may I call you Jack? James wrote often about you and always referred to you as 'good old Jack'. He wrote to me about some of your adventures in and around Sevastopol but I am sure they weren't quite the fun he said they were."

"No, we did have a few scares," I said, and began to flounder as I started to call her 'Lady Broughton'.

"Do call me, Nell," she offered, sensing my discomfort. "After all, you were related to James and I am sure he would want us to be friends."

She had completely disarmed me and I can only think I must have looked very startled at being called Jack and being allowed to call her by a pet name. I had also realised that James would have shared with his fiancée details of who my real father was. Even so, it was difficult for me to forget the gap that existed between us. My place as a social inferior, regardless of my true parentage, hung over me; that I had lived and been brought up in a humble dwelling in the village of Lower Durford after being born on the wrong side of the blanket. Then there was Lady Eleanor's place in society. I tried to force such thoughts from my mind. Twenty-four years of life so far, though, was proving quite difficult to rearrange.

Lady Eleanor then moved towards me and I rose from the warm comfort of my leather chair. I took in that raven-black hair, the soft rise and fall of her bosom, her smooth shoulders and her neck, about which hung a golden chain and locket dangling between those perfect mounds. *Lucky locket*, I thought. Then there were those soft, so inviting red lips.

She stood very close to me, her head barely reaching above my shoulders; a beautiful and quite petite woman but looking no different to that young girl I had seen hurrying into Durford Hall with James all those years before.

Now I felt overcome by the nearness of this lovely if inaccessible woman, intoxicated by this closeness and by the scent of her body.

A small hand reached across to my left breast and lifted one of my medals.

"'For Valour'," she read. I nodded. "Was this for trying to save James?"

"Yes." I gritted my teeth as I silently recalled the events that had led up to the awarding of the medal. "I would rather give up a hundred of them to have him here with you," I added, feeling my eyes watering.

Still standing, she raised herself on tip-toe and her soft lips kissed my cheek.

"Thank you for trying to save him," she said simply and then moved back to her chair. She sat down and bade me do the same.

For at least a full minute neither of us spoke.

"Shall we take tea?" she said eventually, her gentle voice cutting through that solemn moment as she pressed a nearby bell-push.

During that silent interlude, I had been carried back to the Crimea when bullets had ripped into James' elbow, ankle and body and how I had tried desperately to save him.

"Yes, thank you. Tea would be very welcome," I managed to mumble.

"Have you been to the Hall yet?"

"No," I replied, "I can't quite bring myself to do that just yet. Truth to tell, I would feel a little uncomfortable there. You probably already know that Lord Durford gave me a few things. It was only then that I discovered what Captain James had been hinting at during one of our missions."

A maid arrived with tea and delicate little cakes on a silver tray.

"Offer Mr Finch tea, Rosinna," Lady Eleanor instructed.

Once the maid had left the room, I took out the double hunter from a tunic pocket underneath my crimson sash.

"He gave me this watch," I said. "And I must return something that belongs to you." As I snapped open the front cover of the watch, out fell a lock of Lady Eleanor's hair tied with a tiny piece of white ribbon. I offered it to her, hoping but trying not to show it, that I would prefer to keep it.

"Please keep it, Jack, if you wish – but only if you really want to. It does seem to me that we three are inexorably linked and this," she said, offering the lock back to me, "is the link that binds us together. You to James, James to me and now, we two. I am also bound to say that you remind me of him. No, not just the uniform but how you move, how your head turns to one side, rather quizzically. Not surprising really, I suppose. You were, after all, cousins."

"Thank you," I whispered as I held her lock of hair in my palm before returning it to the watch case and snapping it shut, feeling more pleasure and relief than I had felt for a long time. "Do you think it would be all right then to keep this as well?" I was conscious that I had still not called her by her name. I snapped open the back of the watch, the exterior of which carried the initials, J.A.F. These were not only those of James Algernon Fortune but mine too, John Albert Finch. Out dropped another lock of hair. This one was a rich red in colour and was tied with a green ribbon.

"Yes, Sophie would have liked that," she said. "She was my friend you know, but really was more like a sister. We shared all sorts of secrets and like you, Jack, ..." She tried to suppress a giggle. "... she had a love of ponds and rivers. She also knew the identity of a particular young man who took a very keen interest in her bathing."

She looked at me, her eyes lit up with merriment. The charming and disarming manner in which she had disclosed this information dispelled any embarrassment I might otherwise have been feeling at her knowing about that incident when I had watched from the edge of the pond on the Durford Estate, as a naked Lady Sophie entered the water. Lady Eleanor was also fully aware of the circumstances of my birth and childhood, otherwise the incident could have been treated as the unwelcome behaviour of a peeping Tom, instead of a poor village boy drawn like a moth to a flame, watching spellbound in the wrong place at the wrong time.

Polite knocking at the door interrupted these thoughts. At the threshold was someone I took to be a lady's maid. At first I did not recognise Mary, the daughter of one of Lower Durford's families. Life had been very difficult for most villagers, my father had told me. Poor harvests had meant low wages and the introduction of threshing machines had cut out winter work for most of the estate's labourers. He had said Lower Durford had not really recovered even by the '40s. Mary's family, with its eight children, had fallen on hard times but were relieved of the burden of one mouth to feed when a place was found for their eldest at Broughton House. She had certainly grown and filled out most pleasingly!

Mary, with barely a glance in my direction, reminded her mistress that she was expected elsewhere and then hurried out of the room.

"Sorry, Jack, but duty calls. You will call again and very soon. Perhaps we could drive to Durford Hall and see James' family together? I also find it a little difficult now that he has gone, but I could prepare the way for you. Lord Durford has certainly changed. It may be old age or the fact of losing James while Lord Edward remains in Hindustan or – as some people call it – India. Indeed, his own brother, Sir William, is also there helping to govern some state or other, I believe. It will be Edward who will inherit the estate one day if the heat of India doesn't floor him first. I understand the climate is not at all agreeable to Europeans."

I stood up, not really wanting to go. It had been a very different afternoon to the one I had imagined. There had been so much to give me food for thought: a veritable feast or banquet of things to consider. I had not expected such a warm reception from James' fiancée. I was after all, among the very last people that he had seen or had spoken to on this earth.

James had written asking me to visit Broughton House if he did not return from the Crimea. I had only really expected there to be awkward silences and perhaps even a little hostility on my arrival. I was alive but he was not. I had only visited because I felt a debt, an obligation to a man I much liked and respected. The meeting had not, after all, turned out to be the strained affair I had been anticipating as I had marched up the driveway those hours before.

Lady Eleanor clearly still felt the loss deeply, but it had been nearly two years now since his passing and time had gone some way to heal the deep sorrow she must have felt on hearing he was not returning. And although we could only ever be little more than acquaintances, James Fortune would always be the tie that did bind us. Could there be more?

No, Finch, I thought to myself, *be realistic. Go back to what you do well – soldiering – and forget her.*

"Please allow me to call a pair to take you home, Jack," she said.

Apart from really wanting to stay, what I also wanted to do was not to be carried home in a brougham but to leap in the air, run from the room and up the drive, shouting, 'Hallelujah', my chest fit to burst with the joy I was feeling at meeting Lady Eleanor and of falling intoxicatingly under her spell.

Returning to earth, I managed to mumble: "Well, perhaps as far as the river."

"Yes, indeed. Happy memories for you there." She smiled.

She then stood up, moved gracefully to my side and to my shock and pleasure kissed my cheek again.

"To the next time then," she said, "but let me know when your army duties allow and we can go to Durford Hall together."

With that she glided from the room.

The butler duly appeared as if from nowhere and I was ushered from the room, down the stairs, along a corridor and out through a side door. In front of me was a stony-faced coachman with reins and whip at the ready waiting to drive off. A pair of chestnut horses pounded their front hooves on the gravel, impatient to be gone. The coachman continued to stare ahead. I replaced my forage cap on my head, stepped into the carriage and with a sharp rap of my knuckles on the little door, sat back as the brougham moved forward.

Very soon I was thinking back over those last few hours; ruefully comparing them with what the next few hours might bring. How could anything match the joy and contentment I had experienced in the presence of Lady Eleanor?

After a few moments of brisk travelling, the breeze in my face tempered that boyish, lovesick romantic flush that minutes before had made me want to shout and share my oh-so-joyous feelings with the world. By the time we had reached the gatekeeper's lodge a level of sobriety had returned. After all, senior non-commissioned officers in Her Majesty's Rifle Brigade are not expected to behave so rashly. Men at whom I barked orders daily would not have recognised that same sergeant-major during his interview with Lady Eleanor.

We passed from the Broughton Estate after the gateman had unlocked those ornate gates and pushed them wide open. Then we were on the Winchester-to-Romsey road in the direction of the village of Lower Durford. At a point near the river, the coachman stopped. I jumped down and stared rather dolefully into the clear waters of a tributary of the River Test.

Then, as old and much newer memories flooded my mind, I began to feel elated, dazzled by and more than a little in love with the beautiful Lady Eleanor Broughton. There was a decided spring to my step. A feeling of peace with the world remained, better than anything I had felt for years. For a few moments at least I discounted those earlier thoughts of her unavailability and my inferior social position. After all, she had kissed me, not once but twice!

I had always regarded this as my river, regardless of the fact that it ran through the Durford Estate. As it cascaded over the little waterfall and then eddied around rocks on the river bed, it radiated a myriad of colours in the late afternoon sun, just as it had those years before when I had gazed in awe at Lady Sophie Fortune. Then I had been a callow youth unsure of his place in the world, but thinking himself condemned to only a very small part of it.

I reached the cottage, my home for those early years where the two people I had always thought of as my parents had – like so many others in their level of society – struggled to survive. All kinds of hard work and the army had turned me from a skinny boy into a strong, muscled man, five feet eleven inches tall on my enlistment papers. I had moved on. Well at least I had been able to escape a life of labouring, drudgery and years of toil on the estates of others. My parents had managed to get by too. Other villagers, some of whom I had grown up with, had also managed to escape that perilous existence of near starvation during lean years, poor winters and the hopelessness of the workhouse. Many had gone on to drudgery elsewhere, often to the stifling confines of factories for long hours, six days a week.

"Hello, Jack boy," said my father in greeting. Hard work, first as the village baker and then doing all manner of odd labouring jobs on the estate, had left him a wheezing cripple.

My mother dropped her sewing and rushed over to fling her arms around my neck.

"Oh, Jack, it is so good to see you," she said. "You look so well." As she released me from her hugs and kisses, she added: "Look at those medals! Our brave boy."

We sat down to cheese, potatoes, bread and beer while I told them of my encounter at Broughton House and how Captain James had asked me to visit Lady Eleanor.

On an earlier visit to the cottage, when the ship carrying the battalion back from the Crimea had docked at Portsmouth, I had been given permission to visit my parents. So while the rest of the men had continued their journey I had slipped away to Lower Durford. I had told them very little about the Crimea then. They were, after all, honest and simple folk. I decided that telling them about the hardships and horrors of the war would not help them, especially if in the very near future I was ordered away to fight in another war. We also barely referred to the circumstances of my birth and subsequent arrival over the Finch threshold. I had merely thanked them for trying their very best for me and for allowing me to go and seek my fortune in London, a move that led to my joining the army. My mother had always seemed very pleased when the subject of James Fortune had come up. How happy she had been when she discovered that we had served together in the same regiment, and how sorry when she learned he had died.

I stayed the night, though had hardly any sleep. I just could not help but go over the events of the day, particularly the time spent in the company of Eleanor and of course the feel of those soft lips on my cheek. My mind played tricks and I had visions of her in that room in that dress, with her bosom gently rising and falling. It was exquisite torture. The night proved long and testing and all kinds of relief swept over me as the first shafts of sunlight mercifully signalled an end at last from the night's frustrations.

Early rising from my childhood and as part of normal army life meant I was off my bed and outside within seconds. A few moments splashing cool well-water on my neck and face soon wiped away wild thoughts of Eleanor and washed the tiredness, at least for a while, from my eyes.

After breakfast and a few hours catching up with the doings of my brothers and sisters, I said goodbye, tempered with promises to return soon. My parents stood at the door waving and just before I turned down the lane that led out of the village I waved back. Then I set off at my customary brisk pace, still carrying recent events in my head.

I reached the crossroads where village legend has it that – following the defeat of Charles II at the battle of Worcester in 1651 – he had sheltered in a nearby hut before escaping to France and exile. A brewer's dray trundled by, on its way back to a small brewery in Winchester. Once, most villages had their own brewhouses. Many of them were now long gone, as so many families had left the villages in search of work. The draymen turned and beckoned me over.

"Winchester, boy?" asked one, in as thick an accent as

any you'll find in Hampshire but this one flavoured by the beer he had consumed during their early morning deliveries.

"Yes," I replied. "Thank you very much."

I hopped up to share the seat with the two draymen. As I did so I thought how gratifying it was that a soldier's uniform seemed to bring out the best in people. On several occasions when I had walked down the high street in Winchester, people had stepped aside to allow me to pass. A few had clapped when I had been standing by the cathedral wearing my medals.

The draymen seemed particularly pleased to share their wagon with me. The heavy Shire horses seemed to know the way back, which was just as well as the two men (having generously sampled the wares they had been delivering) seemed now to be more interested in listening to my tales of serving overseas than in driving the team of horses.

After a very convivial ride back with the three of us supping beer from a small cask, they dropped me near the cathedral and I marched up the hill back to the ordered life within the barracks.

My original battalion, the 1st Rifle Brigade, had been reduced in numbers from its full Crimean War strength. In the April of last year a new battalion – the 3rd – was formed (or more accurately, re-formed) at Haslar. There had been such a battalion before, but soon after the defeat of Napoleon Bonaparte at Waterloo with no new big wars likely to require the special talents of riflemen, it had been disbanded.

New recruits and men drafted from the Surrey, Middlesex and East Warwickshire regiments were transferred to the 3rd Rifle Brigade. But to provide it with an experienced core of officers, NCOs – including me – as well as riflemen were brought in. This not only boosted its strength but gave the raw recruits some war-hardened men to help turn them into a highly trained, well-disciplined and effective force capable of acting independently: so unlike ordinary regiments of the line. Both 1st and 2nd battalions had received many words of thanks and congratulations for the way they had conducted themselves in the Crimea.

A few weeks after I returned to barracks from Broughton Hall, I was waiting with an escort of riflemen at the railway station for a new draft of recruits and thinking about a certain dark-haired beauty not too many miles away, when I heard a familiar if gloomy voice from behind me.

"What's it all leading up to this time, Sergeant-Major?" droned the London-born Corporal Williams. Many of our new recruits came from London to escape the squalor of that city. I had lived there for a time and knew a little of its vices. Like so many others, Williams had escaped it too, preferring – he had once told me – to face the enemy's rifle and bayonet rather than the daily grind that was the lot of the inhabitants of Whitechapel, struggling in their airless hovels.

As I considered the question I looked at Williams. True, he was a miserable bastard but I had a soft spot for him. In my early days in the Brigade he had helped me and in return when I was promoted I had not always bothered to pick him up on things when he had broken the rules. He was loyal and that weighed well in the scales of how a man was judged in the battalion. Williams was also a tough little man and one I had served with and fought alongside. On several occasions he had accompanied Captain Fortune into Sevastopol and had acquitted himself well. He was also an excellent shot with the Enfield rifle.

I couldn't resist a gentle teasing.

"Have you not heard Tennyson's lines? 'Theirs is not to reason why / Theirs is but to do and die'? You ought to know by now that we just do as we are told, as best we can. Perhaps someone in Whitehall has decided to turn the whole army into one big brigade of riflemen."

He had turned to one side and walked slightly ahead of me. He appeared as though he was about to make a comment in reply to my rather frivolous remark, then he thought better of it and walked down the platform. This just as the approaching train whistled loudly and enthusiastically, the locomotive hissing, wheezing and coughing to a standstill with a squeal of brakes and the harsh, rasping sound of metal wheels on metal tracks. Accompanying this noisy metallic orchestra were clouds of steam and smoke that temporarily obliterated us all waiting on the platform. It also swallowed up the long, low building that served as a waiting area as well as nearly all the carriages that made up most of this latest troop arrival.

Once recruits and escort were finally reunited, I led the procession from the station towards our barrack square where Sergeant Nelson waited ready to issue orders covering the next few days. These included billet allotments, morning parades, kit issue, drill and their first taste of the rifle butts and how riflemen achieve their envied reputation of being the best shots in our own or anyone else's army.

As I stood behind the new men – a company-and-a-half or so – a figure in what I knew to be a footman's livery approached the riflemen who had formed the escort to and from the station. They had been standing around idly while Sergeant Nelson addressed the recruits. The new men, in contrast, were looking increasingly worried with each new order relayed by Nelson.

One of the riflemen directed the visitor towards me and soon I was being offered a letter with a familiar crest emblazoned on its reverse. Just as he passed the letter to me, he rather unnecessarily announced in not the quietest of voices:

"A message from one of the ladies of Broughton House for Sergeant-Major Finch."

This seemed to greatly amuse the riflemen of the escort party and several rather ribald comments floated across that corner of the parade ground and reached my reddening ears. I glanced at them.

"Sergeant Nelson can also find you some drill," I barked. "Get off and take the recruits to the quartermaster's store and then show them to their billets."

My tone had the desired effect and they sprang into action, quickly forming up and marching in front of the three lines of new men. Led by Corporal Williams, they left in some haste – with me glaring fiercely after them.

I then turned my attention to the letter. On the front in

very neat handwriting was written: 'To Sergeant-Major Finch, 3rd battalion, The Rifle Brigade, Winchester'. I guessed who had written it and without really thinking raised the envelope to my lips. Inside was a neatly written invitation to visit Durford Hall in three days time. On the back of the invitation, Lady Eleanor had suggested that we go together. She wrote that James would have appreciated my going there, as it would give the family some comfort especially for 'his dear mama'.

The receipt of the invitation was not entirely unexpected. I had sent a note that had taken many minutes to write because I had been concerned about writing the wrong thing. It had been very difficult to control my feelings. After about the seventh or eighth attempt I was reasonably satisfied with my efforts and that the note indicated no more than my likely availability for an excursion to Durford Hall. I then read and re-read it a dozen times before pronouncing it free from any possibility of misinterpretation and sending it by special messenger to Broughton House and Lady Eleanor.

The following Saturday I was driven to Broughton House by hired driver and gig. There, I found Lady Eleanor as radiant as ever but this time her maid, Mary, was in attendance. Off we set towards my village and to the rambling estate set amongst the streams, meadows and sheep-strewn hills of this part of Hampshire.

On our arrival at Durford Hall, Eleanor dismissed the gig and said the Hall would make arrangements to return us. Mary set off towards the kitchens and the servants' hall. These were locations I knew very well from previous visits delivering bread.

The two of us – Eleanor had requested that I wear my uniform while she was in a soft green (emerald, I think it is called) dress – approached the front door. We were admitted and Eleanor led us to the library. This too was a room of which I had some knowledge. On our way we passed a full-length mirror set in a very heavily gilded frame. I couldn't help but think as I caught our reflection that we looked particularly well suited; one of us in rifle green and the other in that softer-toned fabric.

Today's visit, though, was completely different. As a boy I had come face-to-face with Lieutenant Fortune in this room. After delivering bread from the village bakery I had wandered off and into this same library where for a few happy minutes I had lost myself in books. There, in his Rifles green uniform, James had found me. Now here was I back again; how circumstances had changed! I was now the one wearing the Rifles uniform.

Lady Eleanor was seated in a chair, with me standing just behind her, when James Fortune's parents, Lord John and Lady Durford entered. They were followed by two rather sour-looking elderly ladies both with stooping shoulders. All four of this sombre procession took up seats opposite, but not before Eleanor had risen and embraced each of them in turn.

Lady Durford, as if acknowledging my presence for the first time, looked directly at me. There was a soft gasp and it seemed as though she was about to faint. I moved forward but her husband, not exactly in top physical condition himself, had just enough presence of mind to reach an arm under her elbow and support his wife.

"Such a surprise!" she exclaimed.

"This is Sergeant-Major John Finch," announced Eleanor with what I thought sounded like some pride in her voice, though I could have imagined that.

"So like dear James in your uniform, young man. For a moment you quite took my breath away."

"It was my privilege to serve with such a gallant and honourable gentleman," I replied, conscious of my broad Hampshire tones contrasting with that of the present company.

One of the elderly ladies eased forward, joints creaking as though protesting noisily as she squinted disdainfully in my direction through spectacles that looked ready to plunge to the floor.

"Uhm!" she said, sitting back in her chair but still peering at me.

I wondered if she knew who I was. Perhaps she had been told but had forgotten.

"You shall sit here, Jack Finch," said Lady Durford, patting a well-upholstered leather seat, "and tell me of yourself and my son. We know very little of his final hours. Eleanor warned me that there was something of James about you. I see it too. You must also know by now that he and you were related."

She paused, then added in a very sharp tone: "Do you expect anything to come from this?"

"No," I replied almost as sharply. "I was honoured to serve with him and I deeply regret that I was unable to save him. I have never sought or expect anything as a result of the intelligences that have been disclosed to me. He always treated me with respect and I him as both my superior officer and as a true gentleman. I have also every reason to be grateful to him. He gave me books when I was a boy and encouraged my reading. During all the time that I served in his company he always treated me well and kept me informed regarding the orders we were given. This so unlike the way in which officers in other regiments deal with their men. He was held in very high regard by his brother officers and by the riflemen in his company. The disclosures in his letter to me that we were cousins and the watch he gave me are more than enough."

As I spoke these words I could see Eleanor's face positively glowing with approval, but when I stopped speaking I could feel my legs beginning to buckle. I had been standing almost rigidly to attention as though on the parade ground since the arrival of the Durfords in the library. Apart from my slight lunge to prevent Lady Durford falling off her chair before her husband intervened, I had not moved. I was now wishing that I could slump into the firm, comforting embrace of an armchair. I felt quite drained. Even more comforting but unlikely would be to gather up Eleanor in an even warmer embrace. That would be very comforting.

Then Lord John broke in:

"I wrote my brother William in India. Told him about James and you. What you did. Heard from him. Wants you included in some sort of settlement."

My mind was racing once again. I had certainly not sought nor expected any sort of reward from my link with the Fortunes. Then a sudden recall of our encounters in my pre-army days caught up with me. That was when James had found me in this same library and I had been lost in one of the books. It had been a story by Charles Dickens, 'Oliver Twist'. He had rather dismissed it as a very gloomy tale, though it was about a poor boy who finally makes good. He had then said something which, when I thought about it some time later, had puzzled me: that the same thing might eventually happen to me. Had he known something then?

James' father was still talking.

"Didn't say exactly what the settlement was to be but William should be back from India next year or certainly the year after."

With that he fell back into his chair and mumbled: "Fellow's done his penance," and looked even older and more tired than he had done a few minutes before. Certainly more careworn than when our paths had crossed several months earlier when he had handed me a packet containing his son's watch and the letter that had revealed William, his brother, as my father. That meeting with Lord John at the time of my first visit to my parents' cottage after returning from the Crimea had changed everything. I was the same but everything around me, the certainty of my life just a few moments before that conversation on the road with Lord John, was sending me in a very different direction. Would I – could I – ever remain the same?

"Right, young man, that's got all that out of the way. Now," said Lady Durford, once more patting that same chair she had indicated before 'all of that' had started, "sit here and tell me of your adventures. Nell, stay if you wish."

But with a little curtsey and smile aimed at me playing on her lips, Eleanor left the room.

I looked at Lady Durford a little quizzically as I perched uncomfortably beside her while the other two ladies continued to stare at me unflinchingly. Lord John, now leaning back awkwardly in his chair, was also looking at me closely.

"Spare me nothing. I am the wife, mother, daughter and granddaughter of soldiers. There is little that you could say that will surprise or shock."

Again I gazed at this titled lady. What a strong-minded beauty she must have been in her prime! Her eyes, though bounded by deep lines, still sparkled; for a split-second I could see her son looking back at me, that same twinkle and humour. Such a contrast to James' father. I looked across at the scarred veteran; a man of grim disposition but one who now sat quietly, his body weary and now hunched against the back of his seat. For probably the first time I felt some sympathy for him. An old wizened shell of a man: that he was James' father and had served with the old 95th that became the Rifle Brigade were the only things in his favour as far as I was concerned. But how could I not feel sorry for him? At times he seemed to be fully engaged in the whole proceedings but then he seemed to be just drifting away, lost and far away … but where? That I could not guess.

A vision of South Africa where we had fought native tribesmen came back to me as I sat and thought back over the last four years. I amused my ardent listener – and even the other three seemed to be faintly cheered – by relating her son's shock at first seeing me in Rifle green in the front row of his company. Then I went on to describe how we had pursued the Xhosa across Cape Colony and finally defeated them.

My tale then continued, of sailing from Portsmouth to the Crimea and of our several sorties into Sevastopol. I could feel my throat tightening as I covered that final time for James when, as we left Sevastopol, he had been wounded: how I had tried to bring him back to our lines. In an effort to spare Lady Durford too much unnecessary pain I said that for most of the journey back he had been unconscious and would have felt very little. A lie, yes. He had been in much pain but what could I do? This bereaved mother was clinging to my every word. She had suffered enough by losing him. Telling her just how much her son had suffered would not help at all.

A single tear trickled from her right eye. I followed the little rivulet as it made steady progress down to her upper lip. Both lips were pursed in an effort to keep those deeply felt emotions under control. She now sat bolt upright with her head tilted slightly forward to catch every word.

Lord John remained quite expressionless. As an old soldier he had been amongst death and destruction. The fact that I had been talking about his son made no difference. James had been a soldier and had died doing his duty. A proud father could ask for a no better end for his soldier son.

The two elderly ladies who had also been following my story attentively had been dabbing their eyes at regular intervals.

"Eleanor tells me that this medal," said Lady Durford, indicating the cross (made, I was told by my battalion colonel, from captured Russian bronze cannon) "was awarded for your bravery in attempting to save James."

"Yes," I replied as simply and as softly as I could, hoping that it would not sound boastful.

"And that Her Majesty presented it to you?"

"Yes, during a big parade in Hyde Park. Pinned it to this ribbon with her own hand. Along with other men more worthy of it than me who had also served in the Crimea."

"You are too modest, John Finch. This is just one of the many good things we have heard about you. You do your Queen, your country, your regiment and yourself much credit. What though are your plans now?"

"I did think about leaving the army but what could I do? It would be difficult settling into ordinary life after six years a soldier."

"Will you take some advice from an old lady?"

I had settled a little more at ease in the chair to which I had been assigned after describing the events of the last few years. I now wondered with a little concern what advice was about to come my way from this very strong-minded woman.

"Stay in the army, at least for another year or so. By then William will have returned and the settlement Lord John mentioned may prove beneficial. Then you can plan what the next step should be." Then she added with a little grim humour: "Try and avoid wars. And be sure to come back safely to us."

Her soft tone as she spoke these last words, especially 'to us' pleased but puzzled me. Did this mean that I was accepted not just for what I was, but for who I was? Could it mean that the doors to Lady Eleanor's heart could also be opened?

"Now you must go. Is it back to Lower Durford village or to Winchester? We'll look after Lady Eleanor but I am sure we shall all meet again very soon."

She rose. Her husband and the two elderly ladies, creaking joints almost in unison, followed. As Lord John reached the door he turned, inclined his head slightly in my direction, then moved on.

What another special day it had proved to be in the company of folk who, only a few short years – even months – ago, I would have regarded as my elders and betters. I did, though, consider that James had always treated me differently. Officers and riflemen in the Rifle Brigade were not divided by that same wide gulf that existed between rich and poor in ordinary society. Was it only that 'Rifles' connection and the fact that he was a decent, honourable man who had treated anyone, regardless of who they were or where they were from, with respect?

By the inclination of Lord John's head and the cordial reception given to me at the Hall, was there a growing acceptance of me? Perhaps not as an equal, but now at least I was feeling a few steps up that ladder. John Finch, it seems, does have some expectations – but whether 'small' or 'great' only time would tell.

A pony and trap supplied by the Hall conveyed me to the cottage long regarded by me as my home; a quiet, peaceful refuge to return to after time overseas and to the two simple folk who I had always regarded as my mother and father. With hitherto unknown secret assistance from the Hall, they had managed to bring me up. Life had still not been easy for any of us.

Yet here was I, still a young man and – it seems – a fit, healthy, decorated and respected soldier. Lady Eleanor was still almost certainly out of reach, irrespective of my wishful thinking, but at least I had prospects of some sort. I still had niggling feelings of uncertainty about who I really was and my place in society, any society.

Then I remembered a small dog belonging to one of the other children when I was a boy. It had been a cross between a sheepdog and one of the estate's gun dogs. Most of the litter had been drowned, being of no use to shepherd or gamekeeper, but this one had been spared. It was a mongrel and I began to think of myself in that same light. Part village-boy-turned-soldier and part illegitimate-child-of-the-large-house at the other end of the village.

I made up my mind to make the best of whatever came my way, much like that little dog who had become the much-loved companion of that village child. James had hinted at good things to come and wallowing in self-pity was not my usual way of dealing with any situation.

I had gone directly from Winchester to Broughton House and then on to Durford Hall and this was my first visit home for some weeks. I was looking forward to the security I always felt in the cottage among my family. I pushed open the door.

"I am home!" I called.

My mother rose quickly from the table where she had been mending a shirt. Other garments requiring some attention from needle and thread were scattered across the table and folded over chair-backs. It was a chilly late autumn afternoon and a fire blazed cheerily in the grate. A once-stray black-and-white cat that had adopted the Finch family looked up lazily from its place near the fire, almost daring the disturber of its peace to move it. This was the kind of scene that for a soldier fighting on the other side of the world gave him a reason to fight. It was why I thought of this cottage as my home. That said, aspects of Broughton House or Durford Hall could be equally comforting. Perhaps I was the lucky one, as so many men joined the army to escape their less-than-idyllic home life.

"Oh, Jack!" my mother cried out, "what a handsome figure you make in your uniform."

Then she hugged me, but almost as suddenly released her grip.

"I suppose you will move on and forget us now you

have been up to the Hall and know all about Sir William?"

During my first visit home back in July I had briefly told my parents what I had discovered about my true parentage. Then I realised other details would have been provided by Eleanor's maid, Mary, who still had a few relatives living in what was left of the village. And of course twenty and more years before, they had been party to at least some of my story.

"Never," I said, feeling just a little hurt. "Whatever happens, you will remain what as far as I am concerned you have always been, my parents. This is my home," I added, waving an arm extravagantly around in a circle.

"Some might say we were just paid to do that, Jack."

"Not in my hearing they won't," I said firmly.

I was only too aware of that distance between rich and poor and perhaps that was the main reason I respected James so much. He and the other Rifles officers shared their men's hardships and would eat and drink the same rations. It was closeness born out of mutual respect. Our training to think and act independently made us different to 'ordinary' soldiers. This would, however, never extend to social engagements. It was difficult to see Corporal Williams being invited to dine at the table of Major, the Earl Axelby of Netherborne at his country seat in the depths of Wiltshire. However, could this apply to Regimental Sergeant-Major Finch? Given the chance I would certainly give it a try.

Additional thoughts on my mother's anxiety and the possibility of a complete change to my way of life were cut short by my father's lumbering awkwardly in from the log-store at the back of the cottage.

"Hello, Jack. How do? Give us a hand, boy."

I went off to the room I had shared with Fred and two other brothers and hung my uniform up on some willow hangers that I had made myself years before for my Sunday best. My clothes tally then boasted little else. I replaced my rifle green tunic and the other items with a plain shirt, working trousers and boots.

The gaps in my present wardrobe had been giving me some cause for concern, particularly if I would be receiving more invitations to visit Broughton House.

On several occasions when not involved in army matters I had wandered down Winchester's high street with a view to adding to my very modest collection of clothes.

During one such expedition I reached what I had long thought to be a butcher's premises towards the bottom of the town not too far from the river. Well, it had once been such a shop because I had worked there. Now it was a tailor's, not the bespoke or made-to-measure variety, but one selling garments that were ready to wear. In the window was a display of trousers, quite tight-fitting and long to cover most of the shoe, in a variety of colours including some bright checks. There were also shirts and waistcoats that would stand out in any crowd and to complete the upper body, well-cut frock coats. On a shelf near the back of the window was a row of top hats and a new style, labelled 'bowler' hat. These items were not cheap but certainly less expensive than the handmade dress of the rich. In some parts of town were stalls where the poorer classes could buy secondhand clothes for a fraction of the cost of anything in the tailor's window.

Curiosity prompted me to wander in, although I could not really see myself emerging from this shop dressed in top hat, frock coat, colourful waistcoat, checked shirt and tight trousers.

As I pushed open the door to the shop a little bell rang.

My first question to the man I took to be the proprietor was not about the clothes but to ask after the well-being of the butcher whose shop this had been. I was informed that he had died suddenly and that his widow and children had settled in Chichester where they had other family.

I then declared myself unsure about outer garments, but bought some drawers, socks and a nightshirt.

As I paid for my goods and they were being wrapped in brown paper by a young assistant, I noticed through an open door a workroom with some sort of machines.

"Ah, you're admiring our Singer sewing machines," said the man. "They are from America. They're also going to change tailoring. We can make shirts, suitings, coats, anything and rather cheaper than ever before but of high quality. Come back and see us and we'll be pleased to look after you."

I thanked him and left the shop. That little bell above the door rang again.

For the two days that followed my coming home I happily carried out many of the tasks that I had done as a boy. Repairing hurdles was a job I had always liked, as was anything that included making things from wood. I blocked fences, sharpened tools, and replaced roof tiles now that my father could hardly walk far, let alone go up a ladder and onto the roof. Cutting logs for winter was hard work, but like all the other familiar jobs it was something I sensed I would not be doing every day for the rest of my life.

This physical activity helped to distract my thoughts a little away from Lady Eleanor. Over those two days I had hoped to hear from her, but that was too much to expect: she had her own life, one that was far removed from this Lower Durford cottage or my army life and the barracks.

Assuring my parents that I would take every care and adding that I hoped to return as and when army duties allowed, I left the village – happy to walk on a crisp, late November afternoon. I reached the station at Romsey and travelled lazily via Southampton back to Winchester. This gave me a little more time to think about recent events before returning to my army routine.

Chapter Two

Barracks life continued as before: soldiers require routine. There were daily morning parades and orders for the day, plus a steady stream of new recruits and deployment of trained men to other battalions. It took a little time to turn young men from the towns and villages into riflemen, training them in how to look after equipment and how to use the fixed sword (bayonet) effectively. Then it was off to practise these skills away from the parade ground and the rifle butts and off to the hills, woods and valleys of Hampshire. No doubt some of our activities frightened the life out of the locals around Winchester as we carried out skirmishing exercises and the use of natural cover. Dressed in their rifle green, they were expected to surprise the enemy. Riflemen, unlike soldiers in other regiments who dress so helpfully in scarlet tunics in order to provide excellent targets, were also expected to think and act independently.

Much of the praise heaped on the 1st and 2nd Battalions in the Crimea confirmed the success using our tried-and-tested methods.

Even the chief Russian engineer responsible for turning Sevastopol into an impregnable fortress praised the Brigade for the way it had carried out its attacks on the town. It was a big part of my job to help turn civilians into such a body of men, ones capable of loading and firing accurately twice a minute and conducting themselves at the level expected of riflemen.

Then joy of joys; in the first week of December I received an invitation to visit Broughton House for a musical soirée and dinner. It was to take place a few days before Christmas on Saturday 20th December. The invitation was not directly from Eleanor – or 'Nell' as I was increasingly thinking of her – but from Lord and Lady Broughton. A few doubts swept over me, but when Major Axelby told me that he too had received such an invitation I felt a little relieved. He would be attending with his wife, Georgia. The Major said that he would arrange for us to be taken there during the late afternoon and brought back to Winchester during the late morning of the next day. He and his wife would then go on to Netherborne to keep Christmas and return to attend a ball at the turn of the year. He strongly hinted that it, too, would be held at Broughton House. It cheered me that he would be attending that first function, but realisation of what such an invitation meant began to dawn on me. I hurried after him and he suggested we continue our conversation in his office.

"This invitation, sir," I began, waving the card in front of him. "I am pleased to receive it but it's going to be difficult. I have not been to anything like this before. Don't want to make a fool of myself."

"Don't worry, Jack. I'll be there and so will Georgie. We'll cover each other's backs just like riflemen always do. Sit down and we'll go over a few things. For the soirée, we will be in our uniforms and that will do very well. You will positively dazzle 'em. I'll have a word with the Broughtons, though I am sure Nell will arrange a few things. Anyway, a man who has run at Russian guns won't be put off by a little small talk. I'll sit Georgie next to you – she can talk the hind legs off a donkey, so you won't get a word in edgeways anyway. Other guests will only be interested in our efforts against the Russkies and if I know the Broughtons they won't invite any awkward types."

Then another thought seemed to occur to him and he began to laugh to himself. I looked, I am sure, both puzzled and worried.

"Jack, if you're still worrying about waving the wrong

knife and fork about, just picture some of them handling a rifle and sword. I know who I would rather be standing near when it matters. Just copy me. One other thing, Jack – whatever else anyone may think of you (and why should you care anyway?) how many of them have had our highest award pinned on their chest by the Queen?"

Suddenly I felt very humble but at least relieved.

"Thank you very much, sir, for all your help. I can't tell you what all this means to me."

"We'll talk about this again nearer the time," he added, as I saluted, turned and left the office.

We did speak the day before we were due to go to Broughton House. Really it was to confirm most of what we had discussed before.

The day of the soirée arrived all too soon, but I had been kept too busy to worry that much. After packing a valise with items that Major Axelby had suggested I might need, I went off to the main Winchester station to await the arrival of Georgia Axelby. Major Axelby was engaged most of that morning on regimental duties and asked me to take a hired pony and trap the short distance to the station.

I passed the ten or so minutes' wait just watching the occasional train steam past. I still looked upon the steam engine in some awe, intrigued by that power. Several travellers waiting for their trains lifted their children up to wave at me. I smiled dutifully, patted small heads and saluted parents with appropriate solemnity. This pleased everyone concerned, especially me as I felt quite flattered by this public attention.

Lady Georgia's train duly arrived and I watched as she stepped from a first-class compartment with its rich hangings and comfortable chairs, much better than the plainer décor and wooden bench seats of second class and certainly far removed from those open carriages best described as boxes for the poorer classes in third. Some of these 'wagons' still did not have roofs and the occupants were exposed to all weathers. I usually travelled in second class, where at least the uniform fared better and it was less noisy than the next class down, which was at the very end of the train and out of sight so as not to offend the sensibilities of the wealthier travellers in their more luxurious sitting rooms on wheels.

While a porter struggled to pile hat-boxes and clothes trunks onto a little wheeled cart, Lady Georgia walked along the platform in a steady, deliberate and confident manner. Of course I recognised her immediately. Several photographs of his wife and children were displayed prominently along the walls of Major Axelby's office as well as on his desk.

She was tall, elegant and rather striking overall. Her thick, rich chestnut hair was topped by a dark green hat that matched her coat. Very appropriate for the wife of an officer of the Rifle Brigade.

As she reached me she extended a gloved hand, which I lightly kissed. She smiled.

"You must be Jack. I've heard a great deal about you. You're thought of very highly in many places and I feel honoured to meet such a brave man."

My face flushed but I managed to say: "Thank you, ma'am but I serve alongside many brave men including Major Axelby."

Then she slipped her arm in mine and I escorted her to our conveyance, which was waiting for us just outside the station but was now complete with her luggage. The pony and trap gently jogged the one thousand yards or so to the barracks.

Later that day, the three of us having changed, we set off in a brougham for Broughton House and I enjoyed not only the pleasant conversation but the heartening sight of Major Axelby and his wife sitting side by side. They were a devoted couple and I wondered how he could bear to be parted from her, especially when I knew that he had fought bravely in the Cape and the Crimea alongside his men, often risking his life. Did he need to be in the army? Why did he stay? What would I do if I found myself married or at the very least linked to such a beautiful woman?

We arrived at those strong gates; the gateman, after fumbling with chain and padlock, pushed them open and the brougham continued down the drive. As soon as it stopped several footmen appeared. Our luggage was removed and we were led up the staircase to the front door where Lord and Lady Broughton greeted us.

The butler conducted us to the first floor and opened a door for the Axelbys and then one for me.

"You may wish to prepare for this evening," he said, still holding the door to the room open.

I took this to mean a chance to wash, shave if required and then change into my best uniform. This was just as Major Axelby had said.

Five minutes after the butler's departure there came a polite knocking on the door and I was surprised to see Major Axelby standing there with Lady Eleanor, Nell. I could feel my heart racing.

"Need a quick word, Jack," said the Major. "Forgot to mention it earlier. I know it's not the usual form but while we're here, please call me Robert."

With that, before I could utter a word, he had scuttled back to his room.

Nell moved a little closer.

"So pleased that you were able to come and I am delighted to see you again. It seems an absolute age since we last met. Robert said that you would be pleased to come when mama spoke to him a few weeks ago."

What an understatement that was! Once again I was in Major Axelby's debt. I must be careful not to spoil things.

"The little concert starts at 6.45 pm," said Nell. "Robert and Georgie have agreed to go down slightly ahead of us, if you are happy for you and I to follow." She blushed slightly. "We are also grateful to you for telling us about dear James and this is our way of thanking you. Just a few friends and of course Lord and Lady Durford. We did not want you to feel overwhelmed. Sorry – I don't want you to feel patronised either, but it may …" and she stopped, looking firstly at the floor and then directly at me before continuing. "… It may just be a little difficult for all concerned if our guest of honour felt in any way at odds with the company."

I cut in.

"I understand and really appreciate what you are saying. After all, until a few months ago I was a soldier from a poor village. It's difficult enough adjusting to new circumstances so it is very kind and thoughtful of you to consider my feelings. Major Axelby did say that you would do something like this. I only hope that I don't let you all down, or myself for that matter."

"I don't think there is the remotest chance of that happening, dear Jack. You just impress everyone you meet."

She was clasping her hands together just below her bosom. I reached carefully forward, my hands lifting her hands. I kissed them. This was a spontaneous reaction to hearing those gentle words.

"I'm sorry. I should not have done that. Just wanted to thank you for your many kindnesses."

She smiled.

"No, Jack, it was a lovely thing to do. You act with your heart and you wear it on your sleeve just as brightly as that crown." As she said these words, she pointed to one of the badges denoting my rank that I wear on my sleeves. "You are truly honest and so is the way you behave. Not at all like some of the young men, who should know better."

Best not pursue that, I thought, but it must be clear to many eligible bachelors across Hampshire that she would be a great catch.

Whatever happened I could not bear to think of her married off to some decrepit old man like her friend, Sophie. Perhaps there could be someone like James or another Robert Axelby, both in my experience honourable men. Even then I would not particularly like it, but if it wasn't going to be me sharing her bed then someone like one of them might be acceptable – just!

She tturned to go but after two steps looked back and said: "I hope you like Mozart and Beethoven, Jack."

Well, I had heard of both composers and I think our regimental band had played some of their more spirited music near Constantinople when we had been on our way to the Crimea; it was certainly lively enough. But it was not the efforts of the orchestra that were now crossing my mind. The next test might be the cutlery. Major Axelby had explained the intricacies of place settings and had said that if all else failed just to copy what he and Georgia did. Regardless of Nell's confidence in me and those kinds words, there was still plenty of scope for me to make grave social errors.

I kept these thoughts to myself. Once more she looked to be about to leave but was giving all the appearance of someone reluctant to go.

Finally she added that 6.40 pm would see her waiting at the door for the four of us to go down to the ballroom where the concert was to take place. There was just over an hour to go. As I watched her figure disappearing from view I was sure I had also caught a glimpse of her maid, Mary, hovering in the shadows at the end of the corridor. Perhaps she was fulfilling the role of chaperone, but I turned back to my room and thought nothing more of it. Indeed my thoughts now turned to the pressing need to get ready.

My uniform had already been laid out for me, though one item was missing.

Once more there was a polite knocking at the door and I went to answer it.

"Is there anything you require, sir?" asked one of the servants, easing past me to place my missing shoes – impressively polished and shiny – underneath the bottom of my trousers that were draped very neatly over the side of the bed.

"No, I don't think so, thank you," I replied.

"Well, if you should think of anything please ring the bell," he replied, pointing to a length of curtain-like material that reached just short of the ceiling where it joined a thin wire that no doubt connected it to the servants' hall.

He then backed out of the room, reaching behind him for the door-knob and with practised ease left the room.

For the first time in my life I had been waited on by a servant, my kit set out just as it was for the officers in my regiment.

I could see why the rich and privileged wanted things to remain the same. What they had, they wanted to keep! Any whiff of revolution had always received very short shrift. That it was obvious to me, though, did not make it right. No one in England should fear starvation but it would be a long time, if ever, that life would become a little easier for those in poorer straits.

Leaving these Chartist thoughts behind, I turned my attention back to my toilet and to getting ready for the evening's performance; mine as well as the musicians. Best uniform complete with medals and red sash was put on.

At approximately 6.30 pm there was another knock at the door of my room. This time it was Major Axelby, Robert.

"How are you doing, old fellow? Well, looks as though you're about ready. Georgie'll be along in a few minutes."

Then his wife appeared, positively radiant.

"My my, Jack and Robert, how handsome you both look."

Another minute passed and another figure was at my side in a shimmering, light blue gown. She had curtsied at the three of us. My breath was taken away. I was lost in love.

"Are we set?" Nell asked. "Shall you lead the way, Robert? We'll follow." She lightly touched my arm. "We'll let them go in first, Jack."

We waited a full minute before following the Axelbys, the delay not helping in the steadying of my nerves.

Then, linking her right arm in my left, we set off.

As we reached the door, the little orchestra struck up a few bars of the old '95th' but as we crossed the threshold of the ballroom it stopped. I turned towards where chairs had been set out. There, around a score of ladies and gentlemen were applauding our arrival.

I stopped, quite overcome by emotion tinged with some embarrassment, but feeling an odd wave of contentment. There was Nell on my arm, county quality and lords and their ladies clapping me. I was moving up!

We were directed to seats in the front row of the audience. As I turned to sit I caught a glimpse of the Axelbys and both looked delighted. I was taking in the

Durfords, the elderly ladies, Nell's sisters and several of the local gentry. Lord and Lady Broughton indicated everyone should be seated. They remained standing and Lord Broughton cleared his throat, preparing to speak.

"I shall keep this brief. This young man's had enough shocks already this evening as it is. On behalf of Lord and Lady Durford and our own dear Nell, we welcome both our guests from the Rifle Brigade. To this young man, John Finch, we offer our sincere thanks for his efforts in trying to save James. We know Nell has been particularly touched by his courage in telling us of those tragic events in the Crimea. Please accept this evening as our thanks. May God bless and keep you – Major Axelby, Sergeant-Major Finch and the men of the Brigade – safe from war's alarms."

With that he sat down. This was followed by a ripple of applause.

The hour or so that followed just seemed to envelop me in a warm glow of happiness. I was overwhelmed, not least when the concert was over and even the orchestra applauded me.

Then Nell squeezed my hand. "Let's take some refreshment," she said.

It took a little while for us to leave the room, as many of the audience offered their congratulations. This was beginning to prove too much for a young but still experienced veteran like me.

At length Nell managed to steer me into an ante-room.

"Do sit down, Jack. I hope this isn't proving too much. You look a little startled. I am sorry. Perhaps we should have arranged something else. Don't want to put you off ever coming back here again. Both families wanted to show their personal thanks for all your bravery, but at the same time to mark James' passing, while publicly acknowledging the part you played in these events. We wanted it to be on a scale that would not cause you upset. I am sure it has been something of an ordeal, but we have all been so anxious to show how you are appreciated. Robert also felt that the evening would not be too daunting to a man who has served with such distinction.

I was lost for words.

"May I pour you a refresher? " she asked. "Robert says

rum's the thing to raise the spirits. I have some here." And with that she added a generous amount to a glass.

"Nell, I am so grateful that the families have taken this much trouble, but you really needn't have gone to these lengths. You have given me your thanks and asked for us to be friends. That was sufficient."

But as soon as I said these words I knew that my response was not really how I felt. Yes, at one stage – months ago – mere thanks and friendship might have been enough, but now I wanted and needed more.

A gong sounded, summoning us to dinner.

The hours that followed and the food and wines on offer were not like anything I had experienced before.

I felt full and satisfied as the ladies retired and the talk among the gentlemen turned to old campaigns from the Napoleonic wars to the Crimea.

I had managed to manoeuvre my way successfully through the cutlery at dinner and was soon able to speak, along with Robert Axelby, with some knowledge of events at Sevastopol.

It was very late before I turned in and a more contented man than me would be very difficult to find, except in one particular: it had been many hours since I had seen Nell.

She joined me at breakfast and soon afterwards we walked in the kitchen garden of Broughton House, her arm linked in mine.

Time again seemed to be rushing by. What had someone once said to me? That the hours creep slowly by, but the weeks and months rush past! That didn't seem right to me, especially when I was with or near Nell. When you're with that special person you love, all time rushes by.

Later that morning we returned to Winchester, but two weeks later I accompanied the Axelbys as we returned to Broughton House to see in the new year, 1857. But on that occasion and on several more during the first months of this year there was little opportunity to see Nell without many others being present.

Then, in the early summer of 1857 – nearly a year after our first meeting – came a little note from Nell via a Broughton House footman. I scribbled a reply saying I would be pleased to call on the following Saturday. I added that I was looking forward so much to seeing her again.

The happy news of our meeting was a very welcome distraction, as newspapers were beginning to carry disturbing reports of outbreaks of mutiny in Hindustan.

By July even the Winchester papers contained stories of how around 30,000 Indian soldiers – sepoys – were massacring Europeans and were seizing towns and forts.

Several companies of the 3rd Battalion Rifle Brigade were soon on their way to Aldershot. Fortunately for me, and I hoped for Nell, I was kept back temporarily along with several companies of mostly new recruits. Major Axelby remained too, but confided that he thought he might soon be sent off to assist in the formation of a new battalion, the 4th.

"Don't want to miss the fun though, eh Jack?" he remarked as he handed me a copy of *The Times* newspaper. "Looks as if that reporter, Billy Russell, has been stirring it up all over again. Just like the Crimea. While you're here, Jack, no harm in telling you that we'll be off sometime soon as well to join the rest of the battalion. I reckon it's likely to be us off to India to settle things down there."

He then went on to confirm that indeed another battalion was being raised but that he would be remaining with the 3rd.

I had been to see Nell a few times since that Saturday invitation back in May and had been looking forward to visiting at the end of this particular week, but after Major Axelby's news I realised that matters could easily change.

I asked him how soon 'sometime soon' might be.

"Almost certainly within the next three weeks," he said and with that he went off to round up the other officers that still remained as part of our depleted garrison.

To provide some edge to their newly developing skills I had suggested to Major Axelby that we should hold a competition for the new recruits. He had thought that a good idea and asked me to organise it. He put up a trophy and a two-guinea purse and I added a five-gallon cask of beer.

The men were informed at morning parade and ordered to attend the butts in parties of twenty. We announced that it was partly to celebrate the anniversary of the victory over the French at Waterloo back in June and also to commemorate the action at Ferrol in Spain in 1800, a date regarded as the official birthday of the regiment. The Ferrol date would probably fall as we were bound for India, so it was thought a good idea to celebrate it now instead of struggling to do so on the high seas.

The shadows of that summer's day were slowly lengthening as rifleman after rifleman showed off his newly acquired skills with the Enfield. Eventually a winner was announced and an exhausted looking rifleman, Morrison, stepped forward to claim his prize from Major Axelby.

"Excellent shooting, Morrison," he said.

Corporal Williams, probably the best shot in the whole battalion, bemoaned the fact that NCOs had been barred from entering. Nevertheless, he called out "Well done, lad" to the winner.

Some of Morrison's fatigue seemed to have lifted as he staggered away holding his trophy and attempting to roll his wooden cask in a straight line while still clutching his rifle.

"Nearly as good as me, eh Sergeant-Major?" said Williams a little sourly.

"Ah, but as you trained him you should find your reward in that," I told him.

The merest hint of a grin creased Williams' weather-beaten face. Comments from this usually morbidly taciturn man were praise of the highest order.

As the men dispersed, most likely to the nearest ale-houses, and the officers returned to their mess I wandered back to my quarters trying to focus my full attention on my next meeting with Nell.

As I reached my billet I couldn't help but think again how my life and circumstances were changing. Perhaps only a handful of years or so ago I would have followed the riflemen to the many local public ale-houses. There was much to entertain and divert them other than beer; mostly all aimed at relieving them of their hard-earned pay. Some men would just go to hear music or join in with the singing of mostly bawdy songs. Others went to eat different fare to what the army provided: bread and butter, tasty steak-and-kidney pies, creamy pease pudding and crisp baked potatoes. Some of these establishments were not unlike the penny 'gaffs' I had encountered in London six or seven years before. They provided food, music and even theatrical shows. Other ale-houses had very obliging landlords who provided female company. The army had always found this popular diversion impossible to stamp out and often turned a blind eye, provided the obliging women were pronounced 'clean' after regular medical inspections.

Once back in my billet, I reviewed my still rather meagre civilian clothes and shut the little closet after concluding there was really very little that was as eye-catching as my best uniform.

Earlier in the year I had sought Mr Axelby's advice in purchasing clothes suitable for calling at Broughton House and had appeared several times in frock coat, waistcoat and trousers, but I did not want to fidget uncomfortably on what could prove to be my last visit there before leaving for Hindustan. My uniform was a good fit and I felt more confident wearing it than I did in my civilian clothes. I wanted to feel at ease with the lady to whom I had felt increasingly drawn as the months had passed.

The day arrived, putting an end to that almost unbearable waiting. My wishing away the days in between had not helped.

The driver drew up at the gates with instructions to return at 4pm.

I pushed at the side gate just in case it had been left open, but the keeper rushed forward with that rolling gait of his and unlocked it. He waved me through as he moved to one side to allow me free passage, while at the same time brushing morsels of food from whiskers and waistcoat.

"Here again then, sir and expected too," he said, then turned and hurried back to his humble lodgings and the rest of his dinner.

That familiar sound of crunching gravel continued all the way to the grey stone staircase. I leapt up the steps two at a time, army life and thoughts of happy moments to come contributing in equal measure to my athletic endeavours.

As I reached forward to push the acorn-shaped bell, the door opened suddenly and I almost fell in.

"Follow me, sir," said the familiar if rather doleful voice of the butler.

As on previous occasions we reached that plain door, he knocked and then motioned me forward.

Eagerly, I stepped into the room. Nell was there and although her note had suggested others would be present, I still felt very disappointed not to see her alone. But here she was with her mother and two of her elderly relatives. The latter were certainly looking down their noses at me and with some curiosity. It could be that they were merely short-sighted, but I wondered why all elderly aunts of the aristocracy wore the same expression. Were they related to that other elderly pairing I had first met at Durford Hall?

I suddenly began to feel a little cold. A shivering feeling going down my spine along with a sinking mood was undermining the confidence that had seen me march steadfastly up the steps towards the house only minutes before.

Had I been summoned here to be told that Nell was going away? Or worse still that she was about to be married to some chinless county type? Perhaps my heart had allowed me to be carried aloft on a wave of blind optimism or wishful thinking; that our various meetings, particularly since last Christmas, had witnessed our growing more fond of each other. Was I wrong?

"Come in, Jack," said that vision of beauty, dressed today in a pale red dress. "Please don't look so worried. Incidentally, my father was to be here but had to go to London urgently. Something to do with those horrid events in Hindustan. Do sit down."

When I was a boy, the local vicar – the Reverend Trump – liked to catch butterflies and pin them to a board. He had dozens of them, all colours and all sizes, but for what use, reason or purpose, I could not really say. I was now beginning to feel like one of those trapped specimens. I found it very difficult not to fidget.

Nell, in the moment it had taken for me to recall that childhood memory, had moved from a chair opposite to sit at my left-hand side and was carefully brushing her dress back into its correct shape. That done, she gave every appearance of being very calm and determined as she looked across at the three ladies. Her face radiated a kind of confidence even defiance that I had not witnessed before.

Nell's mother, Lady Dorothea, turned her gaze on me.

"Young man, you have much to commend you and have treated us and Lady Eleanor with concern, respect and humility."

Yet more praise, I thought. *This could turn my head. There must be a 'but' coming very soon. If praise was gold I would be a very rich man by now.*

She continued: "A brave, honest and loyal soldier. A kinsman of dear James and soon, we hear, perhaps likely to inherit a portion of the Durford Estate. Do you plan on marriage?"

Let me rush headlong at the enemy and risk shot and shell. These I had faced and survived, but now I began to flounder. The upper classes did not flinch from direct questions. But what did she mean? When she said, 'marry' who did she mean?

I decided to try and play for time, to put my thoughts into some kind of order so I could be better prepared for what I feared was about to follow. Finally, I replied.

"I have been seven years a soldier and for most of that time overseas," I said. "There has been little time for marriage. Choice has been limited, not least by geography."

Feeling I had little to lose, I added – a little defiantly as that matched the look I could see on Nell's face: "One I should be honoured, if unworthy, to marry is unavailable."

Then, as I looked back in Nell's direction I was distracted by the strangest of thoughts, but perhaps hoping to deflect the kind of reply that would mean my hopes for Nell would be destroyed. *How on earth do ladies manage to sit in those dresses with their hoops and who knows what else? From women of much lower rank, I was fairly familiar on what went on around the area from the waist to the lower limbs – I had, after all, been a soldier for those years away from real or hoped-for home comforts in many places across several continents.* I jerked my thoughts back from those ungracious and (considering the present company) distasteful musings to considering the more immediate and worthy ones.

I glanced again rather furtively at Nell, who continued to smile sweetly. It was just as well that she was unaware of my darker reflections.

"Is this unavailable lady known to us?" persisted my interrogator.

My face was tanned to quite a dark shade after almost constant exposure to the elements. First in South Africa, then the Crimea and more recently skirmishing across the gentle, rolling hills of Hampshire. I could, however, feel my face and the back of my neck warming as I stammered to try and find the right answer.

On each occasion that I had spent time with Nell I had tried to observe the correct etiquette. Respect, honour and barely touching seemed to be the formal way of courtship, though my heart wanted to lay her bare and give myself to her and she to me completely. Best not admit this to her mother and certainly not to her aged, maiden aunts.

We had, as I thought back over previous months, enjoyed each other's company and Nell certainly seemed to be at ease with me. Surely this had not gone unnoticed by others?

But what if they thought I was referring to Mary,

Nell's maid? After all, she was from the same village as me, Lower Durford.

Nell must have been sensing some of my uncertainty and discomfort and mercifully broke in:

"Jack, I have told them all how we have grown fond of each other in recent months. I shall never forget James and neither shall you, but now is the time to move on."

"But," I began, "you are still the daughter of this house. What really am I?"

I was now facing her and spoke directly to her, oblivious of everything and everyone else in the room. "From that first meeting last summer I think I have been in love with you. There, I have said it, Nell, but how can I expect you to adjust to my level? It would surely not be fair to you. What would society think?"

She fixed me with those bright eyes.

"In one of his last letters, James wrote that you were a gentleman in every way that is important. He always believed that you would move with ease into becoming an officer, a view endorsed by Robert Axelby. But you do not have to prove yourself by following such a course of action. In every respect you are a gentleman."

I sat back on my chair more than a little perplexed by the openness of her confession. Then, on an impulse I took her right hand in mine and – still continuing to ignore the others in the room – repeated my earlier declaration of love. I stood up again.

"When I first saw you in your blue dress at this very table I fell in love with you," I said. "But I thought and still think that you are beyond my reach and that I am ever unworthy to step into the shoes of another, better man."

I surprised myself by this boldness and retreated to the warmth of the chair.

Lady Dorothea's eyes drilled into me again, but she looked neither surprised nor upset. Her two companions stared as though they were startled deer in the forest when cornered by huntsmen. Then all three of them nodded their heads in unison.

Nell broke the silence.

"You would not be stepping into his shoes. You would, in your own words, be there on your own merits. I have said before how very fond of you he was and wrote of you as an equal. You have no need to prove yourself as a man or gentleman. Those attributes that James considered you had –you've proved true through your own efforts. Remember, Jack, he had written and said I might see a handsome man in rifle green at my door. That act must have taken some courage also. You must have thought long and hard about the reception that could greet you. As for us," she said gently, indicating with her left hand towards herself and then me, "I sincerely believe he would have wished this to happen. Jack, I love ..." she began and then turned towards her mother. "... Mama, you know I love this man. Jack, you are not a substitute for our very dear James. Together, we shall always keep a little of him in our hearts. I have thought long and hard about this and, dear Jack, I give you my heart."

Having watched the preceding few minutes in rapt silence, Nell's mother at last spoke.

"Nell did observe a suitable period of mourning – a little longer than required, but James was special. We have also been aware of her growing fondness for you but as she is of age thought it best not to interfere. She has a will of her own and is free to choose her own path, though while under our roof she observes behaviour as befits her station."

I thought these to be revealing observations. Yes, she was clearly strong-willed but a woman that society expected to behave appropriately. Which, if I thought too deeply about it, would not include me. Reading Charlotte Bronte might be a lot easier than changing attitudes to how women are expected to behave. Some writers even speak of votes for women. *That will be the day* I had thought. We live in a world of the rich and powerful; a world controlled by rich and powerful men!

"We freely admit that your presence during those first few months was of some concern to us, said Lady Dorothea. "Before your arrival we anticipated a coarse, country-bred soldier hardened by war but tempered a little by having served with James. What we saw as the weeks passed was an earnest, open young man who, it seems, was prepared to sacrifice his own life in order to save that of his officer."

I fidgeted in my seat, wondering where this speech was heading.

"However," she continued, "these are still unusual circumstances. Lady Durford has informed me of her suggestion that you might serve another year. We feel that you should complete your present business with the regiment. I believe you may be bound for India. There you may see Edward Fortune, Lord John's eldest son and indeed, perhaps even Sir William there too. I understand them to be in Lucknow, Cawnpore or some such place. This time will allow us all the opportunity to adjust to the circumstances in which we all now find ourselves. Of course, we do realise this may place you in danger. If though, after that year, you both feel the same then you should go ahead with your plans with the blessing of this House. You may kiss me, John Finch,"

This must all have been extremely difficult for Lady Dorothea to say because it went against her upbringing, her station in society and almost everything else that her birthright had bestowed. I am rarely lost for words nor find my mind and body are sent reeling, but I had fallen back again in my seat as though punched. What a soul-baring revelation this had been. These pronouncements were not only alien but almost unnerving. From that moment of cautiously entering the room anticipating bad news, I had seen an almost complete reversal of the established order. The aristocracy had always – or so I had believed – kept marriage restricted to its own kind and kept its feelings hidden. The reticence about airing feelings in public was based since time immemorial on preserving and keeping what they had to themselves and of keeping the rest of the population – the poor – at arm's length.

Still a little stunned (even Rifle Brigade training does not allow for this) I stood slowly up, gravely bowed at the three ladies in front of me and leaning carefully forward kissed Lady Dorothea on the cheek that was raised slightly for that courtesy. For good measure I kissed the two maiden ladies as well.

I returned to my place endeavouring to control the excitement coursing through my body.

"Shall we take some refreshment?" asked Nell, breaking the silence that had fallen like a heavy curtain on the five of us. "I'll send for Mary. No I cannot, for she is indisposed today."

Then she pressed the bell by the carved oak fire surround and within a few seconds a servant duly appeared.

"Lemonade, I think, Corbin. We are all jolly warm," Lady Dorothea said.

The cool drink was very welcome. Tea, usually taken at this time of the day, would not have helped the 'fever' of desire still inflaming the whole of my body. It also marked that time when I must think of going.

A further fifteen minutes passed before I rose to leave. I stood, bowed and bid the three ladies goodbye. Nell linked her arm through mine and we walked out in the direction of the front door.

I wanted to embrace Nell now, to smother her with kisses and more, but this was hardly the time and place for such deeds. Had Lady Dorothea been able to see into my mind then she might at that moment have reconsidered her view of me and replaced it instead with the thought of me as just a coarse soldier and issued orders for the servants to hide the spoons and lock away the housemaids!

I turned towards Nell, contenting myself with a brushing of her lips, but she pulled me resolutely towards her and we kissed; a long lingering tingling of lips firmly on lips. I could feel the pressure of her breasts thrusting forward into my uniform and could only imagine the more intimate things to come. I wondered if she could feel me rising to the occasion through the layers of material that separated us now, but hopefully one day not too far in the future would not be there to keep nature at bay.

The ringing of the doorbell interrupted those glorious moments.

The butler, having acquired a temporary cough, appeared.

"I'm sorry, milady. It is Mr Finch's driver. He called at the servants' hall but we thought it more appropriate for Mr Finch to leave by the front door."

Those three or so hours had passed very quickly. Slowly, very reluctantly, I said a fond farewell to Nell. I reached the steps and descended with little enthusiasm, though rather buoyed by recent revelations and the progress made during my time at Broughton House.

Off we set to Lower Durford with the vehicle's wheels squeezing pebbles and small stones from its course back down the drive as we sped away. My blood was coursing through my body. so I had instructed the driver to go quickly in an effort to cool me down.

I ordered him to go to the river first. Reaching my favourite part of it I jumped down and for perhaps an hour or so remained just thinking and staring into the cool, clear waters; lost helplessly, blissfully in so many wonderful thoughts. Then, attempting to regain my usual soldierly composure, I stepped back into the gig. The driver – who had all this time been leaning forward in a customary 'waiting' pose, whip and reins in hand – recovered and we continued towards the village. He stopped a few paces from the path leading to the front door of the cottage. I instructed the driver to wait, my intention being to quickly relay some of the events at the House to my parents. Once this was done I would journey back to Winchester, hoping by then to have regained all my calmness.

Still flushed with excitement and the urgent need to pass on my good fortune to my parents, I bounded up the path and pushed the door open wide until its hinges protested. Instead of the usual welcome of my mother grabbing and hugging me and saying, as she did without fail, how fine I looked in my uniform and my father standing but never quite sure what to say or do with his hands, I fell upon a different scene.

There was my mother certainly, seated at the table but sobbing and wringing her hands in some distress.

Before I could ask what the source of her obvious unhappiness was she looked up in my direction and spoke.

"Oh, Jack what have you done?"

Puzzled and not a little deflated I moved to her side, grabbed another chair and sat down. I pulled her hands away from her tear-stained face and attempted to question her about the reason for her distress and whatever my part in it was supposed to be.

"What is it? What do you think I have done? All that I can think is that it is something to do with Broughton House, but everything was calm there when I left a few hours ago. So what is it that has left you in these straits? I had such good news of Eleanor and of me. Why are you not happy for me? Tell me what is it that upsets you?"

"Mary Smith was here. She left just before you arrived. Perhaps to miss seeing you," she said, sobbing. "What she did say was that she is four months gone. She blames you, Jack. You're responsible."

"How? I began to ask, stupidly. "When? I have barely seen her since my return from the Crimea. My duties keep me busy and when I have been to the House I have been in Eleanor's company and never alone with Mary."

That wonderful picture of the two of us, Nell at my side for life and then eternity was fast disappearing. Like an artist's canvas violently having its paints scraped furiously away was how that idyllic scene was fast being erased from my mind's eye. Of the home constructed with the bricks and mortar of love, there remained just discarded materials strewn across my once happy landscape. All that I could see now was Nell standing at the gate sobbing and alone. Her world that had first crumbled on hearing James was not returning, then re-built, was once again in ruins – but not as a result of any action I had taken or had ever wanted to take. Mary was from my village, but there was nothing else!

This conversation with my mother was not the one I had been expecting. I felt demoralised, empty, betrayed and bereft.

My mother continued the sad and totally inaccurate assault on my honour. Her cheeks were now bright red, her nose snotty and eyes still red and wet with tears. Her voice came in short, breathless bursts.

"Says she met you in a hired room. At the Swan Hotel in Winchester. Around the end of February. Where you took advantage of her. With your rough soldier's ways."

At this I nearly exploded and spluttered, spittle going everywhere including into my mother's face.

"That's impossible. Ridiculous. I don't think I have actually ever touched her. Well perhaps when she was a small child in the village and I picked her up when she had fallen over. And," I said, stressing the word, "And I don't think, I *know* I haven't touched her during my visits to see Lady Eleanor. Even when we have shared a carriage I have not even sat beside her. I have certainly never touched her in the way you think. At Broughton House I am mostly in the company of others and she is kept in the background. Has she actually been to the Swan Hotel? If so, was it with a soldier? If she was ever there, she is acting out of spite."

Then a sudden, horrible thought began to haunt me. Mary had been pronounced 'indisposed' while I had been there this very afternoon. Hours had since passed. Suppose this tale was now spreading below stairs and even beyond the House? Ladies' maids are also very close to their mistresses. She may have already been attempting to convince Nell that the story was true. To make this even worse there would be many others – not least in my village – ready to believe any tale and even help spread the poison.

I needed to take swift action and try and kill the rumours before they were able to take hold. Apart from Nell, what would her mother and the two aunts be thinking? Before long, Durford Hall would hear and before the week was out most of the rest of the county. Folk would be pointing me out, not because of my striking uniform but as the low deflowerer of a lady's maid.

"Sorry, ma, I must go. I'll try and get to see you again before we leave for India but I must resolve this mess first."

I stood up. Bent forward and cupping her sad face in my hands, I kissed the top of her head and then moved quickly to the door. I turned.

"Mary's story is just not true. She is lying. I swear to you that I have not been with her. The woman I love and want is Nell."

Then I left the cottage.

❖

I ordered the gig to set off at a furious pace. The driver asked no questions. Perhaps the determined set of my jaw convinced him of the need to remain silent.

In a shorter time than usual we reached those formidable gates to Broughton House. I jumped down and rattled the padlock and chain.

Out from his refuge rolled the gatekeeper.

"Sorry, Sergeant-Major. The family's not at home and I am to admit no one."

With that he checked to see that not only the padlock on the large gate was secure but the one was also locked on the side gate too. That done he turned and with great haste returned to the safe haven of his grey dwelling.

I had no way of telling if they were at home or not. All I could do was to just stand looking wistfully through the painted ironwork and on down the long drive to the house beyond. What should I do? What could I do? A first thought, soon dismissed, was to climb the wall and run towards the house and plead my case. But landowners, no matter who they are, tend not to welcome trespassers. If their gamekeepers believed the rumour (and why shouldn't they?) shots could be fired. I reasoned that the only way I could achieve some sort of response was to return to barracks and there, settle to writing a note to Nell. I could make my case that any accusations against me were totally false and that me fathering Mary's child was a complete lie.

It was evening, around 8.30 pm, before I was able to set to work and write. I was still not completely calm, but recovered enough to do two letters. The first was to my parents, again stating that Mary's tale was untrue. My mother could read a little; I had taught her and as long as I kept it fairly simple then she would cope well enough.

I pictured them both, sitting in silence at the kitchen table wondering just what to believe. At the back of their minds must be the thought that I was, after all, Sir William's son. He was well-known as an impregnator of housemaids and governesses. Was I following in his footsteps? There was little more that I could do at the moment other than assure them I was innocent of Mary's accusations.

The second proved to be more difficult. In an

afternoon I had gone from potential husband to blackguard. How to persuade Nell to even read the contents of my letter? Seizing the pen I stabbed it into the inkwell and set resolutely to work. In a few minutes and over half a page, I had poured out my heart. I made it perfectly clear how I felt about her, how jealous folk might be blackening my name as each hour passed and how Mary's story and all that accompanied it was a lie. I added that if I survived the coming fight (because stories in the news made war seem the more likely outcome in India) then I would return and swear my undying devotion to her and hope that she would accept the word of that fine gentleman that James Fortune had said I was.

Over the two weeks that followed I sent two more notes similar in content, but received no reply.

As I lay on my bed in my quarters in the barracks at Winchester, I attempted to put my own feelings to one side. I tried to see matters from Nell's point of view. Up to a few years ago her future had been mapped out: engagement then marriage to James, with life continuing much as it had begun – sheltered and secure. That had all changed with the intervention of fate in the form of Russian bullets and James' death. Then I had made an appearance and been praised by all and sundry, until fate once more intervened with the rumours about Mary. That sort of behaviour – deflowering young women from the village – would be expected from me, given my background. If only I could see Nell and explain that the rumours were just not true, but I realised that was unlikely to happen. That left me with only one course of action: I must see Major Axelby and tell him my side of the story. He was a fair man and surely would give me a hearing. I was also only too aware that time was running out – India was looming.

The following morning I knocked at Major Axelby's office door.

"Come in," said a familiar voice.

I marched in, saluted and waited.

"What is it, Sergeant-Major? Have you heard the rumours too?"

"Yes, sir but there is no truth in them. I give you my word."

"I'm afraid there is," he said. Then he looked up, carefully studying my face and the concerned expression I was wearing. He realised we seemed to be at cross-purposes.

"Sit down, Jack. You look upset. What on earth is the matter? You had better start at the beginning."

"Sir, you will know that since calling on Lady Eleanor last year to fulfil an obligation I felt I owed Captain Fortune, we have been growing rather fond of each other. I know only too well that there is a gulf between us, but that was proving to be less of a problem with the passage of time."

"Yes, Jack. You'll remember that little concert before Christmas and the New Year Ball? Georgie made a point of saying that you could not keep your eyes off each other. Plain as the nose on your face was how she put it. When you and Nell were dancing The Galop she went on to say that she thought you two were made for each other. Even said your dancing was good too!" He grinned then added, "but you have not come here to discuss your cutlery or dancing skills have you? How do you think I can help?"

"Well, sir, I've been accused, wrongly accused, by Lady Eleanor's maid Mary. She claims to be with child by me. I swear to you on everything that I hold dear that I am innocent. I have barely been near her and not touched, kissed and certainly not lain with her. Now I am unable to get past the gatekeeper to visit the house. I was refused entry. I have written several letters to Nell and have begged to see her. Is there any way you could help me, sir? I do not wish to cause you any embarrassment, as they are friends of yours, but I am left with no other course of action other than to ask. I am not used to begging or asking favours, but know you to be a fair man."

"I'll see what I can do. In all the time I have known

you I don't remember too many occasions when you have asked for anything. Only once, as I recall, when we arrived back at Portsmouth from the Crimea. There are two or three things in your favour: you are a loyal member of the Rifle Brigade, the holder of the Victoria Cross and you helped me out of a tight spot or two around Sevastopol. Incidentally, don't blame the Broughtons. Good types, but a bit on the old-fashioned side. You finding your way into Nell's heart was probably a bit of a shock at first. Other than the girl making that accusation, blame Sir William. Not only did he father you at Durford Hall but managed to do the same to quite a few others elsewhere. Big scandal. Lots of rumours, accusations and all that sort of thing were flying about then, so I was told. Lots of chaps in the big houses seem to think the maids are fair game to see if the equipment works. Other sons get taken by their fathers to certain establishments around Pall Mall in London. That could be risky, though. Easier, cheaper too I imagine, under your own roof. Difficult for the maid to refuse her master's son!"

Although my present concerns weighed me down, the mood had suddenly turned a little lighter. He then added with a smile and a wink: "Course Jack, nothing at all to do with me, such goings on. Now, getting back to your troubles. You must also remember that dear old Dorothea, Lady B, is a little protective towards her eldest gal. Won't want bad talk or anything upsetting Nell. She is a modern woman but still lives quite a sheltered life. And, not to put too fine a point on it, she jumped to the not unreasonable conclusion that you're following in your father's footsteps. That fathering children, whether by governesses or housemaids, runs through Sir William's veins and elsewhere and so it may have appeared to them, through you as well. Not very fair but when has life been fair? You certainly ought to know that, bearing in mind your start in life and what happened in the Crimea. Too many good men, it seems to me, died there for very little."

"Thank you, sir," I replied. The more he spoke, the more the dark mood that had been encircling my head since Mary's accusation began to lighten.

"Think nothing of it. We riflemen stick together."

I stood, saluted, turned and left the office, wondering how he would set about such a task. All I could do was hope and wait.

Orders were received that we were to travel by train to Aldershot in just a few days time, and there we would rejoin the rest of the battalion before taking ship to India. Things were moving on apace.

As acting commanding officer at Winchester, Major Axelby had been informed by telegraph that the 2nd Battalion would be leaving their Dublin barracks soon; also bound for India, in three ships.

This news only added to my despair, but I was still enough of a soldier to continue carrying out normal duties.

Rather than just allowing the men to sit around idly waiting for the day of our departure to Aldershot and beyond, I decided to employ them on the rifle range.

We set the targets at 100 yards. The men were told to report to the butts in their companies; one at 9.00am and the second at 3.00pm.

Each man was ordered to fire two shots in less than a minute, then fix swords and charge down to the butts and check how they had done. There were twenty-five round targets and with five men firing at each target, they should be peppered with shot. Missing was not a consideration. Sergeant Nelson sat on a chair with a telescope mounted on a tripod. He was assisted by three corporals with similar equipment. They were to keep a sharp lookout on the efforts below and to call out 'miss' in the unlikely event of seeing a puff of sand from above, below or to the sides of each target.

I ordered the men to keep firing their two shots then charge to the butts, but after the fourth firing to rush down, remove their tunics and place them either side of the targets; and then charge back to their firing positions, reload and fire two more shots before rushing back down to retrieve their tunics, put them on and return to the start line.

As they settled to their tenth set of shots, a rifleman from the second company rushed up to me and saluted.

"Major Axelby's compliments, sir. You are to drop everything and report immediately to his office. His very words, sir, 'drop everything' and go at once."

"Right," I said and called across to Nelson. "Get them to repeat it again and make it a round dozen and then down to the butts and back, and check the last pair of shots carefully. Oh, and send my tunic and rifle back to my billet in case I am not back. I may not return until this afternoon."

The idea behind my apparently strange tactics was to get the men used to firing when they were very warm. We had done some skirmishing around the county but not every day was as hot as this one and I wanted them to have a taste of the sort of heat to expect in India. I realised it would not be quite the same, but at least it kept the men busy and certainly warmed them up and gave them some extra practice in quick shooting.

As I marched in some haste to Major Axelby's office I puzzled over what it could be. Perhaps a change of orders? At least the time at the butts had kept my mind on army matters and not affairs of the heart. Maybe I had only arranged the whole thing to keep *me* busy and not just the men! I would be doing the same with the other company in the afternoon. Many of our men had yet to face an enemy, let alone fire a shot in anger. The one drawback of the butts is that they do not move or fire back. As I neared the Major's office I mused that soldiers are an odd lot. They usually moan about going, can't wait to get in the thick of it, complain while they are there and miss it when they get home.

A few days before, one of the newer men – keen to just get on with it – had asked what India was like.

"I've not been there," I told him, "but I imagine it to be uncomfortably hot. Temperatures there during the summer can be well over 100 degrees. Not helped by the humidity. Uniform will get hot and feel damp. A bit chilly at night in some parts of that country. They get monsoons. Very heavy rain, just like home. Hope you like snakes, elephants and tigers. A few of them too. Probably a bit like South Africa and like it was in the Crimea during September '54," I added as I recalled the hot march towards the River Alma and the wet and freezing conditions we also experienced during the Russian winter on the heights above Sevastopol. I then said to him: "We survived that. We'll do the same in India."

I reached Major Axelby's office that was situated inside the main barracks and to the left of the Officers' Mess. I mopped my brow and tried to look as smart as I could in my sweat-stained collarless shirt, regretting that, as always, I would not ask any rifleman to do anything that I would not do: I had run with them, fired my rifle then removed my tunic, just as the men of the company had done.

I knocked sharply at the door. No response. If it was that urgent, where was he? I knocked again but receiving no reply stepped inside; there was still no sign of life or any clue as to where he had gone. I sat down stiffly at a chair in front of his desk, which had been covered with souvenirs of the Crimea and photographs of his wife and children, as well as a rather good painting of his home and part of the estate. Now just a lone photograph remained of his wife Georgia and their three children. But where was this son of an earl?

There was a knocking at the door and I briefly wondered why he was knocking at his own office? *Wake up, Finch,* I thought.

"Come in," I growled impatiently, not a little annoyed at being called away from the butts. I was also feeling hot and bothered, out of uniform and thinking I would be better off just returning to the shooting.

In walked Corporal Williams grinning from ear to ear. This was a shock. Usually if Williams attempted to smile it was more likely to end up as a frown. Such a thing was rare enough, but to see him with his face wreathed in smiles was something I had not seen during the seven years' army service I had known him. It was almost too much to bear along with my current frustrations.

"Beg pardon, Mr Finch, sir," with an overwhelmingly ingratiating tone that was so unlike him. His usual talk was gloomy and begrudging. I felt my skin crawling. "Someone to see you."

"Don't just stand there grinning stupidly, man – send him in."

My words seemed to have an even worse effect on him. He started chortling and then still grinning like a half-wit moved back and nodded his head vigorously towards whoever it was outside waiting to see me. By now his head had disappeared beyond the doorframe and I gave up trying to follow his antics. For a moment I thought to get up and just box his ears, but I turned back in my chair to face across the Major's desk once more. Williams moved forward and to his left and very carefully placed my tunic on the back of another chair several paces from the door.

"Rifle and sword back in your quarters, sir," he added, still with that note of ingratiation but tempered with cheerfulness. Whatever his reasons, he seemed to be really enjoying this whole episode.

His moving into the room had allowed the visitor to enter also. I could hear his movement but could not see him, as Williams was shielding him with his own stocky frame. Williams' actions were so out of character. I had watched his movements as he had dealt with my tunic and now I sat looking at him as he beamed back at me with the most radiant of smiles as he lightly brushed my uniform.

I had expected the visitor to announce himself, but perhaps he too had been overwhelmed by Williams' actions. All I could hope was that the visitor was not a very senior officer on some official business, for as far as I was concerned I was improperly dressed and not an example to the men.

Best turn and face up to the visitor and get it over with, I thought. I was about to rise and greet them when a small gloved hand touched my shoulder.

Then I received the happiest shock of my life, for there standing just a half pace away was Nell.

I had barely managed to rise to my feet when she flung her arms around me.

"I have been so foolish and horrid to you. Are you able to forgive such a thoughtless woman?"

Williams remained in the room, evidently still enjoying the whole spectacle, not least in seeing me in a compromising situation. He stood, slightly bow-legged, with his arms at his sides. Without moving them he swivelled his hands through 90 degrees and then raised both thumbs in my direction. A miserable moaning, supposedly humourless, bastard as well as a good soldier he might be – but he was I think just very pleased for me.

I was embracing Nell, my chin resting on her little bonnet which was perched on a low bun just below the nape of her neck. Little ringlets dropped down, covering her exquisitely shaped ears and framing that beautiful face.

"Thanks," I muttered gratefully to Williams and then followed it with a silently mouthed 'get out' as I glanced meaningfully at the door.

Holding his right arm somewhere between a salute and a wave and singing happily to himself he left.

No doubt before long I would be the talk of the whole barracks and beyond, but I didn't care.

As the door closed behind him I said weakly to Nell:

"There's nothing to forgive. It was just a sad, foolish girl, jealous of you and me and probably left to fend for herself. Even though it could have cost me everything, I bear Mary no ill-will. I hope she'll be alright."

"Don't worry, darling Jack. But isn't that just like you? To be concerned about an unfortunate girl. We shall take care of her."

"Well, I can imagine what life could be like for a girl in such straits and don't forget I know what her early life was like."

I sat her down and knelt in front of her, taking her hands in mine. Then with difficulty I began to tell her that orders had been received; that we were about to leave and join the rest of the battalion before embarking for India. I then said that was why I thought I had been sent for, to hear confirmation of our departure date from Major Axelby.

"No," she said. "I asked my father to arrange this

meeting. He and Robert Axelby are old friends. He suddenly appeared a little while ago and spoke to mama and papa. Then he asked to see me with them. Would you believe that he was prepared to swear to it that you had absolutely nothing to do with Mary's condition? If he could have so much faith in you, why couldn't I? This made me feel ashamed, that I could think that of you and not even give you a chance to speak. Please, Jack, say you forgive me once more. I have felt so wretched, but how must you have felt? Wrongly accused! My mother sent for Mary and the truth came out in floods of tears. She begged my forgiveness and we both went to your parents' cottage to lay the truth before them. I must just say, they are a little crestfallen for not believing you and if you do have time perhaps you could spare them a brief visit just to give the poor dears a chance to say they are sorry too. I did say you would not really be cross at them and I think they are as embarrassed as my parents are regarding the whole affair. My parents have the additional burden of having shut the gates in your face. But I am the one most at fault, my darling, for I should have stood up to them and at least allowed you up to the house."

"No," I said, kissing her cheek. "Let's not talk again about this sad episode. I will try and get back to the village. We haven't much time, Nell but I intend following your mother's wishes anyway. I did write this in one of my notes. I'll wait for a year and return. Will you wait? I don't know what will happen in India. It may be all well-and-truly over by the time we get there, or it may just drag on and on like the Crimea. And of course I must face up to the possibility of not returning if we do have to fight."

As I spoke these words, a hand – glove removed – touched my lips.

"Hush, Jack. Please don't even think that. We lost James – I couldn't bear to lose you. I think my heart would break. Promise that you will return to me, safe and well. And of course I'll wait."

She half rose from her chair and kissed me.

"I must, I fear, get you back to the house," I said, though with no desire at all to carry it out.

I was even more disheartened and disappointed when

she said her brougham was waiting in attendance near the barracks' gate.

We kissed again. I could feel her body even underneath that steel-hooped crinoline. I could feel it quivering as I too was caught in a moment of not yet fulfilled ecstasy. Through my cotton shirt I could feel the warmth of her breasts and even the firmness of erect nipples almost bursting from the lightest of corsets and on into my ribs. A wave of desire was spreading from my loins to my fingertips as I longed for the time and opportunity to caress and explore those hidden mounds, folds and curves.

Reluctantly, we both knew that we had to part. Perhaps when later on I looked back to this moment it would be just as well that we were not able to spend more time with just the two of us; blood so heated in the Major's office and Nell unchaperoned. Mary's example was not the course either of us would want to follow! The thought of those hot moments, though, would sustain me through those long, hot Indian days and nights.

She stepped back and removed the gold locket she always wore at her neck. She opened it. Inside was the tiniest of pictures of her.

"Take this and think of me, my love."

I have no words to adequately describe the love and anguish I was experiencing as we walked towards her carriage arm in arm and oblivious of others we may have passed on the way there.

I said that I had nothing to give her in return but she sweetly said:

"Just come back to me, Jack, safe and well."

As we reached the steps of the brougham the coachman half turned and I was heartened to see him smiling at me in acknowledgment.

Nell looked at me, moved forward and kissed me before stepping into the carriage trying to hide the tears she was attempting to brush away. Then she was off!

I followed the progress of the brougham down the hill and out of sight, then in some despair turned back into the barracks. It would be difficult to settle to any task, let alone returning to the butts for the afternoon's shooting.

"Business finished, Jack?" asked Major Axelby in a mild tone and with a look of innocence on his face.

How could I ever thank this officer for what he had managed to do? Thanks to him, at least some of my expectations could still be realised.

"Yes, sir. At least for the time being," I replied, adding with a rueful smile, "thank you very much, sir from both of us. As for me, I shall forever be in your debt."

"No, think nothing of it. As I said to you when you came to see me, we riflemen stick together. Ah, don't worry about the butts. Nelson's taken over. You're probably the talk of the barracks at the moment. Never lasts long. The other big event is Williams who is still smiling. Never thought I'd live to see that."

Chapter Three

The day for our departure to Aldershot finally arrived. Some kit had already been sent on ahead, carried by train and then by wagon.

At early morning parade, final orders for leaving were issued. Our train would leave the station at seventeen minutes past two o'clock that afternoon. All riflemen would carry an Enfield and a sword suspended as usual on a two-inch wide belt fastened by a small clasp, with a pouch folded into his belt with a few rounds of ammunition. Then there was a haversack for a cooking pot and food (today that would be just bread and dried meat), a water canteen, a metal pouch with an additional 60 rounds, a tin box for the storage of up to 100 percussion caps and a canvas knapsack with mess tins. Strapped to its top was a blanket and greatcoat. We were ready for anything.

Four buglers were to sound the quick-step march 'Ninety-five', a favourite of my old 1st Battalion in the Cape, which would lead us to the station. They were to be followed by officers of both companies and then the riflemen, then non-commissioned officers, with me bringing up the rear. Then it was onto the train to Aldershot and before long we would be boarding ships for India.

At 11.30am Major Axelby sent for me just as I was leaving the battalion office where I had left some letters for collection and forwarding.

One was addressed to my parents, another to the Fortunes at Durfold Hall, the third to Broughton House and most importantly, the last of my quartet of correspondence, to my beautiful lady, Nell. To the Fortunes and Broughtons I offered my sincere thanks for the kind things they had said and for allowing me into their homes under difficult circumstances. I signed off by expressing my earnest hope that I would carry out my soldier's duty. For Lord John I included a post scriptum that I hoped I might see his son, Edward and perhaps even his brother, William. I made no mention of recent misunderstandings to either household. Even though I had lately, if very briefly, visited my parents to assure them not to think anymore about believing Mary rather than me I wrote confirming as much and added that no matter what happened in the future they were and would always remain very close to my heart.

My letter to Nell was particularly difficult to write. It was not easy baring my soul at any time, but how could mere sentences describe my love and devotion? It was hard trying to make sure I wrote what I felt: so difficult to commit to paper those tender feelings. Realising that precious minutes were ticking by, I decided I had done as much as I could to convey how I felt. I was also compelled to write that I could meet my end in some dusty, forgotten corner of a remote British Indian possession. I had been a soldier long enough – and had seen more than my fair share of men killed and wounded – not to accept that death was the only reward that so many men received. I added that I would try not to take any unnecessary risks, but did not want to bring shame on those I loved and so would endeavour to carry out my duty. In my final sentence I assured her of my love and that no matter where I served in India she would be constantly in my thoughts and that I would count the days until my return.

"Ah, there you are, Jack!" exclaimed the Major. "Looks like something jolly important for you." He proffered a large, buff-coloured envelope sealed with wax and impressed with a large coat of arms.

As I took the packet from him it crossed my mind that in no other regiment would an officer, let alone an earl's son, have taken so much trouble in helping me overcome that problem with Mary. Not only that, but here he was delivering this envelope to me with his own hand. Mr

Axelby was just such a fine, respected officer and gentleman. I had certainly more reason than most to admire, respect and be grateful to him.

The packet was addressed to 'Sergeant-Major, John Albert Fortune (also known as Finch)'.

Rather lamely I asked, "What is it, sir?" not fully reading or taking notice that 'Fortune' appeared before 'Finch'. I was not really used to receiving packets. I teased and turned the envelope in a bid to gain some clue as to its contents.

"Have a very strong feeling it might do you some good, old fellow," he said. "If you'd care to step into my office, you could open it away from prying eyes. Got a drop or two of rum left just in case".

I followed him into the office now cleared of all but military essentials. Even that lone photograph of his wife and family had gone: it would now be in a trunk delivered to Aldershot. Draped across the leather-topped surface of his desk was his officer's sword in its scabbard on a black leather belt as well as other belts, pouches and sabretache with its patent leather sling. In a holster was his Adams revolver, which in the Crimea he had favoured over James Fortune's Colt Navy model.

The envelope was expensive looking and well-sealed, but I finally managed to break the seal and pull out the carefully folded contents. These proved to be various documents. The top sheet of headed, expensive-looking paper describing a London based firm of solicitors was very neatly written but had a distinctive smell of gas and candlelight about it.

I regard myself as well-read, certainly in terms of books and in having a good command of the 'Queen's English'. Years of reading and an imaginative, questioning nature had helped make that possible. But by the time I was less than a third of the way down the page I was struggling to grasp the business of the letter. Many of the words posed as much of a problem as an unknown foreign language would have done.

"Can you make anything of this, sir?" I said waving the page at Major Axelby.

He glanced down at it while I turned to the other pages

hoping for some enlightenment, especially as to why they had been sent to me in the first place.

One of the other pages caught my attention. The writing on it was spidery as though the work of a shakier, more elderly hand. My eyes glanced down towards the bottom of the paper where there was a large signature, that of William James Fortune.

"Well," said Major Axelby, looking up, "it's very good news. This sheet confirms you to be the son of Sir William Fortune. It acknowledges and affirms your right to the name of Fortune. There is also his personal letter to you confirming what I have just said. I imagine that is the letter you are holding." With that he took the letter from me and quickly skimmed its contents.

"It's quite a touching missive. Hopes to see you one day and explain it all. Oh, and there's a 'thankyou' for trying to save James. It goes on to say something about Lord John having told him what a decent cove you must be. Good show. Old James would be as pleased as billy-o. My warmest congratulations to you, Sergeant-Major John Fortune."

There were a few other sheets, including one that required my signature to confirm the documents had been received. Major Axelby was pleased to sign as witness.

"It gets even better, Jack. These solicitors are holding Sir William's written oath for settling the portion of the estate bequeathed him by his father but assigned to the care of his brother, John while William is in India." Mr Axelby was clearly warming to his task. "Towards the bottom of the page, it is clear that Lord John has accepted you as Sir William's acknowledged son. He has also made some sort of provision for you in his will. In the event of Edward, his only surviving son, dying without issue, the estate would go to William who," the Major observed, "ain't no lively young pup and is far removed from that first flush of youth. He is also unmarried – so John is accepting you as his heir too.

He paused while I tried to take all this in.

"If you die without you and Nell producing a fresh brood of little Fortunes, then the Hall and the estate would be divided between some very junior members of the family." He sniffed extravagantly and added, "somehow I can't quite see Durford Hall without the whole place echoing to the sound of hoards of little Nells and Jacks swarming about."

While much of this had just left me rather dazed, his remarks about a brood of little Fortunes made me smile and reduce the enormity of it all.

From the look on his face I could tell that he was really pleased for me, but his mentoring was not over yet.

"Of course, when you marry Nell and her people pass away, the Broughton Estate – lock, stock and barrel – will go to her save for a few bequests, dowries I suppose we should call 'em, to her two as yet unmarried younger sisters. Bravo, Jack, you could have an estate that'll make mine look like a cottage garden."

His comments – amusing and certainly well meant – succeeded in lifting my spirits. He was also fulfilling one of the key roles expected of Rifle Brigade officers; that of supporting their men. Perhaps, in keeping with the moment, he had exaggerated a little, though James had once told me that his Wiltshire estate was huge.

I sat down heavily, shaken to the core and still unable to fully take everything in. It did, however, seem to bear out James Fortune's prediction of better things to come. There was one unfortunate obstacle in the way: I had to survive India and return, a thought that was also occurring to Major Axelby.

As we sat there, perhaps almost as stunned as each other, he gave voice to this concern.

"It's a pity all this and of course your happy reconciliation with Nell has come so close to our departure. This might all so easily change things."

"It has. It will, sir."

I then told him about my promise to Lady Broughton and an earlier one to Lady Durford, who I now realised was my aunt.

"Some might try and wriggle out of going to India. Who could really blame them? No one would blame you, Jack," said the Major, looking at me with grim sympathy.

"No, sir as I have said before, I am a rifleman deep down. Lady Eleanor would not want me to shirk it. Nor would I want to. It is a matter of honour, so it's off to India come what may."

As I said these words I swallowed hard, thinking quite dark thoughts. I could just give it all up so that we could be with each other, but could we both live with my staying behind while Major Axelby and many riflemen sailed east? It would be an act that would lose me the respect of those I loved and who loved me. India first – then, I sincerely hoped, back home to Nell.

"Make sure that you get back then, Jack," said the Major. "I can't tell you how pleased I am for you."

"Sir, may I ask if you knew anything about all this?"

"Not exactly. I suppose there was more than a hint of something in the wind affecting the Fortunes when I called at Broughton House to discuss your little problem. I was on my way home anyway, but wanted to make it look as though I was passing and calling in out of courtesy. I was also curious to see if Lord Broughton knew anything about our posting to India. He is after all, well connected. There was talk of things moving concerning William Fortune.

"You'll also recall Nell calling here."

I nodded.

"'Course you do," he said. "Well, I was brought into Lord B's plan for her to come to the barracks. If she could be at the gate by such a time I would ensure that a certain soldier would be in my office very soon after her arrival. I ordered Williams to stand by. Miserable he might be, but you two go back a long way and he can be trusted. His smiling was something I hadn't bargained on though! While these arrangements were being made, news came from London. Old Lord John confirmed he had spoken to the solicitors and documents were to follow concerning you. While he was in town Lord John added his own to the packet and here we are. The rest you know." He moved over to the desk.

"Now, if I were you, I'd get this note I've witnessed ready to send off and parcel the rest up." He indicated the other papers. "Enclose a little note to Nell and forward it to her for safe-keeping at the house while we're chasing around after misbehaving natives across the Indian countryside. Sit at the desk and write it now. I won't look over your shoulder," he said, smiling broadly.

He sat down and busied himself examining the Adams revolver while I did what he suggested. I then thanked him for all his support.

"Not at all, Jack. Glad to help. I've said it before, we in the Rifles stick together. I have to say, I always thought there was something different about you. There were times when I saw you and James standing together in the trenches in the Crimea that I could have taken you for brothers." He reached across for the bottle of rum. "But have that drink now. Think I'll join you."

I asked if he wouldn't mind satisfying my curiosity over something else.

"Go ahead," he invited.

"If you don't mind me asking then, sir, why did you join the army? You'll soon inherit the estate and you have – if I may take the liberty of saying so – a beautiful wife and fine children."

"Thanks. Georgie'd be tickled pink to hear that. No mystery really. Axelbys have been in the army since the year dot – or even before. But there we were at Marlborough's side at Blenheim, on the winning side in the Civil War. Come the Restoration one of my female ancestors was great pals with Charles II. We probably came across with the Normans, I shouldn't wonder. Bit of a tradition for the first-born male to do his bit. As long as there's a spare or two knocking about." At which point he laughed and added, "our only rule is that we finish up on the winning side."

He then poured two very generous measures of rum into two glasses in the middle of the desk and handed one of them to me. We raised them in silent salute and drained them in an instant.

I rose to leave, having managed to return the documents into their original envelope and tie it with a length of string that Major Axelby had produced from a desk drawer. I held the ends of the string taut as he half-drew his sword and cut-off the surplus; there was nothing else suitable for the task!

He reached across the desk and shook my hand.

"Good luck to you, Jack. Good luck to us all."

I left the office to arrange for the delivery of this life-changing packet to Broughton House and the posting of the witnessed receipt to the London solicitors.

Then it was back to my quarters and final preparations for departing the barracks, Winchester and very soon after, England.

The army camp at Aldershot, in the north-east of Hampshire, was a large area formerly of heathland divided by the Basingstoke Canal into the North Camp and South Camp. Why the army had chosen this setting near the small village of Aldershot, little bigger than my own village, was unclear at first. I asked Major Gregson who had already been at the camp several weeks awaiting the arrival of the rest of the battalion. He told me that Prince Albert felt the army needed a proper training ground and this was to be it. There was certainly room, but why here? I did wonder how the canal had survived the mania for railways: it did allow supplies to be brought up in lighters in very large quantities but only at a horse's walking pace. As a small boy I had heard stories of the railways to the detriment of canals but local farmers had said – perhaps in hope – that steam would not last. There were stories of cows not giving milk and hens not laying as the result of the approach of a hissing, steaming monster. Such stories had reached Lower Durford, but I could not recall any tales of a horse pulling a cargo along a canal contributing to such havoc among livestock.

As well as the canal, a new railway station and track had been built to receive large numbers of soldiers from all over the country to Aldershot; and then on to their port of embarkation.

As far as the eye could see, the once green countryside was covered in large bell tents, some of them serving as married quarters. A few small children were running about. There were also rows of wooden huts but even the ones for officers were quite basic. Perhaps one day the camp would become a more permanent site and bricks would replace wood to make a proper barracks.

I was not the only one whose mind drifted back to the heights above Sevastopol and the variety of tents – and later huts – that had covered parts of it. Another reminder of the Crimea was the installation of a bell in a tower overlooking the camp; this bell had originally hung in the Church of the Twelve Apostles in Sevastopol.

As we waited in Aldershot for final orders for embarkation, we spent quite a lot of time checking and cleaning equipment. This was an essential but tedious task for men poised to sail off and risk their lives. So it was a welcome relief when we were instructed to attend a special parade.

Although the camp was not the best place for him to do so, our colonel had decided to give the men some idea of why the battalion was being sent to India and what to expect there. This would have been quite unusual for an ordinary regiment of the line, where officers and men were clearly divided, but was typical of the Brigade. We were certainly no ordinary regiment.

The first thing the colonel told the parade was that intelligence of a general dissatisfaction among soldiers in India had started to reach England by telegraph and ship.

It seemed that some Indian troops – or sepoys as they were known – blamed the good old Enfield, or rather the animal grease on the cartridges it used. Smeared with this grease, the end of the cartridge is bitten off and powder from it is poured down the barrel. The grease helps the cartridge to be pushed down the barrel after the powder. This use of animal fat managed to offend not only Moslem sepoys, who consider pork to be unclean, but also upset Hindus, for whom the cow is sacred. Rumours had apparently spread around the East India Company's cantonments like wildfire. The incident that turned a minor local incident into a full-scale mutiny was down to the actions of a disgrunlted sepoy at the arsenal at Dum-Dum back in January. Before long, discontent was spreading across the Oudh Province.

Apparently many Hindus also believed that the Europeans were attempting to do away with their religion and replace it with Christianity. There was already growing unrest in some quarters because several of their customs had been swept away. One, we were told, was suttee – the practice where a widow is thrown live onto her dead husband's funeral pyre. Infanticide was another Indian custom that had also been outlawed in some provinces.

Other Western influences such as the railway and the telegraph were viewed with deep suspicion and resentment as they spread quickly across large areas of the sub-continent. Europeans looked upon such inventions as the natural march of progress but many Indians believed it undermined their way of life.

"It may have just been coincidence," the colonel continued, his voice straining to reach the back rows of rifleman, "but they appear to have chosen to mutiny around three or so months ago, when the heat is intense, funnelled by wind, and dust is everywhere. Many Europeans tend to be lethargic and go in search of shade, some preferring to leave their bungalows and spend the hotter days of summer in the hills.

"The mutiny also took place at a time when native Indian regiments outnumbered our people by around six to one, this down to our involvement in a certain action that involved numbers of you."

He went on to detail some of the things that had happened that might have proved to have been the last straw for the Indians.

Back in March at a place called Barrackpore, a sepoy of the 34th Native Infantry had been hanged for wounding a non-commissioned officer. This led to the spread of discontent during the weeks that followed and further disbandment of regiments of native units had been carried out as a precautionary measure to deprive them of a ready supply of weapons.

"By disbanding these regiments," the colonel continued, "it was hoped to nip the revolt in the bud."

I was standing at the back of the battalion and was therefore some distance from our commanding officer but I could see him starting to frown as he added:

"This didn't work and seems to be having the opposite effect."

He told us that, at a military station at Meerut, attempts

had been made to calm the situation. The sepoys had been told they could tear open the cartridges rather than bite them before forcing them down the rifle barrel. Many simply refused. A punishment parade was set up for the next morning, the 9th May. The sepoys were disarmed and the defaulters marched off to the cells.

"Cavalry troopers, sowars of the 3rd Light Cavalry, later attacked the gaol where the defaulters were being held," said the colonel. "All the prisoners were set free, not just the defaulters. Many were men of bad character or 'badmash' as they are known locally. These criminals, having nothing to lose and happy to vent their anger on any Europeans, joined in with the excesses that followed. A large mob was being encouraged by the Indians of the town to attack the bungalows and all the property in the European parts. Men, women and children were slaughtered in their hundreds. Then Delhi was attacked and more outbreaks followed in many of the military stations of the East India Company across central India.

"At Cawnpore a fellow called Nana Sahib, trusted by our people, turned on them and lay siege to the town, pouring shot and shell on the Europeans and loyal troops who had remained there. A truce was agreed but the mutineers broke their word and most of the defenders, although promised safe passage, were butchered. Many of the bodies of the women and children were thrown down a well."

I exchanged glances with the men standing to either side of me: this sounded a much more dangerous situation than we had thought we were being sent to deal with.

The colonel went on to describe the situation in much of the rest of the province of Oudh and why many of the sepoys there had mutinied. In Oudh, he told us, Indian princes had been deposed by the Company who had taken over the running of the province, a move whose outcome could surely have only been to upset the people even more. Most disgruntled of all were those local men recruited to serve the British who now found themselves posted hundreds of miles away from their homes. Earlier agreements to keep recruits locally were being ignored.

Soldiers in Lucknow, the capital of Oudh, flatly

refused to accept the cartridges and discontent continued to spread across other provinces. At Lucknow, Brigadier Lawrence had seemed to have matters under control, but the city was soon under siege, then relieved and besieged again. The colonel said that, according to the latest reports received by telegraph, the situation continues to this day.

"Our task is to land at Calcutta," he said, "move north with all possible speed and assist as required. The climate may be hot and many of the people hostile, but it's nothing that we have not met with before.

"Remember, we are facing not just one kind of rebel: some are mutineers but others are civilians using the mutiny to settle old scores against the Company and the presence of any Europeans. Then there are locals who hold grudges for one reason or another against their own princes, tax gatherers or land-owners. Finally, you may face religious fanatics, the Ghazi. These Moslems say they are defending their faith against the evil of the infidel." He paused. "Us!" he said, adopting a look of feigned hurt and surprise.

This brought a ripple of laughter from his audience.

"Our task is to carry out our duty without fear or favour," he said in conclusion. "Whatever their – and it could be argued some may have a point – we face a dangerous enemy. I am confident we shall succeed with our usual diligence and before too long quash the rebellion. If you have questions, refer them to your company commanders. Other information will be issued at company level."

He then saluted solemnly and moved off followed by senior officers, leaving junior ones and non-commissioned officers to dismiss the parade.

Soon clumps of men were walking off the make-shift parade ground. The colonel's words had given them much to think about and there was discussion ranging from the very serious to the very light-hearted, with cursing and nervous laughter mixed up in it all. It was good to be kept informed, but sometimes too much information could be unsettling. Before long, however, we would be embarking and there would be other things to occupy us.

As I moved off in the direction of the small hut that

served as my quarters, Corporal Williams caught up with me.

"If I was a disagreeable, miserable sort of chap, which of course I am not," he remarked, "I might say that it's us again interfering in another country's business. What's India got to do with us?"

"Bit late for that," I said. "The East India Company controls well over half of it. Still, don't let the colonel hear you say that." It was a warning, though issued in as pleasant a tone as I could muster. I was, after all, a regimental sergeant-major and he merely a corporal, albeit a very good one. There was also much in what he was saying and although I would not admit it to anyone, I was generally on his side. He came from a rough background and there had been few favours shown him by those with power and wealth. It was also pleasing that he felt able to confide in me.

"It is a good job I know you, Williams. Some people might think that you don't want to go. India helps us to stay strong and keep the Russians' noses out. What about the massacres the colonel told us about? Don't you want to help avenge them? Anyway it will give us all a new experience. I'm told it's an interesting place."

He looked at me with the sort of expression that suggested he knew what I could do with such experiences, saluted, and turned and walked away.

I gazed after him and thought once again that for many men born like him in the squalor of the big city, India meant very little. Only the very rich with a few spare sons to make men of them and help run the country would see any profit or gain in India. Or, I reflected grimly, men who had fathered children and had been advised to go there to avoid the disgrace and lose themselves in this large corner of an overseas British interest.

From what the colonel had said and from my earlier talks with Major Axelby, it seemed to me that the Company had brought some of the actions of the mutineers down on their own heads. The Company had certainly made mistakes and if they did not change their ways control of India – if it were to remain British – would pass into the hands of the British Government in London.

❖

The day of departure came all too soon. We marched from the camp and boarded the train for Portsmouth. Our battalion was divided among three ships, each able to take around 350 officers and men.

I boarded the 'Sutlej' that same afternoon, Wednesday the 22nd July. Colonel Glyn's party had left a little earlier on the 'Barham'. I didn't see the departure of the third ship or catch its name. I only heard later that it and the 'Barham' were steamships.

The voyage was long and the seas rough: not all riflemen made good sailors. We left the calm of the Solent for the more testing seas of the Bay of Biscay and soon after, the South Atlantic. As I had already sailed around the Cape of Good Hope and had hoped never to have to do it again, I was not looking forward to repeating the experience. During that first time my battalion, the 1st, had been bound for Cape Colony and for long marches and fights with native tribesmen. Now we were bound for India … and who knows what else?

The journey seemed endless and as we rounded the Cape a fearsome storm crashed over us. Mountainous seas caused our ship to roll perilously. Lightning lit up the masts; sails were taken in to save them from being shredded. Several sailors were swept overboard and lost. Seawater poured across the decks, through hatches and down companionways. Give me trees and hills to being caught below decks! Nature seemed determined to take out Her anger on us. Steam engines would no doubt be straining to drive the ships forward that were carrying the other two parts of the battalion. The 'Sutlej', however, was a sailing ship and seemed to be completely at the mercy of those strong winds roaring across the southern ocean. The three ships, not surprisingly, lost flag and telescope contact with each other.

Then the storm seemed to have just worn itself out and we continued on through the more tranquil waters of the Indian Ocean.

Finally we reached our destination, Calcutta, on the 8th

November. One of the other ships, the 'Barham', arrived soon after but there was a delay in their men disembarking, an outbreak of cholera rumoured to be the cause. Whatever the difficulty was, Colonel Glyn's ship had fared very badly during the voyage, running into a hurricane at the end of October. This, after facing the severest of weather as they had rounded the Cape several weeks before. Three of their ship's crew had even been struck by lightning!

Once ashore, the detachment under Colonel Glyn left Calcutta. We later heard that by forced marches and train they reached Allahabad and after more marches got to within 30 or 40 miles of Cawnpore. They had pitched tents there, but even though they were fatigued they were ordered to strike camp and move nearer to Cawnpore. Soon they and the 2nd Battalion would be engaging the enemy.

Calcutta squats on a tributary of the Ganges called the River Hooghly but is many miles from the sea; perhaps seven or eight hours steaming from the Bay of Bengal. We seemed to come on the city very suddenly. For mile after mile along the banks of the river there were stretches of dense jungle broken occasionally by mud-hut villages. Heat and poverty always seemed to be constant companions and it appeared to be no different here.

Then there was Calcutta! Landing places and jetties were cut into the jungle with palm trees waving briskly in the hot wind that seemed to be funnelled up along the river all the way back to the Bay, to catch everyone in its path in a brain-searing haze.

It soon became very obvious which part of Calcutta was the European quarter. There were grand houses and bungalows, gardens full of exotic trees and shrubs of the deepest green, and flowers as bright and as colourful as an artist's palette. Birds of every hue chattered excitedly in the trees or flew past like a feathery rainbow. Then there were the native areas, which teemed with all manner of human life. Small, naked children splashed in the river; gaily dressed women were at their daily tasks; men wore loincloths. I was told later that this simple cotton garment was called a dhoti and many native men wore very little else. There were beggars and cripples everywhere.

The harbour was a buzz of activity as porters scurried to and fro between decks and docks. Blue-jacketed sailors and red-coated soldiers poured down companionways, doubtless very relieved to be away from the uncertainties of the sea, cramped conditions and meagre plain rations. There were ships of every kind; steamers of every size. Some vessels were like my own, others bigger and grander. There were warships and merchant craft and – flitting in and out between vessel and shore – were flimsy native boats.

Overlooking and rather overshadowing the whole harbour was a collection of solid, permanent-looking buildings. This, I was soon to discover, was Government House.

Once we had disembarked we expected to soon be on our way like other new arrivals, but our departure was delayed for twenty-four hours. Once off our ship, we formed up a little away from the crowded quayside. Instead of marching off as expected, we were ordered to march in full kit in the direction of those impressive buildings.

This, we were later advised, was to be a show of strength to remind the local natives which side they were on. There had been some wavering in respect of their loyalty when the mutiny had first begun and a feeling of unease among the European element of the city. A few of them had found urgent business to take them off to the south; that part of the country still untainted by rebellion. Our marching into the compound might just be enough to stiffen the resolve of those who had remained behind.

Morale-boosting and impressing the natives completed, we were deployed to a nearby barracks to eat and rest and to await the arrival of the remainder of our kit and more ships carrying soldiers and other reinforcements. By the following day we would also be heading north.

❖

I had eaten, overseen the men to their temporary quarters and was standing on a terrace overlooking the harbour, when rifleman Dickinson appeared in front of me. As he stood at attention and saluted, perspiration poured down his face.

While contemplating the industry in the harbour I had been thinking about events that I knew about in Calcutta's past. There was the incident of the 'Black Hole', which had occurred just over one hundred years ago. Around 100 Europeans had been cast into a stiflingly hot, small room and left to suffer. A third or more succumbed to thirst, suffocation and exhaustion. Looking at the rifleman's sweaty face, I realised that thinking back on the story might not be a good omen.

"Sergeant-Major Finch, sir, the colonel sent me to find you. There's someone wants to see you. It's that bungalow over there, sir," he said pointing to a small, if rather grand-looking, building set a little apart from the rest but still overlooking the harbour.

Off I walked, wondering who it could be that wanted to see me, but coming to the obvious conclusion that it could only be either Edward or William Fortune. As far as I knew there was no one else outside of the Rifle Brigade likely to not only be in India but also wanting to see me.

I approached the front door after mounting the steps with some caution, not knowing quite what to expect. Servants busied themselves with a variety of tasks.

One – a tall, heavily bearded, turban-wearing fine figure of a man – pointed towards a door.

"Through there, sahib," he said most agreeably, though looking with some concern at the rifle I still carried. Among the general orders given before departure from England was the issue of a sensible one to all riflemen: always go armed, just in case!

"I was told you wanted to see me, sir," I said as I knocked and entered, the coolness of the room a pleasant contrast to the heat of the day outside. Like every other European's residence and those of wealthy Indians, long grass reeds were placed over the window shutters. These were kept constantly wet by what they called water-wallahs, the servants whose job it was to keep a flow of water poured over them. It did go some way to cool the hot wind that seemed to be ever-present, though despite their efforts the temperature still hovered around 100 degrees.

The figure, whose back had been towards me when I had first spoken, turned. The bright rays of the sun pouring through one of the shutters he had opened threw light across his face. Twenty and more years in India had taken its toll, but there was no mistaking the family likeness. Though lacking the vivid scar that crossed his brother's face, he was unmistakably William Fortune. He was dressed in the uniform of a brigadier in one of the East India Company's regiments.

"You one of my bastards, boy? Though by all accounts you have done well for yourself."

This was not exactly the sort of greeting I had expected and I felt dismayed and annoyed. I'd not take such a slight from many men, though the plain truth of it was that is just what I am. Not that it had been my fault.

"Step forward and shake your father's hand."

I took that to be some sort of apology for the odd way in which he had greeted me and for the twenty-four years that he had apparently ignored my existence.

He had been leaning against the shuttered window, but now he straightened up and turned fully to face me; proffering his right hand. He was about my height, or I his. For all his years, he carried the wearing of a uniform well, which was probably down to his breeding. He had those same piercing blue eyes of both Lord John and his nephew, poor James, and for all his sixty-plus years he had a very firm hand. He did wince a little and said by way of explanation, "an old wound."

"I am pleased to make your acquaintance, John, or is it Jack? I trust you bear no ill will? Too bad if you do! It's a little late now, what with the mess we've made in India making for more pressing matters."

"I am pleased to meet you at long last, Sir William," I replied.

I was not really sure what I should say, but thought it best to remain calm if I was to stand any chance of getting some answers to my questions. At least here he was in front of me: I had waited a long time for such an opportunity. My soldier's training had encouraged me to expect the unexpected, to be prepared and hope for the best in case events turned sour.

He waved me to a seat but remained standing and seemed to be deep in thought.

I felt that he was either wrestling with his conscience or wondering just how much to tell me.

At length he spoke.

"You have received details of the proposed settlement?"

"Yes, sir and I thank you for it. But I have to ask – why me? Why me?" I repeated.

"It's true there are a few others, but you have proved most worthy. However, that's not entirely why I asked my brother to see that you had some education and the Finchs didn't starve. You can thank nephew James for some of it too; especially your education going on longer than originally envisaged. Instead of leaving it once you knew your letters and could write, James insisted that your opportunity for learning was encouraged."

He looked at me, his face screwed up a little, and added: "Probably as good as his was at Eton! I heard about your encounter in the library. He said there was something about you – not merely because you share blood and more than a passing likeness between us all. That and the fact that you were farmed out to a local family and not to the workhouse or worse, meant that if you did prove to have the character then you could be steered in the right direction. Which," he added, "would not necessarily have been in the direction of Durford Hall. What was a big surprise to us all was your following in James' footsteps in the Rifle Brigade and doing well."

This seemed to be the perfect moment for me to ask Sir William something I had been wondering about for years.

"I have a question, Sir William," I said.

"Probably can guess what it is. Your mother?" he said, fixing me with those piercing eyes.

I nodded.

"Beautiful young woman. Jane was her name. One of John's children's governesses. Caught her one day bending over the piano. Couldn't help meself. Been out with the hunt. Blood was up. Before I knew it, there we were, me with breeches down and she with her skirts up and soon she was undone in every way."

Perhaps realising that this might not be what I had wanted to hear even after all these years, he stopped abruptly. After all, I was the outcome of this heated encounter.

"Do you know what happened to her?" I asked, anticipating the very worst.

"Lord John's wife packed her off to some distant relatives in Salisbury until her time."

"Then?"

"Don't know for sure all the details. It seems her own people disowned her. I did settle some money on Jane. Couldn't very well marry her. Different station and all that you see. Particularly then."

At this I think I may have blanched a little. That did not bode well for the plans I had for Nell.

"But ..." He frowned, then seeing the look of determination on my face, continued. "... She was found floating in the River Avon about six months after you'd been born and passed to the Finch family. I did not know about her death until much later. It had been suggested to me that I go away as soon as possible. John was owed a few favours in the East India Company so off I went."

He looked a little crestfallen. Perhaps he felt sorry for what had happened to my mother. Perhaps he felt sorry for himself and the cloud that had hung over him causing his 'exile' to India. He may, of course, have been thinking back to that encounter with Jane. He must – or should have been – considering that he had been responsible for a birth and, ultimately a death. If that was indeed the case then he did look very sorry for what had happened, unlike so many men in his station in life who took advantage of such helpless girls who had little choice but to succumb to their advances. This apparent display of humility was difficult for someone like him and rather a surprise to me with my background of living at the wrong end of the village looking up at the gentry in the big house.

I had questions for my own conscience to wrestle with as it was. Would it be acceptable if he was trying to buy me off to thus allow him to salve his own conscience? It had not been the only occasion he had brought ruination upon servant girls or governesses in Lord John's household. He had also, according to rumour, scattered some seed below stairs at Broughton House.

I did tell Sir William that his brother felt he had done his penance for past sins. At this his face softened and he nodded his head as though offering thanks for me telling him this; especially as I was the offspring of one of his victims.

On the other hand he had had many years to get over those rather self-inflicted difficulties. My mother had not. Her exile in a suicide's grave was rather more permanent.

Perhaps the settlement was part of this. Should I refuse it? But what good would that do? A soldier's pay would not be enough to keep Nell, even if I decided to become an officer. This latter course of action was unlikely: there were too many cases of lieutenants up from the ranks who had fallen so easily into debt trying to keep up with the lifestyle of brother officers, who almost to a man came with money and title behind them. I had struggled previously with my conscience before accepting anything. My upbringing had convinced me that you don't get something for nothing at my level of society. My parents in the cottage had worked all their lives, like so many others. What had hard work done for them? What did they have? Living in a cottage that could see them evicted on the whim of the estate's owner. Not that, all the time I had breath in my body, would I see them homeless.

To refuse the settlement, however, would almost certainly mean I would have to give up the woman I loved. I had very soon rejected the thought that if a man and woman loved each other, nothing should stand in the way of them being together. This may be the stuff of books but not of real life. It would not be fair to expect a woman born to wealth and security to gamble on a man too proud or too stupid to refuse a change of fortune.

I tried to look at things from a different point of view. Perhaps it was not something for nothing? My mother had not been given the opportunity, but I could. And in some ways I had earned it, for according to many people keenly disposed towards me I had behaved correctly and with honour.

Sir William had sat down while I had been considering matters and certainly looked quite relieved, as though his telling me had absolved him and lifted a large burden from his shoulders.

He asked if there was anything else, but by now I felt quite drained and said "no". I was too stunned to delve any deeper and hear more revelations concerning Jane. Let her rest in peace. Perhaps one day I would discover where she was buried.

I now required a little time to think over everything I had learned, though in truth it was not as easy as that. Here was I newly arrived in India facing the unknown. Those other feelings would have to be put to one side, but as soon as I had a spare moment I would write to Nell and tell her of this meeting. We had indeed promised to write but accepted that communication would not be very easy, especially as I was likely to be marching back and forth across India in pursuit of murderous sepoys.

Sir William turned his thoughts to England and asked questions about the estate and about the two families, the Fortunes and Broughtons. Then we shifted to more immediate problems.

"Always felt a bit out of touch here. How are we really doing? I hope that you don't believe all that you have been told about why this whole mess started? A bit more than just cartridges. Place is like a tinder box. There's a thousand miles between here and Delhi. Rivers, hills, jungle and everything else in between, as well as this infernal heat. Never got used to it. And lots of towns, villages and forts. Easy for armies of sepoys to hide."

I attempted to explain the part we were hoping to play in quelling the mutiny and that we were soon off to Cawnpore and then on to Lucknow.

At the mention of the last name, he said, "You may find Edward there."

He told me something of the events in Cawnpore five or six months previously and how he had ended up in

Calcutta. He said he had been based in Oudh Province for some years. There, he added, it had been difficult to single out a particular problem that might have caused the Company's difficulties, other than a growing resentment of the presence of Europeans. Then it seems in Oudh the ruler had been deposed and the Company had taken over the running of the whole province. This action was not welcomed by the local population.

"I was ordered first to Lucknow then on to Cawnpore by the Governor to assess the mood," he said. "As the largest station in India it was regarded as crucial to maintaining a firm grip on European and therefore British interests across the country."

"What's Cawnpore like?"

"The station is an odd shape. It runs along the left bank of the River Ganges for miles. Then there is the city itself. To the south a canal, the Ganges Canal. The senior official is a clever cove, General Wheeler – he sensed there could be trouble so he was quick to move everyone inside the cantonment. It had two large barracks, a kitchen, a couple of privies and a well. We did, after all, have many ladies and some children there. The cantonment was turned as best it could be into a defensive position just in case trouble broke out."

He sniffed, "I might have chosen to build my defences further up the base nearer the magazine and a lot more convenient for bringing in help from the river, but," he said, shrugging, "I was not the one in overall command. The general ordered a trench to be dug all round the cantonment with the excavated earth thrown up to form a low wall, about one yard high. If mutiny did break out then it wouldn't stop bullets, let alone shell and grapeshot, but it heartened the women and children and the rest of the civilians.

"He also decided on the 21st May, rather than just wait for things to happen, to send to Lucknow to see what the situation was like there. Had it already fallen? If not, then perhaps they could spare Cawnpore a few companies of men. Edward, who had been in Cawnpore on some official Company business or other, decided to return to Lucknow and so accompanied the detachment."

"Did you get some help?" I asked.

"Yes, Lucknow sent a small contingent of the 32nd Foot, then a few days later another small force reached us. Soon after, the situation changed. A spy reached us to say that Lucknow was under siege.

"After completing his business Edward, just before the rebels cut the city off, had taken a company of the 32nd to occupy a former Company cantonment called Jumna-ki-Serai a few miles east of Lucknow, between the Gumti and Ghaghara rivers. For reasons known only to themselves, the rebels in moving against Lucknow just by-passed this station completely."

"If mutiny was suspected, couldn't steps have been taken to crush it before it broke out?" I asked.

"Perhaps yes, if we'd had enough Europeans in the army or knew exactly who we could rely on and who we couldn't. Some regiments were disbanded and their weapons seized, though in some cases this action made things even worse."

"Yes, our colonel told us as much."

I then asked Sir William to tell me a little more about India. He said that over one third of India still lay outside of British influence. The Honourable East India Company controlled what was referred to as the 'three presidencies' of Bengal, Bombay and Madras. Each presidency had its own army, each with European officers and men. There were also much larger numbers of native regiments with European and Indian officers, though Indian officers had lower status. There were a few regiments from England here even before the outbreak of mutiny. Besides the various armies there were many clerks, including Indians, to administer the presidencies as well as tax gatherers to raise the money to pay for it all.

In short, he told me, about twenty- or thirty-thousand Europeans had control over 250 million Indians – with the help of many of the locals prepared to be in the pay of us, the foreigners.

"Fortunately, at least so far," he continued, "it's mainly Bengal that has been giving us the trouble. There has been the odd, isolated problem elsewhere in Bombay and Madras. I also think, as do others, that some rebels want to bring back the Mughal Empire of old and resist us. But the present emperor is old and doddery and more content with his nautch girls and his opium than in lending an army to kick us out."

"Nautch girls, sir?"

He waved away the question, looking a little irritated at my attempts at interrupting.

"Then in the first week of June the mutiny crashed about our ears in Cawnpore in Oudh province. It seemed to be the 2nd Calvary among the troopers, the sowar, who started things. Then most of the sepoys of the 53rd and 56th followed soon after.

"Shells began to fall all around us. Put the wind up the women and children, I need hardly tell you. After taking this for several days a few men disguised themselves and crept through their lines and managed to put some of their guns and gunners out of action. Boosted the rest of us. Caught them napping. Mutinous sepoys, not knowing where the action was coming from, blazed away in all directions."

This last remark made me smile for it reminded me of nights slipping into Sevastopol causing similar confusion.

"Word was coming down to us about a massacre that had taken place a little way upstream. One hundred or so civilians including women and children had been captured, lined up in trenches and killed. This fed more rumours that the situation across the country was reaching fever pitch.

"Matters were certainly moving towards the panic stage in our meagre defensive position. A couple more of our soldiers tried again to disrupt the rebel forces that were swarming around Cawnpore and what had been the strip of land containing our military base along the river, but they were captured and killed.

"Every day more rebels were arriving on the Ganges. What was even worse was that our intelligence said that rebels of both religions, Moslem and Hindu, seemed to be acting together to push us from our trenches and barracks. One of our greatest fears was the possibility that some of the more fanatical among the Moslem community might manage to turn the mutiny into a holy war and enflame and engulf the whole country. Our spies were estimating the force all around us to be at least 5,000 strong while we had barely 300!

"Shelling continued and then one of the barrack roofs caught fire. The rest of the building may have been brick but the roof wasn't a pukka one. A thatched, rather than a tiled, affair. Soon the whole block was ablaze. As men, women and children fled from the burning wreck, murderous sepoys began to shoot them. There was little the rest of us could do to help. A few defiant shots were loosed off at the sepoys but many innocents either died horribly in the flames or were cut down in a hail of bullets."

"How did you manage to get away?" I asked.

"Well, there was talk of trying for a truce because one of the rebel leaders was considered to be an honourable man, Nana Sahib. He agreed to allow us to pass without interference to the Ganges where he had even arranged for boats to take us to safety. I was not feeling too well and was carried by litter, a doolie, down to the river. What a shambles! Boats were there but it took a long time to persuade the sepoys to bring them in close enough to board.

"Eventually some of us did manage to get into the boats. I had a little craft to myself, save for the three sepoys who were to act as crew; one to steer and two to row. A similar crewing arrangement was taking place in the other boats. Then as we moved towards the middle of the river ready to go down the Ganges the crews of the boats jumped overboard."

"You'd been betrayed by Nana Sahib?"

"Yes, a callous betrayal. My boat all but capsized and I gulped in mouthfuls of the river fouled by the bloated corpses of the earlier massacre upstream. Just as we began to realise what they were doing, sepoys began shooting at the women and children while the sowar began to slash at them with their swords as they tipped from their boats or made pathetic attempts to run through the shallows into deeper water in a desperate attempt to escape. Above, black shapes began to appear as vultures flew in ready to take advantage of the opportunity.

"By some good fortune my little boat had righted itself and was soon caught in the current. Firing by the sepoys continued, but they must have thought that my craft was empty. I had indeed slumped into the bottom of it and must have been out of their sight. I was just able to see and hear their bloody work on the bank and in the shallows, but I could only bear silent witness to these horrors."

His face now showed signs of strain and helplessness, just as he must have been feeling in the bottom of his boat as the whole tragic scene had unfolded before him but with him unable to do anything to help. His cheeks looked hollow, his face gaunt and grey regardless of his 20 years of exposure to the heat of Indian summers. Those fierce blue eyes had softened. Life in this country, waited on hand and foot by hordes of servants, had probably left him – for only the second time in his life – with a feeling of uncertainty. There was a vein of uneasiness running through every aspect of a European's life in India.

I recalled an incident in South Africa. We had been on a forced march and I had miscalculated the distance between several rocks as I rushed forward. I had landed heavily and twisted an ankle. I was allowed to travel the rest of the day on a commissariat wagon, which was some distance behind the rest of the supply train. The driver had been a very cheerful man but when he told me that the wagon contained powder for the Royal Horse Artillery and that a spark or stray bullet could blow us sky high, I think all colour had drained from my face.

Looking at Sir William I felt that he too had found himself in a similar life-threatening situation and that India seemed to be the powder keg with British interests sitting on top of it all. He had been caught up in an outbreak of mutiny that could be one of the sparks. It explained why those Company administrators I had seen only a few hours after arriving in India in and around Government House looked more than a little nervous.

"Please go on," I said.

"Not all Europeans were shot or butchered with swords," he said. "Some escaped. A few were taken prisoner, including the young daughters of Company officials. What fate awaited them, I shudder to think. Then several pairs of hands appeared on the boat's sides. I was powerless to do anything – I had no weapon. But I was relieved to see there were European faces above them. They clung onto the boat, which in the current was making good progress away from that dreadful place of death and treachery. One of the poor fellows lost his grip and was swept away. The other managed to pull himself up and over the side of the boat.

"We must have spent several days in the blistering heat before the craft hit a sandbar. That's where a friendly patrol found us. The next thing I remember is waking up in this same bungalow; burnt skin on fire, eyes and head aching and the driest of throats."

"A remarkable tale," I commented rather inadequately but feeling something very akin to respect and sympathy for this man, my father but whom I barely knew.

"So it's time for you to bring these treacherous dogs to account. I have had a difficult time, but many others have had it far worse. The screams of the dying haunt my sleep and cry out for justice. Defenceless men, women and children murdered …"

These last few words were mumbled and I had to strain to hear. It seemed to me that the very act of saying them had caused him much distress. In Lower Durford he had been regarded as a selfish, heartless man but there was little trace of that in front of me now.

"What are your plans?" I asked.

"Remain here and wait for the good news that the ringleaders and especially that treacherous swine, Nana Sahib, have been captured and hanged. I don't think I'll leave India. Been too long. Besides," he added, even managing a smile, "got a better man to go back in my place. Do well, Jack. Go back, but don't make my mistakes. Get this mutiny over and go home. Now it's time for you to leave. Back to your duties. I don't think we shall meet again, but goodbye and good luck to you."

With that, he turned back to the shutter, closed it and with a sigh sank into a chair. No doubt he had much to think about; of recent events, of our meeting and encounters long ago and of an England he would never see again. How very sad it all was.

It had crossed my mind over the years to wonder exactly what sort of man he was. Some of what I had expected had been based on my view of his brother. I had now met William, heard his story, found out a little more about Jane, and heard of his brush with the sepoys. As a consequence of this meeting I would regard him rather differently.

I stood there for a few moments just looking into the gloom of that now darkened room at this man I had met for the first and probably last time in both our lives. Then I turned and left the bungalow, thinking as I ran down the steps that a chapter of my life had closed but that a new one lay open before me.

Chapter Four

I returned to my quarters, passing many of the rifleman busily attending to their rifles and other equipment.

Before very long, companies of riflemen of my battalion were sent north to advance on a broad front. I was part of one of these detachments that left Calcutta on the 10th November.

The first part of the journey was by railroad until we reached the terminus at Raniganj where further construction of the track had been postponed indefinitely. Then it was along a road, 'The Grand Trunk Road', by bullock-cart and horse-drawn wagons and forced marches through many hot, dusty villages to Benares on the Ganges' west bank with its fort of red sandstone, like so many that we were to see on our marches over the coming months. The walls of this Reminagar Fort rose menacingly from the river's edge.

There had been an outbreak of mutiny here back in June. Shots had been fired, so attempts had been made to disband a native regiment, the 37th Infantry, whose loyalty had been challenged. Dozens of natives had been hanged.

Benares, we had been told, was a very holy place for many Hindus. Where possible we were encouraged to respect holy sites. This city, it seems, was special to Siva – one of their more revered gods. As we passed the fort or garh, where the Ganges meets the River Assi, we saw an example of one of the forms Siva takes: a 'linga'. It would have been difficult to miss it! It was a fine example of that part of a man that when aroused is very precious to all men and even welcomed in that state by some women.

Then we continued towards Allahabad. This was a very large garrison town sitting where two rivers, the Ganges and the Yamuna, meet. According to myth there is a third, the Sarasvati, or so Hindus believe. What really impressed us, though, was the red sandstone fort above the banks of the rivers. Someone had chosen the site of this fort and the one at Banares with great military care and skill.

We reached Fatephur by midday on the 30th, when we were informed that one of the columns that had left earlier had been urged to march on with all possible speed. We were put on alert to be ready to move off at a moment's notice as enemy troops were massing beyond Cawnpore.

A messenger arrived riding a camel, much to the consternation of some of the men in the company who had not seen such a creature up so close before. It is, I am bound to admit, an odd animal. It moves in an ungainly fashion, not at all like a horse. It also regards the world with a look of disdain on its face.

We pressed on towards Cawnpore and before long could hear the sound of guns.

Eventually, after all the long marches which left even hardy riflemen reeling with fatigue in the oppressive heat of north-eastern India, both rifle battalions hoped to be ready by the 6th December to face the enemy. One company had managed to march over 50 miles in around 24 hours. We headed off, preparing to attack a rebel army said to be about 15,000 strong gathered in and around Cawnpore.

Before leaving England, company commanders had shown maps of India to the riflemen in their companies. Remembering how useful Captain Fortune's little map had been, given to him by a French officer in the Crimea, I made my own sketches.

Could be useful, I thought to myself. I like to know where I am going and to get to know the lie of the land.

We had been instructed to pitch tents and then rest. As the men prepared to carry out the order we heard a very welcome sound. A band was playing the '95th'. We were tired but this bucked everyone up, though I was very pleased to turn in after checking that our camp was secure and sentries posted.

The next day was the 6th. We breakfasted on biscuit, tea and a little rum and made ready to leave.

I accompanied riflemen as they moved through jungle chasing out the many mutineers who had taken shelter there. This was my first real sight of the enemy.

As we got within a couple of miles of the town we were ordered to fan out in a broad line with swords fixed. Slowly, methodically we began to clear woods while small parties of riflemen were given the task of shooting at rebel gunners as they prepared to fire their captured artillery in our direction.

We continued our advance into the rebel-held town of Cawnpore, clearing houses between a canal and the town itself. This clearing of the ground was necessary before we were able to attack the main body of mutineers.

The 2nd Battalion were slightly ahead of us and to our left. They had managed to clear sepoys from one of the enemy camps a few hundred yards from Wheeler's entrenchments. As we moved on between the canal and the town, we came upon about 200 sepoys with heavy guns. As we ran across open ground, round and grapeshot was fired at us but screamed over our heads. Fortunately for us, the guns were set too high. The 93rd, those dependable men from the Crimea campaign, chased the mutineers while we continued with the clearing of more houses and trees of skulking rebels. The area between the Grand Trunk Road and the Ganges Canal was now clear as we passed through the city's suburbs and up towards a landmark known as Subhadur's Kund or Tank.

The rebels had suffered many casualties but still resisted. They had two or three heavy guns to both our left and right flanks. These were protected by walls and earthworks. Soon our own guns began to pour in shot at them. While this fire kept their heads down we hoped to move up and capture their artillery. It took us time to advance across the walls and scramble over the rubble and although we managed to capture the guns, the sepoys were able to make good their escape.

❖

Night was falling fast. We felt cold after the heat of the day and hungry too. Some men managed to capture and cook a bullock. Others searched the native huts we were now occupying for any scraps of food. As was usual, we had left our supply and baggage trains miles behind as we had made fast progress. An officer sent a half company of foragers off to see what they could find. The huts produced nothing, which was hardly a surprise – most natives struggled to survive. The foragers did return with a range of meat, including more bullock. I suggested to the company commander that we best not ask too many questions over the origins of this bounty.

During the following morning we heard that we had been in very good company: none other than Sir Colin Campbell. He had brought a force of several thousand men to help clear Cawnpore. It had been Sir Colin who had commanded the red-coated Highland Brigade against Russian cavalry attacks at Balaklava. There was also another Crimean War veteran there too – he had for a short time been in command at Cawnpore, but overwhelming rebel forces had forced General Windham to quit the city and leave it to the tender mercies of the mutineers.

Two or three days later I began to hear wild rumours that General Windham had just given up trying to resist the rebels and had surrendered the town far too easily. There were questions to be answered. This all seemed so unlike the man I had briefly met above Sevastopol. I could just not believe that through his action, or rather inaction, the mutineers had just walked into Cawnpore instead of having to throw themselves at its defences. After Nana Sahib's capture of the city the rebels had been thrown out and it had been reinforced. Windham's failure – if that is what it proved to be – had just handed it all back. If time allowed I hoped to seek out the truth behind Sir Charles Windham's too-quick departure.

The only excitement during the night of the 6th was when a party of mutineers had blundered into our camp leading a dozen or so camels laden with ammunition. The sepoys managed to run off but we seized their supplies, spilled out the powder and were greatly entertained when it was set ablaze. As for the camels, they were to wait for our supply train to catch up and be added to its strength of pack animals. Rifleman Wightman lead the speculation on what camel meat would be like if supplies ran short again.

We then watched as the 2nd Battalion marched off to the camp of the main British force about four miles away. We were ordered to follow the next day. As we left we received news that the missing remnant of the 2nd Battalion had arrived at Calcutta: engine trouble had delayed their ship, the 'Sussex'. So with a few forced marches, the rest of the battalion should reach Cawnpore around the 14th and 15th December.

Sir William's description of the city of Cawnpore had been quite accurate. I still found it difficult to think of him as anything other than Sir William.

Most towns and cities in India that I was to visit during this campaign were divided into two, sometimes three, distinct parts. The first, the native quarter, was easily identifiable, consisting of mostly mud huts teeming with people and a scene of poverty all around them. The European section tended to have brick-built houses and offices, with the addition of a well-appointed brick and stone built residency. These were often surrounded or protected by barracks. Or, making up a third portion, a separate cantonment also with barracks but sometimes even with gun foundries. Troops patrolled while artillery pieces very often poked through embrasures.

We were delayed while the rest of the 2nd Battalion caught up with Sir Colin's camp.

Then I heard some disturbing news regarding the safety of one of the stations.

A patrol was sent to check on the well-being of this outpost; the one at Jumna-ki-Serai and as I had heard that it was where Edward had been temporarily assigned, I asked to accompany Lieutenant Streeter and a company of riflemen.

We left Cawnpore with our customary caution, as we did whenever we entered possible enemy-held territory. Identifying rebels in the villages all around us was no easy task. On several occasions already I had found myself in circumstances when it was almost impossible to judge who to trust in a village. Not all disloyal sepoys had discarded their uniforms in favour of other dress, though traditional clothing of a light cotton tunic and dhoti seemed to be much more comfortable because of their looseness, unlike the European style of military wear inflicted on Indian regiments by the East India Company.

As we passed through the village of Bithur only a few miles from Cawnpore, we came across a 20- or 30-strong party of sepoys. Only two or three of them managed to escape. Then we began to skirt to the north of Lucknow, even more cautiously passing the village of Sandia. We crossed the River Gaghara and approached Jumna from the north-east.

About a mile from the station we dropped into a nullah, a dried-up river bed emerging from a tope or clump of trees some 200 yards from our objective. Lieutenant Streeter surveyed the area in front of us through his telescope.

"Seems peaceful enough, Sergeant-Major. What do you think?"

I borrowed the brass and leather instrument and examined the walls, the roofs of the barracks and the gates that overlooked a wooden bridge, which crossed what had once been a moat. It all seemed to be normal ... yet something did not appear quite right.

"Best send in a few men to scout the post first, sir. Just in case. I'll take six men on over if you agree, sir. I'll send five men forward and left in a skirmish line as cover, while me and another man head straight for the gate. I suggest you wait here. You'll hear soon enough if we find trouble."

Mr Streeter had not long been in the Rifle Brigade and this was his first campaign. He had settled in well and much was expected of him. All he lacked was experience in the field. When I had asked to accompany this patrol the colonel had seemed pleased and had asked me to assist this officer as much as I could. Lieutenant Streeter had also appeared relieved when I had joined his company as it prepared to move off.

We got to within about 100 yards when two sepoys suddenly appeared at the gate. Our covering skirmishers moved closer and two of them lined up on the two men standing at the gate, ready to shoot. Then a very young-looking European officer moved between the two sepoys and called us forward.

We advanced very carefully so as not to move between the three men and the riflemen covering them.

I walked over the bridge, my rifle muzzle still pointing in their direction and passed through the fort's entrance, which was normally closed by two heavy wooden gates. So far, it seemed they had kept out the rebellion that was going on not too many miles away, perhaps 40 as the crow – or in this country the eagle or vulture – flies.

As old habits and a sense of survival die hard, I told one rifleman to wait at the gate while the other six of us moved towards the barrack block and a small collection of bungalows. These, I guessed, were originally for the families of the officers and Company administrators. A few minutes later we stood facing a larger building that I took to be a Commissioner's Residency.

I remarked to the officer about the general look of desertion hanging over the fort. He merely said that they did not have enough men to cover the fort's walls effectively so they had adopted a different strategy. If an approaching force proved to be friendly, guards appeared at the gate, just as we had experienced 10 or 15 minutes before. If on the other hand the force looked hostile, the soldiers in the compound would keep out of sight and pray the enemy continued on its way without even bothering to check inside the fort. It seemed to have worked so far. But to my taste it was too much of a risk. Perhaps they should just abandon the station altogether?

As we moved towards the Residency I noticed several artillery pieces pulled back from the embrasures.

"Easy to run 'em out if our plan fails. We intend selling our lives very dearly," the young officer said.

We had certainly seen no sign of any guns on the fort as we had moved in or any activity at all as we had scanned the walls.

"Go on towards the Residency and you'll see our last line of defence," he said before walking off in the direction of one of the small bungalows.

Well it was certainly a different approach to defending a position than anything I had come across before and it did seem to be working.

While I continued towards the building I did think it was a pity the fort was not being put to better use. But as Cawnpore and Lucknow had both grown in importance, this smaller fort of Jumna-ki-Serai had declined in strategic worth. Even as a stopping place for sepoys and travellers generally, it was no longer considered worth maintaining at full strength.

That accepted, it would still pose quite a problem for would-be attackers if properly garrisoned. The fort rose quite spectacularly, topped with thick, high walls above the parched boulder-strewn plain. At one time waters from the river would have filled a moat all around it. Spanning the dry moat was the bridge, about 25 feet across, to the gated entrance. Instead of water, which had posed even more difficulties for attackers, much of the moat contained human rubbish of every sort as well as the decaying carcasses of animals.

I noticed a few stables just beyond the bungalows but not enough for a full troop of cavalry. The stable-block also looked neglected.

I was still moving with some caution. There had, after all, been reports of renegade Europeans posing as officers, though the fellow who had greeted me certainly appeared to be the genuine, or as they say in these parts, 'pukka' article. But as an old soldier had once said to me, "trust no bugger but your own feelings and you'll live longer."

At length I came to a sturdy but neglected two-storey building, the top floor of which had shutters in place. Doubtless this was also part of their plan to deceive potential enemies. Along the front of the building at ground level ran a verandah, also showing that look of neglect. Without really thinking about it I sent two pairs of riflemen to the left and right to check that all was as it should be. A fifth man was ordered to remain at the foot of the steps that led up to the building's entrance. As an additional precaution I kept my sword fixed. Then I heard something that stopped me in my tracks. A few examples of their last line of defence? No! I could hear the sound of happy and excited children and the accompanying voice of a woman.

As I prepared to enter the building I looked along the line of this dwelling. I could clearly see a handful of rifle barrels tracking the two riflemen moving to the left as well as me. I supposed the two men to the right were also being followed. Were my worst fears about to be realised? I moved my rifle preparing to fire.

A cheerful voice broke the tension.

"Advance and be recognised, Havildar-Major, sahib."

Behind a very heavily bearded face and dressed in the uniform of a Native infantry man stood an Indian sergeant, a havildar. He was soon followed by a second and a third man, who now carried their rifles at the slope rather than levelling them at us.

"How many are you, Havildar?" I asked.

"Twenty-seven, sahib including the colonel who is very bad," he replied. As an afterthought, he said, "five sahibs, eleven women and some baba-logs."

This last word, 'baba-logs', I knew to mean children. At this intelligence I groaned inwardly. Just how long could they continue to deceive marauding rebels? The presence of the 'very bad' man, the unwell or injured colonel and the women and children made me think that was the only reason why they were hanging on in this fort. But the Jumna station had no telegraph in operation and they had no way of knowing what the situation was like at Cawnpore and Lucknow. As far as they knew, one or both of the stations had already fallen to the enemy. They could not therefore risk heading off, unaware of what lay ahead. There was no guarantee of reaching either city anyway. They could just as easily be caught in the open or run into one of a number of bandits or mutineers at large in the area.

"What happened to the rest of your detachment?" I asked. "We believed that you at least had a full company."

"Called away to Lucknow, sahib, but Colonel Fortune has been promised the 32nd will return when things are easier there."

If you can survive that long, I thought, but thanked him for the information and turning, called out to the rifleman at the foot of the steps.

"Give Thomson a shout at the gate. Tell him to signal

Lieutenant Streeter to bring up the rest of the men. I'm going inside to see if I can find this colonel the halvidar told me about."

Moving on and into the building I came to a large bedroom, in the centre of which was a big raised bed. It reminded me of one of those huge tombs I had seen in a cathedral somewhere. Across the bed suspended from hooks in the ceiling was a large, dusty, greyish-red net that brought to mind a very finely carved stone tomb whose mason had chipped away so skilfully as to leave the impression of gentle folds of a mantle worn by the lady lying by the side of her husband, a knight who had fought in the Crusades.

As my ears were on the alert and my eyes were growing more accustomed to the gloom, I raised my rifle. I had heard a noise – a creaking sound – and very nearly stumbled over the dozing figure of a punkah-wallah. He was seated cross-legged to the left of the bed. So used was he to carrying out such a boring task that he probably continued to do it while fully asleep. My nearly crashing into him seemed to have little or no effect. He did not stop or even stir, but his hand continued with its work. He carried on gently pulling at the string, the end of which was attached to a square piece of cloth, one edge of which was fastened to the ceiling. This served as a very simple but effective fan to stir the air and help it circulate.

Recovering my balance, I walked over to the bed. A corner of the linen had been lifted to one side. There, alternately wheezing and panting, lay Edward Fortune.

"Who is it?" he croaked, his voice struggling up from the depths of a very parched throat.

"It's John Finch of the Rifle Brigade."

There followed even more laboured sounds of tortured breathing as well as the rustle of cotton as the figure in front of me struggled desperately to raise himself into an upright position from where he was slumped uncomfortably on the cushions. A small oil lamp threw light across his face.

"Oh, so you're Jack Fortune. You don't see me at my best, but you on the other hand look very much as James described you."

He had referred to me as Jack Fortune, which confirmed that he must have known something about what was being planned for me by Sir William. This I found rather pleasing. Then I looked down at him. How he was able to see my face was beyond me! The little lamp was just enough to illuminate him but little else. The whites of his eyes looked a bloodshot ivory in colour and he could scarcely keep them open. The rest of the room was quite dark and he would not have been able to see me as I was framed against the door through which I'd entered. Perhaps word had reached him that I would try and see him if at all possible and he had realised that his visitor was indeed me, in which case his comments on my appearance were probably based only on reports about me.

No doubt the shutters, covered in lengths of grass, helped keep out that hot, dry, energy-sapping wind that seemed to be everywhere. They also very effectively kept out the light. I had been assured that the weather at this time of the year was nothing compared to that of the regular daytime temperatures around April to July.

I turned my attention back to the bed as Edward, gulping in air, managed to ask me to let some more light into the room.

My attention was distracted from this task as I heard the sound of boots on bare boards. Two riflemen clattered in.

"You all right, sir?" one asked while the other turned to face the open door with his Enfield at the ready.

I felt a glow of pride. It's true what Major Axelby and others say: we riflemen, officers, NCOs and men stick together.

"Yes, I'm fine. Call the others back and ask Lieutenant Streeter if you can stand down and brew tea. I will be back presently."

Once again I looked down on the poor man on the bed, who motioned towards a small table. On the tray above the three bamboo legs that supported it was a carafe containing a cloudy looking liquid and beside it, a single glass.

"Pour me some, Jack."

For most of this time I had been holding my rifle across my chest. I moved to a chair close by the bed and placed the rifle by Edward's feet, but not before unfixing the sword and replacing it in its scabbard.

Then I poured a measure of liquid into the glass and moved back to Edward. I placed my left arm across his bony shoulders, lifting the glass to his parched, cracked lips with my right hand. He managed after several seconds of painful slurping to drain the glass.

While this was taking place I had time to have a really good look at him.

He was tall, like his younger brother James, but there the physical similarities ended. The face was gaunt. Grey skin was pulled taut over cheekbones and jaw. What I could see of his body under a sweat- and fever-stained nightshirt looked wasted. His arms were little better than sticks. He was, I feared, not very long for this world.

"Thank you," he gasped. "Don't know if it does any good. Certainly tastes foul. Wounded a couple of times on the way back. May even have been bitten a few times by snakes. They kill hundreds, maybe even thousands each year. Can't think why the Indians hold them in such high esteem. Vile, deadly creatures. Avoid the king cobra, Jack. Ten or twelve feet of nastiness. Hindus, though, have got a snake god. If it's to keep them away then it certainly doesn't seem to work!" His words revealed a little touch of that same humour his brother James had shown.

"On the journey back from Cawnpore, had to hide in a ditch full of some long dead corpses, though not before they had received attention from a few of the neighbourhood's vultures. Bodies of the dead a blue-grey, bloated but with great lumps and their eyes missing after the carrion had taken their turn. I must have caught something nasty. Can't keep anything down. A bullet went straight through, but the sabre-cut I also received not so good. Just won't heal!"

He managed to turn, if painfully and pull the front of his nightshirt down to reveal a vivid red slash wound typical of a blow from a sabre. It had left a furrow across the top of his ribs from one collarbone to the other. He was right; it wasn't healing.

"What happened to the force that went back with you?" I asked.

"Not too sure exactly. Heard some rustling in the bushes. Took three men to see if it was just a wild animal or a party of rebels trying to ambush the whole column. As we moved into the undergrowth the rest of the men were attacked. Shots were fired. Then my little group was set upon by a handful of sepoys. After about ten minutes we returned to the track where we had left the column. Somehow we had lost contact with each other. By the time we had returned to our starting point the rest of the men had gone. All we found were the bodies of five of our side and a similar number of dead mutineers.

"Then we saw a large force of rebels heading in our direction and that's when I decided to hide in the ditch. Eventually Lucknow did send out a patrol to find us. They brought the two of us who had survived here, but my poor loyal companion died soon after. A company of the 32nd was left to man the fort. Unfortunately, very soon after, matters at Lucknow must have deteriorated and most of the company was recalled. The women and children and a few civilians who had also accompanied the original patrol remained here as well in case Lucknow fell. If and when things improve there, reinforcements will be sent back to us."

"Yes, the halvidar explained that. He seems a very good man."

Edward had made a great effort to tell the story. For a minute or more he lay back on the bed, gulping as he breathed. Then he seemed to recover a little and turned his head to look directly at me. Perhaps the drink or the chance to tell his story had helped him.

"Whatever you do, young Jack, get out of this hell-hole as soon as you can. Look what it's done to me. Stop here long enough and it might do the same to you. The country gets into your bones. Takes you over and after a while there is no turning back. Tell my people, our people, that I am sorry I could not get back.

"If the vapours don't get you, the Indians will. Don't believe what they tell you. The Indians want us out. No, not all of them but some of the rajas do. They call us 'feringhi' – foreigner – behind our backs but it's how they say it!

"We've made mistakes; built up resentment and

brought some of the present troubles down on our own heads. Some of the provincial governors do a good job but others haven't helped at all. This mutiny could be just the start. If they had been able to plan it better and some of our military not acted as quickly, then I think we would have faced being kicked out of India. How the Russians after the Crimea would have applauded that. It's only the loyal sepoy, a few good chaps like Brigadier Nicholson and the arrival of new regiments like yours that might just allow us to damp this one down."

There was a very long pause after this expansive summing up of the present situation. His body after this effort convulsed in pain. This was followed by another fit of coughing. Eventually it too subsided and he managed to wipe his mouth on the edge of a sheet.

An Indian servant suddenly appeared and said:

"Burra-sahib must rest, sahib."

"I'll not be much longer," I replied.

"A jolly decent fellow," said Edward. "Bit more cheerful than the mournful butler at the Hall, unless things have changed in the years I have been away. This fellow flaps around me all the time. Now, Jack, listen carefully." He wheezed a little then regained his breath. "Go as soon as you can. Marry the Broughton filly. Yes, I know all about it. James wrote in the summer of '54 that if he caught a Russian bullet he hoped that you would look after her. Letter from Pa in August this year caught up with me too. Usually it takes a devil of a time for news from home to reach us here.

"Here's my hand, Jack. Hope you don't catch anything, though." He chuckled grimly and certainly painfully, again that hint of humour briefly lifting his mood.

"Wished we'd met sooner. Last time I saw you was when you were about eight. Times have changed us both. God bless you and keep you safe," he managed to gasp out.

His grip was limp, like that of a child.

I stood, preparing to leave. Just as I was about to bid him what I thought would be a final farewell, a small figure – that of a little girl – appeared by the side of the bed, then another and another followed by their nanny, their ayah.

He managed to raise his head once more.

"Yes, my baba-logs, my children. Not sure papa would approve but ..." He paused as if reliving the moments of their conceptions, "... not much else to do here on chilly nights and those long hot days. Exposure to some of their temple friezes is certainly a great help to a chap. And the women here are much more accommodating than our own womenfolk, who just lie back and hope for a painless loss of maidenhead. Don't worry though, Jack – the children will be taken care of when I'm not here anymore."

The appearance of his three children seemed to revive him.

"Just before you go, tell me a little about the estate. Oh, how I have missed the river, the trees and even the rain. The monsoons here just throw it down and everything floods. Not at all like our soft, gentle sort in Hampshire."

I pulled the chair I had been sitting on back into position near his head and sat down again.

I began to talk about the village; his people, Durford Hall, the Broughtons and about my own walks near the river that he loved and missed so much; that we both loved so much but which he would never see again.

He nodded his head slowly as memories of happier times came back to him. I looked across at his face. He looked at peace, contented, with the faintest of smiles touching his lips. He had fallen back onto his cushions and seemed to be asleep, yet still wheezing gently.

I stood up again, looked down at him, touched his shoulder and whispered softly: "Goodbye cousin Edward." I left as quietly as army footwear and the bare boards would allow, to rejoin the men gathered around the steps at the front of the Residency. All the while I was reflecting sadly that I had now seen the second of two newly discovered cousins in dreadful straits and what would almost certainly prove in Edward's case to be the first and last time.

As I rejoined the rest of the company squatting in whatever shade they could find, some under a small clump of banyan trees, Thomson handed me tea. I took a couple of hard biscuits from my pack and sat beside Lieutenant Streeter.

"Pity we can't stay. Looks as though they could do with some help," the young officer commented.

"Yes, sir," I agreed. "But if we leave within the hour we should be able to get a good part of the way back before dark. There's an abandoned village we passed on the way here that we should be able to reach before nightfall. Then move off at first light tomorrow. As you say, sir, there's nothing more we can do here. Just hope the rebels leave 'em long enough for help to get back here."

"I'll go to the colonel on our return and see if we can't telegraph and speed things up a bit. Perhaps Sir Colin can send some men down from our forces around Lucknow," replied the lieutenant.

We set off, managing to return unscathed towards the late afternoon of the following day.

While we had been away, the 3rd Battalion and a company from the 2nd had been occupied pursuing rebels who had been attacking nearby loyal villages. About a week after our return from Jumna-ki-Serai they too returned, bringing with them rebels they had captured from a splinter force that had left a large band of mutineers heading east towards Lucknow from Gwalior. More importantly and certainly very worryingly, one of the captured sepoys was found to be carrying letters to Nana Sahib. He was now being sought desperately by the Governor-General for the part he had played in the massacre at Cawnpore, that same massacre from which Sir William had barely escaped. The letters were urging a sustained attack on all forts around Cawnpore and Lucknow with the latter as his main target.

Our force had crossed the River Yamuna and searched for rebels in thickly wooded country, but – as before – they managed to evade our men and seemed not only to disperse but to melt into the very terrain. The only success had been that capture of a few rebels. Even the 9th Lancers were unable to catch up with the disappearing sepoys. It would be my view, and increasingly my experience, that there were many villages sheltering or supplying food to mutineers. In June, in and around Benares, many had been hanged, accused of aiding and abetting rebels. I was grateful that we were not pursuing such a policy, as this surely would only serve to feed even more discontent among the local population.

Regular patrols were being sent out in all directions and the company I had gone with to check on Edward's station at Jumna was ordered out again, this time to support part of the 2nd Battalion. We caught up with the 2nd at Etawah whose fort was built on a small bank on the River Yamuna. It boasted strong, square-shaped bastions at each of its corners.

I joined the 2nd and 3rd Battalions in rushing the fort. The gates were blown open and in we charged, but were prevented from taking over the fort completely by very stubborn resistance from a determined group of rebels in one of the towers. As we moved on the tower a troop of enemy cavalry suddenly charged down from it. Major Axelby and a score of riflemen who were providing covering fire against the gunners in the tower were suddenly faced with horses charging directly at them. As I moved up the slope towards the enemy bastion I saw an enemy sowar with sabre raised above his head ready to bring it down on Major Axelby. I raised my rifle, took hurried aim, fired and the trooper fell dead at the major's feet. He turned and waved his arm in my direction in acknowledgment. At least I had been presented with an opportunity to return one of the many favours that Major Axelby had done for me.

We finally captured the tower and several of the defenders as well. One of our prisoners boasted about a plan to destroy all forts and massacre the inhabitants. One of the places he described where the feringhi were doomed was not too far away: from his description it sounded very much like Edward's command at Jumna-ki-Serai. I spoke to the senior officer, a colonel of the 2nd Battalion, who said there seemed to be a lot of rebel activity all around; just the sort referred to in those letters to Nana Sahib that his men had intercepted earlier. Rebels had been sweeping east towards Cawnpore and Lucknow and could easily include Jumna on their mission to destroy all loyally held stations.

He suggested that it would be advisable to check, just in case. Captain Galbraith and his company had joined us at Etawah and he agreed to lead the mission. After his men had eaten and rested we set off at a brisk pace.

Advancing as swiftly as sensible caution would allow towards the outpost at Jumna-ki-Serai, we skirted to the north-east of Lucknow.

We left Captain Galbraith in that same nullah where I had first left Lieutenant Streeter. I approached the gate with 20 riflemen, stopping near the bodies of rebel sepoys and loyal men of the 32nd as well as some Europeans including that young officer. More bodies, those of gunners, lay across their guns. Reinforcements had arrived but not enough to keep the enemy out.

I signalled riflemen to check the other buildings while I headed up the steps of Edward's residence. Parts of it and other buildings showed signs of being torched and roofs had fallen in on some of them. The bodies of four loyal Native infantrymen, including that of the Havildar, lay just in front of the verandah. I was only able to recognise him by the three broad stripes on his tunic: he and his companions had been badly mutilated. The date was the 28th December and we were supposedly in the season of goodwill.

Leaving riflemen to cover my back I moved slowly and very carefully towards Edward's bedroom. A trail of dried blood led to the body of the children's ayah. Then I was in the room itself, but fearful of what I might discover there. The children – children related to me – were by the bed where I had first seen them not too many days ago. They had been happy and giggling and near their father then: now they were just bodies. *Yes*, I thought grimly, *they had certainly been taken care of.* In the bed were the butchered remains of Edward. He had been hacked mercilessly to death. An arm was severed and where his head had received a heavy sword blow it had fallen forward, with just skin and his windpipe preventing it from rolling away completely.

I felt helpless; we were just days too late. All I could do for him was swear revenge and cover his tortured remains with a piece of cloth.

Across the bottom of the bed was the body of his butler, his trusted khidmatgar who – judging by the amount of blood around him, a broken sword still clenched in his right hand and the bodies of three rebels – had gallantly attempted to defend his master to the very end.

I stepped back, stunned. Why all this? Just what good had it done? I then recalled Edward's words urging me to leave. Yes, I would but there was still dangerous and bloody work to be completed before I could return home, honour intact and duty done.

Returning to the front of the Residency, I ordered a burial party to deal quickly with the remains of the three children and their dead father. They were buried in the Residency garden in a shallow grave covered with stones to deter vultures and wild dogs. Captain Galbraith said a few appropriate words over them. The bodies of the loyal men were gathered up, wrapped in sheets and taken to a small bungalow near the garden. Wood was gathered along with more flammable materials and set alight. We considered this suitable for our brave loyal sepoys, who we thought were all of the Hindu religion. As for the dead mutineers they were left where they had fallen for the attention of the vultures, dogs and the fiercer of the country's wild beasts.

Some minutes after we had attended to the dead and moved off, we heard shots and the screams of women from not too far away carried on the wind.

Three groups of ten men each were sent off as skirmishers, one straight towards where we believed the sounds to be coming from, while the other two groups went to the left and right in flanking moves.

I led the spearhead force and we soon caught up with a group of rebels. We hid in some trees and waited for the captain and the rest of the company.

It looked as though the mutineers just ahead were part of the larger force responsible for the murder behind us at Jumna. There were bodies of several Europeans among the sepoys and it seemed as though their deaths had been neither swift or clean. Among the men were also the bodies of women in varying stages of undress.

It was too late to do anything for them other than avenge their deaths.

Silently, Captain Galbraith joined my force and the two flanking units and signalled the 30 men to fix swords.

He waved me to lead them and we soon fell among the rebels. No quarter was given.

The main rebel force must have included artillery pieces, judging by the extensive damage done to Jumna's walls and most of its buildings. Although they had quite a start after moving off from the splinter force we had just destroyed, Mr Galbraith felt we might be able to catch up with them.

"They could be part of this same large group that left Gwalior and crossed the Grand Trunk Road," he said. "The artillery pieces will slow them down and they may not be in any particular hurry, as they're waiting for even more rebels to join them for a concerted attack on Lucknow. And they won't be expecting us in their rear – they will be more aware of what's in front of them. They will also be feeling confident after destroying the garrison at Jumna-ki-Serai."

"Sir, I'd like to take a small force on ahead to see if I can locate them and then send word back to you," I said, anxious to avenge the victims at Jumna – especially Edward and his children.

"Very well, Sergeant-Major. I suggest you take 20 men, but eat, drink and rest for an hour before you go. In the meantime I'll arrange to have these Company men and these poor, violated women decently buried. Then we'll follow."

I produced one of the copies of the maps I had made and showed him the route I intended taking.

"They are probably heading for this bridge across the Ganges at this spot here," I said, pointing at the heavily creased sheet. "We'll veer slightly north and see if we can get just ahead of them. That way, if they have left a rearguard we should be able to avoid it. I'll send a couple of men back to you. If they are making for that bridge we'll cause a little damage to slow them up and keep them busy at the eastern end of the crossing, while perhaps you can harry them from this side, the western bank."

"By then," said the Captain, "the 7th Hussars should have caught up with us. The colonel had asked for them to follow and cover us as soon as they could. Should be here anytime now. In the meantime, Sergeant-Major, it's a good plan. Can't think why you're not an officer. You could, though, send a couple of men down to locate one of Sir Colin's patrols once you've secured your side of the bridge. Then we could really squeeze the rebels."

After a short rest and tea and hard biscuit we moved off, just as a troop of Hussars rode into camp.

We made good progress, moving as quickly as the rough, rock-strewn terrain would allow and found a very large force of infantry and gunners hauling ten artillery picces. A party of mounted men, sowars, trotted casually alongside this motley band.

I sent two riflemen off to warn Captain Galbraith that we had located the enemy.

We hid in a small tope, a grove of trees. *How these plants survive the heat is beyond me*, I thought.

I decided to move down into a dried-up riverbed. My plan was to move along this as far as possible, skirt the enemy force and beat them to the bridge.

Then matters began to go a little awry. Just behind and to our right we could see around 20 sepoys running. It looked as though they were being pursued by a similar number of enemy troopers, but it took a few moments for it to become obvious that rebels were the ones chasing loyal infantrymen. If this chase continued along the same line they would be bound to crash in among us. From a distance, our uniforms tended to mingle with the foliage of the trees, even those dry Indian ones. If the infantry attempted to shelter in the tope where we were hiding we would soon be discovered.

Our only hope was to try and reach the gully. There at least we would have some good cover if later they decided to rush us.

"Keep as low as you can," I instructed and gestured for them to leave the trees and head for the nullah.

"I think they've seen us," grunted Corporal Williams.

The pursuing troopers, having caught up with about half of the infantrymen, then turned their attention towards us. The surviving sepoys just tumbled into the dried-up riverbed. They quickly explained they had been part of a larger patrol, had become separated, ran out of ammunition and then – to compound their misfortune – had run into another force of rebels who had decided to chase them.

Fortunately they had not discarded their Enfields, so we were able to provide them with some of our ammunition.

While this had been happening, I had been positioning the men along the nullah. It was just the right depth for the average rifleman to use as a firing platform.

Telling every other man to hold his fire so as not to give our true strength away immediately, the rest of us prepared to engage the 20 or so rebels now running straight at us. I told the men to open fire when the enemy were 80 yards away. Without me having to order it, the men had fixed swords.

"Fire!" I shouted and eight or nine sepoys fell. A small troop of sowar had managed to ride around our left flank and a similar number of them were also shot.

As the surviving enemy cavalry attempted to breach this flank a further score of sepoys had left the main force and was now rushing our front.

All riflemen and loyal Indians were now fully engaged.

Several braver or more ferocious rebels managed to evade our rifle shots and had dropped into the nullah waving their swords. Several of them had vicious-looking lathi -- clubs covered in nails that could easily crush a man's skull.

Around 40 minutes had passed since our first shots and I half-expected them to be over-running our position by now. Fortunately, for some unfathomable reason, no more of them had broken away from the main force. Perhaps the fact that our small number had accounted for so many of them in such a relatively short time in hand-to-hand fighting had dampened their enthusiasm. Or, if they were concentrating on capturing Lucknow, they did not want to be diverted by anything else and had just given up. Or – and perhaps more likely – as they were composed of so many different regiments they could not agree on what tactics to use against our small unit.

We weren't faring too badly as a result: just a few wounds as riflemen had fended off sword thrusts and sabre slashes.

Then those remaining decided to charge in again. Sepoys rushed forward alongside mounted rebels. A couple of artillery pieces seemed to be aimed in our general direction too. But either they were too hasty or the gunners were inexperienced, because the shot flew over our heads and bounced harmlessly away.

Once more I shouted "Fire!" and 20 enemy fell. Yet this time their attack seemed more determined. Six or seven sepoys dropped into our temporary trench. A sowar managed to guide his horse into the gully and was heading straight at me just as another rebel raised his rifle and bayonet ready to strike. I moved my Enfield and sword ready to stop the sepoy, catching him just below the ribs. Before I could withdraw my weapon I saw the trooper towering above me on his horse and raising his sword ready to slash at me, the sun glinting on its curved steel blade.

A figure at my side pushed me out of the way. He thrust his rifle and sword up with great force at the fellow as the sabre descended. There was a sickening crunch as steel sliced through cloth and then hit bone, followed by a scream of pain from both assailant and victim, Corporal Williams. The sowar fell backwards, the rifle and sword beginning to pull away from the fatal thrust that Williams had managed to inflict on the man who had been intent on killing me. The corporal was doggedly maintaining his grip on his own weapon.

I retrieved my own rifle as the full weight of Williams began to slide down my left leg and finish in a bloody, crumpled heap at my feet. I glanced over the edge of the nullah. The rebels had once again pulled back, partly as a result of our efforts and partly because of a bugle call from the troop of Hussars and the rest of the rifle company coming to our aid. The rebels, not wishing to see how large this force was, began to disperse in some disorder.

Corporal Williams had somehow managed to slide from my boots and lean against the base of the nullah. He still gripped his rifle firmly with its blood-stained swordblade. He looked up, half smiling, as I fell to my knees by his side. A great gash ran from his collarbone down and across his chest, splitting several ribs. Blood was spreading over his rifle green tunic.

"I'm done for, Sergeant-Major Finch ... or Fortune ...

or whatever you call yourself," he said with much difficulty.

The damage to his chest was not only causing him severe pain but great difficulty in breathing and speaking.

I looked at him in surprise.

"Yes, Jack. We all know about your good luck, your good 'fortune'. All pleased for you too. You're a tough 'un but always played it straight."

"Why did you do it? You threw yourself in front of me. That sabre should have been mine," I said despairingly. His selfless action had almost – and I find this difficult to put into words – reduced me to tears, not for myself but for this odd, brave little man.

"Why not? You've got everything in front of you. If I were you I'd get out of this dump as soon as you can and get back to your lady." At this he chuckled or tried to, but blood began to froth around the corners of his mouth. He mumbled, "Major Axelby's office. Lucky old Jack!"

"Don't talk, George," I said, plucking his Christian name from somewhere deep in the recesses of my mind. I don't think I had ever used his first name since I had first met him in a barrackroom in Kent soon after I joined the Brigade.

He was an old veteran soldier even then and I remember one of the other riflemen saying, "Don't mind him. He's a miserable bastard."

True, but he had kept something of a fatherly eye on me in those very early days and had taught me how to shoot. He had passed on to me something of the speed and skill with which he had handled first the Brunswick, then the Minie and for the last year or more, the Enfield. Thanks in large part to him I had survived South Africa and the Crimea, but I was now helpless in being able to do anything for him.

"Do me a favour, sir ..." he began.

"Yes, anything."

"If," he began, then corrected this to 'when'. "When you get back, go to Whitechapel. It's 63 Clive Street. Yes," he tried to laugh, "funny weren't it? Called after Clive of India and here we bleedin' well are and he's welcome to it. Thanks, Clive! Tell them about me. Haven't seen 'em for years. Maybe all dead. The old man probably drunk himself to death years ago. Maybe all dead," he repeated. "Spot of cholera never too far away. Got a sister and four or five brothers. I've put some money aside. Didn't spend it all on whores. Haven't even had a chance to see those nautch girls dancin' here neither."

At that, some of the old truculence returned, albeit just for a few moments.

He continued to stare at me but his eyes were glazing over.

At least I could carry out that one small favour for him. It was little enough payment for a man saving my life.

"Don't talk, George. We'll get you back." Even as I heard myself saying these words I knew that it was all up for him.

"Give 'em me medals too. Might be able to sell them. Thanks, Jack Fortune. It's been ..." but his voice trailed away. He had gone. I could only wonder at what the rest of his sentence might have been.

I looked down at this brave little man, a true rifleman who had sacrificed his own life to save that of another.

Straightening up, I looked at the sun-browned face for the last time as I ordered men to carry off our wounded and bring our dead back to camp for burial. I did not want vultures tearing at their bodies.

By this time the Hussars and Mr Galbraith's company had returned to the nullah. Very quickly I reported to the captain all that had happened; how the plan had not worked quite as well as we had originally hoped.

"Sorry about Williams and the others," he said. "All good men. Had those infantrymen not blundered into your party, then in all likelihood you would have beaten them to the bridge. Still, the Hussars and the rest of the company have upset their progress."

Chapter Five

As we resumed our march back, a small troop of Lancers caught us up and gave the captain some urgent despatches. The rest of the battalion would catch up with his men at Lucknow. I was ordered to assist another officer on a reconnaissance mission: I was told that I would be accompanying Major Axelby and six picked riflemen.

Our task was to slip through the enemy's lines surrounding the fort at Khamasgarh on the River Yamuna. The garrison there was really hard-pressed, according to reports brought back by spies. The major would then assess the situation and if necessary call for help. Apparently we did not yet have enough soldiers in India to react to every siege or situation and soldiers would only be taken from around Lucknow if it looked as though the Khamasgarh fort would be overrun by rebels.

The spies had reported – though not all spies had proved to be reliable in this campaign – that heavy guns were pounding the walls and mutineers had already made several assaults. So far, they had been driven back and had suffered heavy losses. They could decide just to move on, lift the siege and thus save the need for the fort to be reinforced. There still seemed to be no rhyme or reason about some of the tactics the sepoys deployed: at times they would stick doggedly to besieging a fort or a town, then when it seemed about to fall, they would just leave. This did seem to bear out the view that the mutineers lacked an overall plan and were disadvantaged by having a divided command. Their shortcomings did help us, though.

We managed to slip into the fort through their rather haphazard siege lines without too much trouble.

The following morning I decided to reduce the effectiveness of the besieging artillery a little more by picking off a few rebel gunners.

I moved down to the south wall and for five minutes watched the enemy artillerymen as they prepared to fire what looked like a couple of 18-pounders. I loaded and was about to raise my Enfield to my shoulder, ready to permanently remove one of the gunners, when a voice from one of the other infantry regiments manning the fort called my name.

"Follow me please, sir. The commissioner and your officer want to see you urgently."

He then ducked low and rushed off. Following, I was soon bounding up the steps of the Residency and being ushered into an office. So far it seemed to be free from the attention of the besieging artillery. There was still plaster on the walls and ceilings, with no apparent damage to mirrors and other hangings.

"Ah, just the man," said an officer in the uniform of a brigadier in the Company. He waved me to a seat and then moved to stand in front of a large wall map.

"Major Axelby tells me you've some experience of spying and moving in and out of besieged towns."

"Yes, sir, that's true but we usually did it the other way round. We were the ones besieging."

Again that feeling was returning; the feeling I get when contemplating a full, frontal assault on an enemy position.

"This is Havildar Singh," he said, waving an arm at a tall, neatly bearded man standing stiffly to attention. "His loyalty is beyond question."

Once again there was the build-up to a forlorn hope of some sort, although I did feel a little reassured in the fact that my likely companion was to be a Sikh. Their loyalty had been a crucial factor in the Europeans holding on to some of the towns where mutiny had broken out. Then, thanks in large part to their support, it had been put down in some places very effectively.

"You have obviously concluded that it is only a matter of time before we're overrun here," said the brigadier. "You and the major and the riflemen could, of course, slip back out, though I am sure that with your previous experience, getting into a besieged fort is easier than trying to break out of one. Enemies tend not to expect soldiers trying to break in. Telegraph is down and several of our attempts to break small forces out have failed. You have heard what happened to one of our men they captured."

I did know and so did the rest of the garrison, the civilian clerks as well as the 50 or so women and children in the fort. The rebels had tied him to the barrel of a field gun and blown him to pieces. We could expect no mercy if captured. But we had to do something and soon. I was about to volunteer to break out and go for help when the brigadier spoke again.

"We want you to accompany the Havildar here and get help. He speaks Hindi and if you go during the early hours you might not even be challenged. Then it's off to one of our stations, Cawnpore, Agra or Fatehpur. You might also run into one of our cavalry patrols around the Grand Trunk Road. A troop of Hodson's people and the 3rd Light Cavalry down from Delhi should also not be too far away."

Not to mention, I thought, *the possibility of running into hordes of sepoys and sowars moving across from Gwalior where they seemed to have strong support.*

Fortunately I was sitting down, otherwise the enormity of the situation might have floored me.

"We're asking you," said the brigadier, "because of your experience and level-headedness in a crisis. We cannot order you, but believe you and the Havildar here to be the best men for the task and certainly our only salvation. It is, of course, always just possible that a patrol might arrive and see our predicament and call up reinforcements, but we cannot rely on such chance, can we? What do you think, Sergeant-Major? We appreciate this places you in something of a dilemma."

"I don't really think there is much choice, sir. As you said, the compound is likely to fall to the rebels unless drastic action is taken and I have already seen evidence of their treatment of women and children. But I don't really look the part. The eyes will give me away if we are stopped. What about this man? Does he know what to expect? If we are both captured he'll probably be treated even worse than me … *if* that's possible." I said.

"We've thought about that. You two are – as near as damn it – the same height, though you are broader. We can kit you out in old uniform tunics, the short cotton variety or a long robe-like garment. Or, if you prefer, a dhoti like most of 'em outside seem to favour. Or these very loose fitting 'pyjamas' as they call them and a pair of slippers on your feet. If you do have to walk for any length of time, they may give you a few blisters; not what your feet are used to."

He had produced a very soft-looking pair of those slippers with slightly turned-up toes and brightly embroidered tops.

"We've a sword and its shoulder-belt scabbard and Mr Axelby suggested you borrow his revolver. Should fit under the tunic or robe, whichever you prefer. Pull this turban down a little. Should keep your eyes shaded and away from all but the closest of inspections. And," he added cheerfully, "not all Indians have dark brown eyes."

Not many Indians I was thinking, *have eyes as blue as mine, or have I been unlucky in not coming across those blue-eyed Indians yet?*

"For those parts of you that show, we've been experimenting with this," he said, pointing to a little bowl with dark pieces of what looked like wood floating in it. "It's burnt cork. Your face is quite brown already and most of the sepoys outside are bearded, so running this over your moustache and jaw should give some depth to your beard. Perhaps leave it to grow and cultivate a heavy growth when you get back, just in case you go out on other missions. Also your hands, wrists, lower legs and feet. Obviously your travelling companion does have something of an advantage in this area of disguise," he added.

I don't know whether his last remark was intended to be a humorous observation, but the situation we were in did not merit it.

"Will you go, Sergeant-Major? Do you think the two

of you can pull it off?"

"We'll certainly try, sir. We'll go out as soon as it is dark. Better stay here in case they are keeping a close eye on our comings and goings. Also, we had better eat and drink before we go – can't weigh ourselves down carrying too much. It could prove to be a long, dusty trek tomorrow … if we get that far." I added this view of how realistic I felt about our chances of success: we would do our best but I did not want to raise any false hopes.

Darkness comes quickly in this part of the world. We slipped out of the compound, dropping from the lowest part of the north wall and on to a sandy swathe of the bank of a stream. I managed to avoid contact with any water in case it washed away some of my disguise. We crept around to the southern part of the fort. This was the point near where the Grand Trunk Road was at its closest to the outpost.

As we moved towards those same guns that I had been looking at this very afternoon, we could hear the excited chatter of sepoys. We quickly dropped to our knees. The Sikh moved to one side and I took the other as we shuffled past a gun's wheels. Suddenly, a tulwar flashed in the light from a fire as it descended and caught my companion across the back of his neck, killing him instantly.

I stood up and – from the other side of the gun – began yelling, "Feringhi! Feringhi!" as loudly and excitedly as I could, while waving my sword and pointing away from the gun. This proved just enough of a distraction. They moved off to follow my gesturing. I then ducked down as low as I could and ran towards a cart. Returning my sword to its scabbard but holding my borrowed revolver, I crawled under the whole length of the wagon. The excitement and – I hoped – confusion caused by my sword-waving and shouting would give me just enough time to get clear of their lines and reach the relative safety of a stand of trees near the edge of what I hoped was the right road.

Once again, their lack of a chain of command had allowed me to progress better than I deserved. My only regret so far was that I had been unable to do anything for my erstwhile companion.

Had the mutineers had a regular command structure, rather than men from many units as well as criminals bearing grudges but with no single person in overall charge ensuring basic military duties were being carried out, they might not have all just rushed off so quickly following my shouting. Had they questioned the wild figure who had yelled 'feringhi' then I might have been recognised and killed or captured. About the only thing they did seem to have in common was the desire to kick all Europeans into the sea.

Managing to merge into the blackness of the night I moved north-west, hoping that I had not lost my sense of direction as a result of the recent burst of dangerous excitement. At first I had thought of heading south and east towards Cawnpore but was very mindful of the movement of many sepoys and sowars heading for Lucknow from Gwalior and the area around Jhansi.

I found the road I was looking for, the Grand Trunk, and began to hurry along it. Several troops of cavalry and native infantry were picking their way along it carefully, going – I surmised – to either Lucknow or to assist in the anticipated massacre at Khamasgarh. I was forewarned of their approach if not by the sound of horses' hooves than by the chatter of rebels hellbent on the slaughter of foreigners. On three or four occasions I hid behind boulders or found a ditch to roll in. At the time I thought little of snakes. It was only later that I considered I was lucky not to have confronted a cobra or that human form of snake, a mutinous sepoy.

The hours passed and I began to feel delirious. Travelling in the gloom, having exhausted my small canteen of water and being constantly on edge for fear of running into an enemy force, made me wish my journey was over.

Then, suddenly, it was! Strong hands grabbed me and threw me to the ground. Something sharp was at my throat.

"Shall I kill the mutinous dog, sahib?" shouted the voice of a Sikh.

Just as I was about to beg them not to finish me off,

another voice – a European one – broke in.

"No, we'll take him on to Agra for questioning before they string him up. Tie him to your horse. If he flags, prod him with your sword."

My throat was parched, my head dizzy, but I managed to stammer out:

"Could I not just walk beside your troop, sir?"

"Well I am blessed. He's one of ours. Who are you exactly?"

"John Finch, Rifle Brigade," I wheezed out just as I felt like fainting.

"Ah, heard of you," he said. "What exactly are you doing here? And not quite in your usual uniform."

"Slipped out of Khamasgarh. Place is under siege. Can't last much longer. On my way to get help. Did think of going to Fatehpur or to Lucknow where my battalion is based but considered it too far to go. By then the siege might be over and everyone dead. Too much enemy activity towards Lucknow anyway, so thought it best to strike north instead."

"You've done jolly well," said the officer. "Must have travelled 30 miles in the last day or so. Had to cross a couple of rivers by the look of you. Very good going in the dark surrounded by marauding mutineers, not to mention wild animals. You look a mess. Do you ride? Always carry a few spare mounts. We'll get you to Agra and organise the relief column."

So for a time I rode with a troop of Hodson's Horse whose status as scouts, fighting men and men of independent action had spread across central and northern India. One of their particular talents was discovering the position of the enemy's forces. Hodson also had a network of spies and agents across most of the sub-continent.

Their leader, Captain William Hodson – having survived some earlier scandals – now had a well-deserved reputation for his exploits. His men were a mix of European officers and loyal Sikhs from the Punjab. I had seen him at the head of his men a few times, a tall, fair-haired officer whose flamboyant character encouraged his men to follow him anywhere. He had also insisted that the usual scarlet cavalry tunic be replaced with a loose-fitting overall. This was dyed a dusty yellow green called in Hindustani, khaki. To complete the uniform, loose pyjamas were worn instead of the tight-fitting trousers of the regular cavalry. A scarlet turban was adopted, giving the unit an overall very distinctive look.

My horse trotted along obediently but I could barely keep in the saddle. I will admit to not being a good horseman. Bareback as a boy was all that I had really done. I now felt myself to be falling forward or to the left and right and was only kept in the saddle by the close attention of the two Sikhs; one on either side grabbing me and propping me up as the need arose.

A couple of hours later – I really don't know how long exactly because I was riding fast asleep certainly for a fair part of the journey to Agra – I slid with much relief from the saddle. The two flanking Sikhs propelled me into an office, that of the Deputy Governor of the province.

"Poor fellow here," began my rescuer, "is Finch of the Rifle Brigade from Khamasgarh. Compound there is in danger of being overwhelmed. They desperately need help. I managed to divert a small force heading to Lucknow to help out at Khamasgarh, but they'll still need more reinforcements if the rebels are to be dispersed or defeated."

During this time the two Sikhs had planted me in a chair indicated by the Company official. I must have looked a sorry sight. My clothes were torn and caked in dust. My arms were limp in my lap and I could feel my head just lolling forward, but without my really being able to control it. I was tired and fought to keep my eyes open. The turban, a key part of my disguise, had fallen to the floor.

Water was splashed over my head, neck and face. A cold, metal cup was pressed to my cracked lips. No invitation was needed, however, for me to gulp down the contents.

I could hear voices but they seemed far away. In my trance-like state it was all just washing over me. Orders were being issued and it seemed as though a force of cavalry, artillery and infantry was to leave immediately to relieve a besieged station. Another order was rattling around my head. Soon I felt myself being lifted. I was floating gently away. Later I discovered the two Sikhs had carried me to a quiet room where I was placed on a doolie, a mattress. There I remained for many hours, oblivious to everything going on around me.

It was growing dark by the time I finally awoke. I had slept for more than a day, but apart from a headache I felt alright – if very hungry. Thoughts soon turned not just to food but to wondering how the relief column was faring.

As I sat up to try and get my bearings I found I was wearing little other than a dhoti.

An aide-de-camp entered the room.

"Jolly good effort, Finch. With luck, our force should be among them before too long. By this time tomorrow we should have word. Anything you need? Well ..." he laughed, "... apart from a good wash and some clean togs."

"Sir, would it be possible to have some food? I don't think I have eaten for three or four days."

"We'll see what we can do. I'll send the khidmatgar in with something."

He was as good as his word and soon a variety of items appeared before me on a tray, including cold soup, potatoes, vegetables and spiced chicken.

One of the Residency staff poked his head round the door.

"We'll have clean clothes sent in soon, Mr Finch," he said. "Then when you feel up to it the Deputy Governor, Mr Carnegie and a few other officers including Captain Hodson want to see you in the office. Take your time though. You've had a rough few days."

Clothes duly turned up. Not, as I had hoped, my rifle green uniform somehow spirited in from Lucknow but a loose skirt-like garment and pyjamas or churidar. If pressed I might begrudgingly agree why such clothing was favoured by the local population; because it was light and comfortable. I moved to a washstand and poured cool water into a bowl from a jug, washing luxuriously my face and other very important parts of me in melon- and lemon-scented water. I managed to remove all traces of my skin colouring efforts from face, hands, arms and legs. The burnt cork had proved to be quite effective! A glance in a large, ornately decorated mirror still revealed a rather fierce bearded face. My complexion did seem to be a deal swarthier than the last time I had looked. Perhaps, as Edward had remarked, the country does get inside you. Looking at the beard made me think a razor would be a good idea. But even after a careful search of some drawers I could not find one. Perhaps if there had been one it had been removed to prevent me from removing my facial disguise. It had, after all, been suggested that I could be employed on similar missions.

The khidmatgar appeared at the door and I asked him to direct me to the Residency office.

A group of officers were standing around a mahogany table. The aide-de-camp, seeing me hovering at the door, detached himself from the group and came over to meet me.

"Well done, Sergeant-Major Finch," he said, grabbing my right hand and pumping my arm like a villager drawing water from the old well in Lower Durford. Releasing his grip, he steered me towards the gathering.

"A lot of people in Khamasgarh owe their lives to you," offered the gentleman standing at the head of the table.

"If it hadn't been for me blundering into a troop of Captain Hodson's Irregulars, sir, things might have been a lot different. Is there any news then, sir?"

"Yes, a rider from the relief column brought intelligence a short time ago that the bagheelogs – the mutineers – have been scattered. Probably heard of the approach of our main relief column and decided to slink away. The force that Lieutenant Mason of Hodson's Horse asked to divert from going on to Lucknow did manage to give them a bloody nose. By the time the main reinforcements arrived, the rebels seemed to have lost heart and fled. Captain Hodson here and his troop will chase them early tomorrow morning with his usual verve. Pleased I am not in rebel shoes! They won't get far. The plan is to prevent them from joining up with the main rebel force at Lucknow. Oh, and your Major Axelby has just ridden in. A good horseman; should be in the cavalry."

I heaved a sigh of relief. By now I had been thanked and congratulated and was just waiting to be dismissed before rejoining Mr Axelby and then it would be back to the rest of the battalion; my spying days over, or at the very least, suspended. No, not quite, as it turned out.

Instead of being dismissed I was invited to sit down again by the Deputy Governor who was leaning across his desk positively glowing in anticipation of something or other.

"Do make yourself comfortable, Sergeant-Major. Care for a glass of something?"

The khidmatgar weaved in and out of the assembled company dispensing a variety of beverages.

"Gentlemen, will you join me in a toast to the brave efforts of this young man? I have already notified his commanding officer and the Governor-General of his exploits. Ah, here's Major Axelby. Just in time, Axelby,"

I had opted for rum, and after their toast and more accompanying words of congratulations gratefully drained my glass and waited to be sent on my way.

There seemed to be an awkward silence. Major Axelby looked a little uneasy. He seemed to be sensing that something was about to happen that was not what I would want.

At length the senior Company official cleared his throat and spoke, while looking keenly and directly at me.

"Sergeant-Major Finch, by your recent action you have proved your devotion to duty by carrying out your orders magnificently."

Here we go again, I thought, *something's heading straight at me!*

"We have a task," he continued, "that needs to be carried out with some urgency. We think you are the very man to carry it out to a successful conclusion. But," he added, his expression darkening and worryingly so for my taste, "like most of our action during this present emergency it is not without some considerable risk."

He proceeded to outline the 'task', but as he went on to relay the details he looked up at the other men in the room at intervals. It did appear that he was not trying to play down the dangers of it, or – if it was possible – to exaggerate them.

"We are concerned, and here I speak on behalf of and with the full authority of the Governor-General, to ensure that the leader of Jhansi, the Rani, Laksmi Bai, remains loyal. She is surrounded by rebel factions and could be said to be wavering in her loyalty to us. She is a widow. After her husband's death, Jhansi was annexed. She has petitioned for its return on several occasions but instead was given an appreciably large pension and a palace. She seemed until recently quite content to live peacefully and not fall in with mutineers.

"What has not helped in keeping the Rani content to live quietly and beyond the spread of revolt are agents of Nana Sahib. There is suspicion that the Russians may also be spreading money around and in Nana's direction in order to bribe wavering loyal princes to join the mutiny. This would serve to add to that unease among the general population. It would undermine our influence across the country, perhaps even to the extent of the Russians replacing us in India. Their influence would then extend from land along the Afghanistan frontier right across the sub-continent and on to who knows where else.

"I am sure Nana Sahib's name is known to you for his cowardly actions at Cawnpore. Indeed, I hear one of your own kin was affected by this man's treachery. There are others who have also been trying to undermine the Company and other European interests, not merely the Russians. I need hardly to remind you that last June a number of Europeans were murdered. The Rani, though, has given us assurances that this tragic incident was the work of renegade sepoys and not those under her direct personal command.

"We propose sending an honest representative to her palace with our written guarantee of British good faith. There will also be a letter in Hindi introducing our envoy – you – and insisting he be accorded all due respect and safe conduct in and away from the palace.

"She is, however, a very resolute character and the task to persuade her to even consider our proposals will not be easy.

"We could of course send a regiment or two into Jhansi but this was discounted. A show of force at this stage might have the opposite effect."

The aide-de-camp took up the plan just as I began to feel more and more trapped: a victim of my own success.

"You'll not be alone. We propose sending you into Jhansi with two of Captain Hodson's trusted Sikhs. Their task is a little different from your mission. You will seek access to the palace, while the other two men will go on to the fort. Efforts have already been made by other agents to convince the sepoys that returning to us is the only solution. That is, apart from those men who have committed rape and murder. The Rani is in the middle of so much confusion and rebels there have many ideas besides a general desire to kill all feringhi in sight. If we can drive a wedge between even a few of these groups, that can only relieve some of the pressure on us while we consolidate our forces. If the Rani sees dissent she may decide to keep clear of anything likely to reduce their chance of victory and so return to her quiet life within the walls of the palace."

The Deputy-Governor took up the briefing.

"Since about last August, because the Company's attention has been elsewhere, Jhansi has been rather left to its own devices," he said. "We cannot, however, let matters drift any more. Our apparent lack of interest could convince the Rani and others that we are powerless to do anything. It could also turn out that if the rebels repeat their ideas often enough the balance of power may be tipped in their favour rather than ours."

He paused and looked at me, eyebrows raised quizzically ready for any questions I might have. So far I was content just to sit and wait for the whole scheme to be revealed. It was not, however, improving with the telling of it. This all sounded rather desperate, not to mention a last dangerous resort. I had been trying to distract myself from the likely dangers by conjuring up images of home; the river, the cottage … but mainly Nell. I involuntarily shook my head, which caused the speaker's eyebrows to rise even higher. I supposed he had interpreted my action as a possible refusal to go on the mission. What it really was, though, was me trying to pull myself away from those warm thoughts of home. It had had the effect of reminding me that I had so much to lose if it all went wrong – mainly my life!

I did manage to glance at Major Axelby, whose face was showing signs of strain. Captain Hodson, however, looked eager and ready to charge off himself: such was his character. Several other officers and Company officials maintained their expectant looks.

Two Sikhs dressed in Hodson's Horse livery had by now been ushered into the room. More volunteers, I thought rather sourly.

"We plan," continued the senior official, "to have you disguised and – accompanied by these two trusted guides – be escorted by Mr Hodson and a troop of his men to Datia, which is a few miles short of Jhansi city. They will be preceded by a scouting party who will check to see if there have been any developments that could upset things. The troop will remain at Datia for three days for your return."

"Do you have any questions, Sergeant-Major?" asked the aide.

"Just two, sir. With respect, why don't those agents who are already probing the area and who will be familiar with the terrain just continue with their work? And, secondly, when is this to take place?"

"In answer to the first, the agents are beginning to raise suspicions and some of them are only employed for money and may sell out to the highest bidder. We could not in all honesty expect them to carry out such a sensitive mission effectively. In short, we do not trust them. Some agents have taken our money and either vanished or passed on information instead of collecting it. Your two companions will get you close enough to the palace, as they are familiar with the area. If you agree to undertake this you will leave early morning, the day after tomorrow. That is the 14th January. By then Captain Hodson will have returned from his harrying mission.

"You may be wondering what the rest of your battalion will be doing while you are on your travels."

I nodded expectantly.

"They are going to engage a large force of mutineers on the east bank of the Ganges, then will move back towards Lucknow and protect its approaches. This, we hope, will also work in your favour as mutineers will be heading from Gwalior to confront Sir Colin Campbell's forces. As the enemy has just lost Khamasgarh, largely thanks to you, we are assuming they will be heading east in some haste. And, of course, that's why your mission to keep the Rani loyal is vital. There is still some rebel activity not too far from Jhansi, however."

"Well sir, at least we know what to expect. We'll go off and prepare."

"Good man and good luck to the three of you," said the aide and the sentiment was repeated by the officers around the table.

The three of us were led off and I was escorted to the room I had first occupied. On the dhullie was a selection of native clothing as well as a sword and a bowl of burnt cork.

Although our departure was not for many hours, I decided to change into my disguise in order to get used to the feel of the clothing. The ones I had been given earlier were too clean and sweet-smelling to be of much use.

Then Major Axelby entered the room.

"Jack, what can I say? Had I been here earlier I would have tried to persuade them to send someone else. The truth is, you have been too successful. Doesn't make me feel good, though, about you going on this mission."

"Sir, I beg you not to give it another moment's thought," I said. "It would have been difficult to refuse. And we are soldiers. We both know only too well that it could all end any time, anywhere; a stray rebel bullet, a shell or some grapeshot. Bound to be some risk somewhere. Doesn't mean I like it, but as a soldier I accept it. And if it does work it could save lives in the long run, especially ours, eh sir? And perhaps get us home all the sooner."

That seemed to cheer him a little and before leaving the room he added: "I hope you will take my revolver again. What else can I say but wish you good luck and see you when you get back."

Twenty or so minutes later I was standing in front of the mirror. Yes, I might just pass for a sepoy. At least I believed I looked more convincing than I had done on my last foray into enemy territory. My beard did look suitably wild.

I spent some time before our departure talking to the two Sikhs and felt reassured by them. I pulled out a copy of the little map I had made and congratulated myself for having taken the trouble of making several copies. The best one I kept with the rest of my kit in the battalion luggage.

Agra to Jhansi is some distance but we could travel the first 30 or so miles by cart, down the road that linked Agra, Gwalior and Jhansi. Just before our departure I noticed that both Sikhs had also adopted a disguise. Realising that most Sikhs in the land had remained loyal, they had changed into turbans, tunics and trousers that were more typical of the average mutineer than their usual very smart attire. Even their usually carefully groomed beards looked wild and unkempt.

Keeping a safe distance behind us would be a troop of Hodson's Horse. Another troop of these Irregulars had set off in pursuit of the rebels dispersed at Khamasgarh but had not yet returned. It occurred to me that even if Irregulars were spotted near Datia, it would not be regarded by the rebels as anything particularly sinister. Hodson's men had the reputation of suddenly appearing, attacking and then moving on before the enemy could re-group and counter-attack.

As we progressed, the three of us barely talked. They spoke Hindi and although I was picking up the odd word here and there I could not risk talking whenever we moved among the villages on our way south to Jhansi. English, although spoken by some Indians, mainly the educated ones in the employ of the Company, could not be risked among ordinary villagers.

We managed to reach and cross a river, the Chambai,

but our wagon – a hackery – and the bullocks pulling it made the timbers of the bridge groan in protest.

What kept me alert as we made steady but slow progress was the constant movement of sepoys and sowars all around us, but there were also many other travellers as well as camels and elephants carrying all kind of loads.

I did have one frightening experience. We had come across a tributary of a river we had recently crossed and were allowing our animals to drink. Something in the long grass by the side of the track we were on caused our bullocks to veer off suddenly. There, on one of the flat rocks scattered among the coarse grass, was a snake basking in the ever-present heat of the sun. Disturbed, it reared up. Instinctively, I reached inside my long, white cotton tunic for my borrowed revolver just as this hooded serpent – now reaching almost chest high – prepared to strike.

One of my Sikh companions was more than equal to the task. In a flash of steel his tulwar removed the cobra's head. The rest of the snake just flopped back onto the rock leaving a streak of blood.

Grinning broadly, he remarked: "You are lucky, Havildar-Major, sahib, that I am Sikh and not Hindu. They revere such vile creatures."

I thanked him, but for the rest of the day kept a very wary eye open for other cobras.

We reached Gwalior. The fort there was impressive and seemed to straggle over a couple of miles. It was cleverly positioned on top of a sandstone hill about 250 feet high, and the walls above this hill rose a further 25 or 30 feet.

We had by this time abandoned the hackery. We had noticed with some alarm that there were many sepoys moving down the road, who – when they drew level with a cart – just climbed up on it and were usually allowed to remain on board. Our hackery could have easily taken two or three more men. But we couldn't risk them being in such close proximity, so we decided we must draw off the road and abandon the cart. We returned to the heat and dust of the road but hoped not to draw attention to ourselves. There were many such travellers, mostly too hot to glance too keenly at fellow walkers. Before leaving the hackery we had unhitched the bullocks and as we had walked away they had just stood there looking bewildered, before they too moved off in search of water. If they were lucky they would steer clear of the many tigers said to be in the area.

We joined a group of merchants with elephants and camels heading towards the gates of the fort, thinking there might after all be safety in their company.

Inside there was a maze of streets, with several small palaces and temples decorated with friezes of brightly coloured tiles with scenes showing every kind of animal including peacocks, elephants, tigers and crocodiles. We were not there, though, for the undoubted beauty of the place. Gwalior was said to be one of the main centres of the mutiny and as we wandered around we saw there were many sepoys present.

Just before darkness fell we slipped out of the fort just in case the gates were locked overnight. Then it was down the hill to an abandoned hut we had found on the way in. Now was the time to rest up. We took it in turns to keep watch.

After a simple breakfast and just a few sips of water we prepared to move on, keeping close by the road.

Before reaching Datia we stopped overnight once more. There, using the fringes of a tope as cover, a small force of Hodson's Horse surrounded us. An officer told us they would wait for us out of sight until our return and then escort us back to Agra. He added that the rest of the troop was not too far away.

Even though Datia was loyal, there would be spies everywhere and that was the reason we had originally taken a wagon so that we could mingle with the local population.

Heartened by our meeting with Hodson's men we headed off in the direction of Jhansi, the fort and the mahal or palace.

My two companions veered off in the direction of the fort while I looked around for a point where I could slip into the palace unnoticed. I walked around the walls but, concerned that I might just attract the attention of anyone above me taking the trouble to look down, I affected a limp. Perhaps my moving awkwardly would make me look less like a British soldier.

The gates to the palace looked to be heavily guarded, so I inspected the walls more closely. I came across a gully that served, I guessed, as drainage for when the monsoons turned the flat expanse below into a flooded plain. At one point I found that some of the stonework had fallen and I managed to scramble up and onto a verandah. From there I made my way past several rooms that were very richly decorated with rugs of every hue on the floors. Walls were hung with silks. Then I heard loud voices and a female screaming.

As I passed another khirkee, a window, I saw two men attempting to force themselves on a young woman. Part of me said *ignore it. This is not your fight*, I told myself. If two rival groups wanted to hurt each other, that served to reduce the odds I might have to face later. But I couldn't just walk by. A woman was about to be dishonoured. I quickly clambered into the room. The men flung the woman – who was naked from the waist up – to the floor and attempted instead to take their frustrations out on me. Fortunately I had the advantage of surprise.

I drew my tulwar and rushed at them. They were slow to react: their hands had been occupied elsewhere. I slashed one across the throat and he fell choking to the ground, his blood adding to the rich colour of the floor coverings. The other was still struggling to remove his sword from its scabbard but took to his heels before I could bring my weapon up to deal similarly with him. I started after him but a heavy blow from behind knocked me senseless to that richly endowed floor.

Time had passed but I had little way of knowing how much.

I was being held firmly. Two men gripped an arm each behind my back. The left side of my jaw was pushed down hard to the marble floor. A third man held the point of a sword rather too closely to my throat. I could, from this somewhat restricted and uncomfortable position, just make out the figure of a woman. Not the one, however, who I had jumped through the window to rescue.

Then I saw her too. She had entered the room, her soft shoes gently flapping on that part of the cold, hard floor not covered by a rug. She was now clothed, the once exposed small breasts covered. She stood just a pace or two behind the other woman, who now began to speak.

"You saved one of my household and are a very brave man, ferenghi," she said in English, "but a fool."

From my rather vulnerable position I judged her to be around thirty years of age; and she stood proud and erect. Whatever pose she adopted it was certainly better than my present view of the world.

A fool, I thought, *and soon a dead one!*

But then she motioned the sword-waver to move back. He looked bitterly disappointed at not being given the order to finish me off rather than being told to spare me, at least for the time being. The two other men had been ordered to raise me to my feet and then let go of my arms. I fell forward while my freed arms took a little time to regain their feeling.

"All the other renegades, the bhainchutes, have been killed or driven off," she explained, "but why are you here?"

For a few seconds I hesitated, unsure how to respond. I was, after all, disguised, wandering abroad in unfamiliar territory and certainly looking less like a peace emissary and more like one of the bandits of the hills or those murderous sepoys or – as she had described them – 'sister-violaters' who had tried to ravish a yakshi or femle servant. I only hoped that the woman, now restored to some dignity and with breasts covered, could intercede with the speaker if she had not already done so, to extend that same courtesy to me!

The speaker was certainly elegantly dressed in fine muslin with exquisite jewellery at her throat, wrists, ankles and around her waist.

"You are a very brave man, feringhi soldier," she repeated, but this time with a trace of humour in her voice. No doubt she was amused by my attempts at disguising myself. "But," she added with a grim smile, "a foolish one to pass through the land of the bagh, the tiger!"

For the second time I thought that I was a dead man and not merely a 'foolish' one. It was sending cold shivers down my back that I could so easily be killed, my body then dumped among the rocks for the vultures. Who would know? I'd probably be posted as 'missing presumed dead' and that would be an end to it.

"Do you not realise that all around are sepoys and badmash who are using the present unrest with the British to steal, rape and kill? You have just met some of them. Part of a band who managed to somehow slip past my bodyguard. You were very nearly mistaken for one such evil man."

While she had been speaking I found my eyes drawn to one of the jewels around her neck. It seemed to be a silver torque necklet braided with many twisted lengths of that same precious metal. Set into the silver were what appeared to be diamonds and rubies. Apart from the renegades' plans to attack members of the household they would have grabbed other handfuls of riches. On tables and sideboards were various jewels. The woman who had done the talking so far also wore brooches, rings and had glittering stones in her hair. Her servant was almost as richly bejewelled.

"Why are you here?" she asked.

"We have heard in Delhi and Agra that certain sections of the rebels nearby wish to discuss giving themselves up, or are at the very least hoping to rejoin the Company's army," I said. "There is also an important person I need to seek out and hand over certain documents. I believe I have found that person, madam, but require confirmation of this." I looked directly at her while at the same time carefully reaching inside my tunic and then tearing open a specially sewn pocket where papers had been concealed.

As I did so one of the guards started forward and I half-turned towards him to show him that I was not reaching for a hidden weapon. I then continued.

"There is concern that the royal person in question may be wavering in her original desire to support the Company. If she should choose to follow one path or the other, such a decision will almost certainly persuade other princes to follow her example. I am to make contact. Then if I am able to discover how others, still unsure what path to follow, will take, I am to offer all concerned a chance to return to supporting us. My superiors believe that this is in the best interests of all parties, as it will prevent further disaster and bloodshed. Princes and sepoys wishing to return can be escorted under a flag of truce and onto Agra.

"I have also been instructed to say that, although it may take time, British forces will prevail in the end. My superiors are anxious to avoid unnecessary conflict."

"Why should anyone believe anything that the British promise? Your people have taken our land. You ignore our religion, our customs, take the women for yourselves, steal our taxes, even many of the state jewels of Jhansi have gone. Then you force us to take your merchandise. What do we get? A foreign master, the sahib-bay."

This was said with a tone of derision in her heavily accented English. She continued with her condemnation of British influence.

"Your people also seem to be encouraging the pro-British local princes of Orcha and Datia to invade what is left of my land as my punishment for a massacre of Europeans last year and for my consorting with rebels. What they fail to say is they want my castle for themselves. The British do not accept my word when I say the massacre was not my doing."

I did not particularly want to argue. There were many rumours about the way the two sides behaved. From what I had seen of India there seemed to be some truth in what she was saying. Other people had told me that the Company had handled some things badly and that rich people at home had grown even richer because of links with India. Yet a lot of Indian people seemed content to work alongside Europeans. Outsiders did provide employment and paid wages. On the other hand, if the Indians did not accept such jobs, what else could they do? Who would pay them and how would they feed their families? It crossed my mind that the Russians would be happy to step in, replace us and employ those same Indians who supported the Company. I could also have said to her that Indian society – with its castes, cultures and traditions – served to keep the country backward, though if she ever visited London or any city in England she might use a similar argument about the gulf between the rich on their estates and in their town houses and the poor in squalid hovels, as well as the uncounted forgotten in the workhouses of England. And who produced the goods that were sent to India? Thousands of men, women and even children slaving away in the foul, 'dark satanic mills' of England's factories, as the poet William Blake described them.

I thought it best to merely content myself by saying: "I'm a simple soldier. I obey orders while others decide the fate of millions."

This brought a wry smile to her lips.

"You are not quite a simple soldier, I think!" she said.

I decided to press on. "But you have me at a disadvantage. For, madam, you have not said who you are though I can guess."

"Yes, you are indeed correct for I am Jhansi-ki-Rani Laksmi Bai, the Rani of Jhansi, born Manikarnik Tambe but named Laksmi to honour the goddess of that name. My family held the land from here to the sea and to Rawalpindi and beyond in the north and to Delhi in the east. Then it was stolen when my husband died. My petitions for its return have been ignored. My son, Damadar Rao, has been denied his claim to Jhansi. We have *thus far* remained loyal to the British in India in spite of the many provocations. Many of my people and those around favour our joining the rebels, as some regard the present conflict as a cry for our independence. We shall remain loyal but only for as long as it serves our purpose rather than yours. Take that back to your chiefs."

She may have greatly exaggerated the extent of her husband's lands but with regard to the other particulars they seemed, from what I had heard, more or less an accurate summary of what had happened to the town, palace and fort of Jhansi.

Then she fixed me with an intense look.

"What to do with you in the meantime?"

Let me go quickly crossed my mind, especially as she had mentioned about going back to report to my superiors. I suggested I should return to Agra and describe what had taken place here. I also thought that with so many rebellious sepoys marauding not too far away, the situation could change at any time. India had been described as a keg of powder. The spark could come from anywhere. The Rani seemed in control, but for how long?

How were my companions faring? It seemed very unlikely from what Laksmi Bai had been saying that anyone beyond the walls of the palace could be trusted.

"Now you must tell me who you are," she said.

"My name is John Finch. I am a Sergeant-Major, a Havildar-Major, 3rd Battalion, The Rifle Brigade," I said with some pride and stood to attention as best my loose-fitting native clothes would allow.

"You greatly impress me, my bahurdar, my hero," she replied. "If all British were as honest and loyal as you, then perhaps all would prosper. Had that been so, however, our paths would never have crossed. Your two battalions of riflemen would never have needed to land in Calcutta two and more months ago."

This surprised me and it must have shown on my face.

"Common knowledge among many princes, who have spies and agents everywhere – just as the British do," she said. "You will take refreshment and rest. Then two of my men will escort you to the borders of Datia where you will no doubt catch up with Irregular cavalry."

Again, I could not help but show surprise. For someone who seemed to be living a quiet life she seemed very well informed. It would also make her a very useful friend … or a very dangerous enemy.

"At the border," she continued, "my guards will leave you, for they risk capture. But before you go I must reward you for your action in saving the life and honour of my servant." With that she removed the diamond and ruby silver torque necklace that I had been admiring earlier. She handed it to me. "You seem to like this," she commented simply.

"I thank you ,but cannot accept such a fine gift. It is a beautiful piece of jewellery and I am not worthy of it."

"You can and you will accept this or anything else you may receive while under this roof," she responded, her eyes shining, "or do you wish to offend me?" This was added in a very sharp tone. "It has been passed down through my husband's family. Once it adorned the neck of a mughal emperor's wife." She then added rather dryly: "the British usually have no problem in taking whatever they want in this country. This, however, is freely given with our thanks."

"I thank you most sincerely, but this was very different. I did what any man should do for a lady in distress," I said and bowed while tucking this unexpected gift under my native tunic.

She rang a little bell and the khidmatgar entered the room.

Speaking in Hindi, she gave him instructions. He left, only to return a few minutes later carrying a tray with an assortment of fruit and other food and some drinks.

"Refresh yourself, John Finch, and then rest. It is too late for you to leave and wander around a strange land in the dark. Go tomorrow instead. May you sleep contentedly. My khidmatgar will show you to a room where you will find peace."

After I had indicated that I had completed a very welcome repast, she rang the bell for the second time.

The butler returned. Again she spoke to him and off he went, returning soon after with two of those same men – her bodyguards – I had encountered earlier. The Rani spoke to them and they left.

"I have ordered them to return at sunrise and bring you to the Datia border. Now go. Rest and allow your senses to be restored. Tomorrow you go with our blessing. We shall not meet again, for if we do – who can say what might happen?"

This last remark was said in a very careful, measured tone and I noticed her brows furrowing as though she was contemplating some deep concerns. Did this mean, after all, that she might have to resort to fighting us instead of staying loyal?

Then she turned directly towards me and bade farewell. She raised her hands, palms together. the tips of her long, slender, carefully manicured fingers just touching that part of her forehead above her nose and her long eyelashes on turquoise lids briefly closing.

I bowed as solemnly as I could, but as I stood upright again I found myself wondering just what she would do. Once more I was left feeling a little bewildered by this formidable, certainly remarkable, vibrant and beautiful woman. I hoped that we would not end up on opposing sides one day.

The khidmatgar had been standing at a respectful distance while that final scene had been played. He gave a brief cough and with a sweep of his right arm invited me to follow him. This I did and we passed many richly decorated rooms until we came to a smaller one with fine wall hangings, sumptuous rugs, dhurrie, and simple native furniture. Just below the single shuttered window was a large (and after some of the rough nights I had recently experienced, very welcome looking) bed. It was covered in colourful linen and inviting cushions. A punkah hung from the ceiling. A cord ran from the bottom of the punkah and up through a small, square aperture set halfway up the far wall. I imagined a punkah-wallah on the other side of that wall would be gently pulling on the cord when the fan was required.

The Rani's butler left, softly closing the door behind him, while I moved across to the shutters and eased one of them open. I glanced out; I needed to know what lay outside just in case I needed to leave in a hurry. Six or seven feet below was a finely tended garden and the scent of flowers, of jasmine particularly, reached my nostrils. Looking to my left I could just make out in the thickening gloom, the forbidding walls of the formidable Shankar Fort that towered above both the palace and the town.

Removing the tunic and placing my sword across the seat of a chair, I washed my face and hands in lightly perfumed water, which I drew from a jug on a bamboo table. I gratefully gulped down some cool water from a large lota; a cup favoured by high-caste Indians. The brass of the lota did leave a metallic taste slightly tingling my lips. Then it was necessary to use other vessels placed behind bamboo screens. Rather better than some of the latrines I had used elsewhere!

I moved to the bed and began to settle myself. I looked around the room, making sure I knew where the window was – just in case. I then blew out the oil lamp on the little table by my bed and lay back, ever alert for threatening sounds of movement. But other than the odd whistling of the fox-like dhole or wild dog and the occasional screech of peacocks, I could not hear anything to cause me alarm. I was also trying to convince myself that if they had intended doing me harm there had been opportunities aplenty earlier. So why bother to wait for the dead – an unfortunate word! – of night?

At last, having finally convinced myself that I would be safe, I settled back on the cushions, though I kept my borrowed revolver within reach. With my hands behind my head I stared up towards the ceiling and thought back over the events of the day. Uppermost in my mind was my encounter with the Rani, her maidservant and the bodyguards.

It was very difficult not to focus on just the Rani. When she had been describing her views of the British she had sounded particularly bitter. There did seem to be an atmosphere in and around the palace and one I could cut with my tulwar.

The more I thought of it, the more I began to consider that she had good cause. She had, after all was said and done, been effectively deposed. She lived in the family palace but others held the real power. I was glad I was a soldier and followed orders rather than having to issue them. Once again, if pressed I might admit to a sneaking regard for this striking looking woman who had put her case well. As I lay there in the all-embracing darkness of that January evening I could feel myself agreeing more and more with her, as well as having been rather intoxicated by her physical presence. She was, however – I rather ruefully concluded – ultimately doomed if she took that fatal step of supporting the rebels. What to tell them in Agra? She might, she might not, stay loyal. At that moment as I lay on that bed in Jhansi Palace I hoped that she would remain on our side. My interview with her so reminded me of the times I had embraced Nell and been overwhelmed by the warmth and nearness of her body. The Rani, whose close-fitting garment had done little to cover her charms, would be a very difficult temptation to resist. No doubt there had been times when she had been forced into using those charms to good effect. I also thought that she must be very brave in the way she had dealt with rebels, her own people and the Company.

The day's events, the evening air, and the scents wafting over me were slowly, steadily numbing my senses into a feeling of euphoria. Lids were heavy, sleep would soon take over.

I was drifting away in that sensation of floating … thoughts of home, of India and its horrors and then back to Broughton House and loving, reassuring memories of Nell. My head was scrambled but contentedly so.

At least sleep must have captured me, for I awoke a little startled in my head but more alive in my loins as a hand began to lightly caress my member into the sort of life I had seen represented on temple walls. An intoxicating scent began to fill my head as lips followed hand across my belly and down and down. Who was this? For a moment I thought that it might be the Rani herself. But why would she seek out a rough rifleman? After a few more seconds of exquisite pleasure I realised it was the maidservant whose honour and life I had protected.

What could I do but lie back and think of Nell as waves of ecstasy and delirious pleasure swept over me. I struggled but then managed in my head to ask Nell for forgiveness.

My visitor had turned completely around with her back to me and was easing her lithe body to accept my very ready member.

This did not prove to be too easy, but as I slipped into her she let out a soft cry while her body trembled. Then she began to rise and fall, taking in most of me.

Her arms stretched back and I could feel her wrists on either side of my hips, the palms of her hands soon flat on the dhurrie. Her head was tilted back and her unpinned hair soon fell to my belly.

Without thinking I reached up and with my hands cupped small, firm breasts; then exploded inside her. A long felt need was certainly fulfilled. She called out as waves of pleasure seemed to affect her too. Then she fell back before rolling off me and silently leaving the room.

Again I thought of Nell. But what could I do? What would any man have done?

When we are finally together it will be our love that joins us. This was not love, and I had not sought this coupling, but it had certainly provided a much-needed outlet for the frustrations I had been feeling for many months.

But I was alone again and before long was drifting back into sleep.

Just as the sun begun to rise the khidmatgar knocked on the door, entered and opened the shutter to allow light to stream in.

"It's nearly time, sahib. I shall return shortly."

I used this time to wash – not only my face and hands but other parts that had been in nocturnal action – before I began to carefully replace tunic, dhoti and turban.

Then a thought struck me. In washing myself the previous evening I had removed the dark from my face, neck, hands and lower legs. A mirror with a massive gilt frame filled most of the wall at one end of the room. I moved towards it, dreading what it might reveal. Overall, I looked as unkempt as many of the rebellious sepoys I had come across. My beard was certainly past the straggly stage and no longer as light brown in colour as it had been those first few days in India. But it needed help if it was to pass as that belonging to one of the local natives. The other parts that protruded from my sepoy 'uniform' and which were burnt by the Indian sun might, in a poor light, pass for that belonging to a sepoy. Standing there, I cut quite a comic figure. If my army career failed, then I might be forced on to the theatrical stage. I stroked my beard and gazed at my reflection.

"Apply this, sahib to darken your beard," said the Rani's man, offering me a bowl containing a measure of very dark thick liquid.

I took it from him, sniffed the contents of the bowl and asked:

"What's in it?"

"Call it a special brew of tea, but it will make your beard more like mine," he said in an amused voice.

I dabbed it on and soon my whiskers turned the colour of coal.

"Thank you," I said gratefully.

He left me but soon returned with a small tray covered in simple food. I ate several chippatis and drank some tea before turning to him saying that I was ready to leave.

The two bodyguards appeared in response to a wave of the khidmatgar's arm.

Following these two men, I passed those very opulent apartments and then it was on and into the heat of the day.

I turned to take one last look at Jhansi Palace and the ramparts of the fort and reflected that I would not want to be a part of any force sent to storm those walls.

The back of my neck still had the uncomfortable feeling that danger was not too far away. The sight of my two guides just a few paces ahead of me was doing nothing to allay those fears. Would I make it to the meeting place? I had survived a night at the Palace and not merely survived; quite the reverse. I had been very pleasurably entwined rather than fighting for my life. That night I had dismissed the possibility of being done to death while I slept, so what would be the point of it now? Unless my two companions bore a grudge or we ran into some rebels I should be safe enough.

I turned to other considerations. Would the Irregulars still be there? If they had been recalled for some reason. I would have a very long, dangerous walk back to Agra. How much had the situation changed over the last couple of days? What of the two Sikhs? How had they fared?

As we crossed a dusty track I saw a small patrol of Hodson's Horse riding into view. Without hesitation and barely a glance at me, the two – also catching sight of the khaki tunics, red turbans and sashes of the irregular cavalrymen – decided not to wait for me to exchange pleasantries with the riders. They turned and ran into a tope. No doubt the reputation of the khaki-clad horsemen had prompted the Rani's men to swiftly disappear.

"Everything all right, Sergeant-Major? Barely recognised you," said an officer, fondling his horse's ears.

"Yes, sir. Mission accomplished," I answered but muttered, "I think. Sir, do you know how the other two men got on?"

"Bit of a rough time but they are back safely. Found most of the people around Jhansi just waiting for an excuse to cause trouble. Natives got a bit upset apparently when our two fellows moved among 'em and tried to persuade them to stay on our side."

After quickly-taken refreshments I clambered into the saddle of one of their spare mounts and we set off.

The riding was heavy going as we crossed rough country with the late afternoon sun still beating down relentlessly on us. The horses protested as they sank into dry sands bordering a river, which I think was the Sind. At regular intervals the horses had to be rested, but after three days we reached Agra.

Once there, I was ushered swiftly into the Residency. Mr Carnegie stood alone behind his desk as I prepared to make my report.

"How do you assess the situation at Jhansi, Sergeant-Major?"

This after I had relayed events at the palace; well most of them, but particularly my meeting with the Rani.

"I think it's very confused, sir," I began. "There is a strong feeling of something about to happen. The Rani is a determined woman but in my opinion after speaking to her, I must reluctantly conclude that she will join the rebels before very long."

"You passed on our assurances, of course?"

"Yes, sir, but she was very bitter and feels let down. She was also under a great deal of pressure from those trying to persuade her to rebel. She also feels that we could be doing more to protect her from the ambitions of the rulers of Orcha and Datia. Sorry, sir, but that's how I think things are."

"Thank you, Mr Finch. I'll pass this on to the Governor-General and to Sir Colin Campbell and Sir Hugh Rose."

No doubt between the three of them they'll decide the best course of action, I thought; but I was now ready for my bed.

"Had word from your colonel," he said. "Wants you to stand down for a couple of days. You've had a pretty active time since arriving in India. Once again you have done your duty well and I congratulate and thank you for all your hard work. I have made some arrangements for you to have a bungalow put at your disposal for the next three days. Have a rest, Sergeant-Major. You have earned it. Oh, incidentally, the colonel suggests that you keep your beard the way it is. At least for the time being. Never know, might be able to use the disguise again."

I groaned inwardly but thought it best to say nothing on that subject. I contented myself with thanking him for the use of the bungalow.

Chapter Six

Having rested, I returned to camp dressed once again in my familiar rifle green uniform. As I passed Captain Galbraith's company I was given three rousing cheers.

During my late adventure, both battalions had been kept busily engaged fighting the enemy among the lands along the Ganges north of Fatehgarh. Four companies of the 3rd Battalion were then sent to protect the road between Cawnpore and Lucknow.

To catch up with events and return his Adams' revolver, I walked across to Mr Axelby's tent.

He stood up and shook my hand.

"Glad to see you safe and well, Jack. Wondered if you'd care to accompany me to a reception in Cawnpore? The station is slowly returning to normal. The Company's officials and their families are moving back in to carry on where the poor souls massacred by Nana Sahib left off."

"Yes, I'd like to accompany you," I said. "Is the town secure now?"

"Half the battalion is protecting the road and there's a heavy protective ring of infantry and artillery standing by. Once Lucknow's secure we'll control most of the territory fringing the Grand Trunk Road from Delhi to Allahabad. Just a few villages around the River Yamuna are still sheltering mutineers."

"Who is attending the reception?"

"A number of people, Jack, who would like to see you and thank you for your help at Khamasgarh and Jhansi. No need for you to stay long. Just drop in, say 'hello' and go. Knowing you, I expect you would prefer to keep out of the limelight but as it's for the good of the regiment the colonel thought you'd not think twice about attending,

"A carriage will take us in and fetch us back here. Quite a trek but we'll have Hodson's Horse escorting us. Billet overnight and then back. We leave in an hour."

"Dress uniform?" I ask, fingering my beard, which after a lot of effort, was now reasonably tidy.

"Yes, or the best you've got with you. Understand you have been advised to keep the beard. Makes you look older," he added grinning. "Don't think Nell would recognise you in your dhoti. Hope you're going to keep it as a souvenir."

"Looks as though I might need it again," I replied.

Just over an hour later we set off, to be bounced and thrown about for hours keeping mainly to the Grand Trunk Road which – after the constant passage of feet, human and animal as well as artillery pieces and all manner of carts and wagons – was not in the best state of repair. We arrived at our overnight quarters and after a wash and last adjustment to our uniforms we hurried through roads patrolled by men of a loyal infantry regiment. We reached Duncan's Hotel: like many of the buildings in Cawnpore it had suffered considerable damage from artillery fire. Hardly a wall was not peppered with grape- or musket-shot.

We walked in through a reception hall and on into a large dining room, the way in marked by Lancers at attention. Around 40 or 50 officers and Company men and their ladies were already assembled.

I endured about 15 minutes or so of shaking hands, receiving thanks and nodding my head as various people spoke to me, though above the buzz of conversation and background music from a small military band I could not always hear what was being said. It was easier just to give the impression that I did.

About time I melted away, I thought, and looked for some rum or beer to while away the time before returning to the billet with Mr Axelby. He had suggested that I wait around the hotel entrance at 10.30pm. I felt inside my tunic and was comforted by the solid feel of my hunter watch. This precious timepiece and its dear contents held so many memories.

As I turned to slip away, the sight of someone at the other end of the room brought me up sharply. Instead of creeping off into the anonymity of the night I decided I must speak to Major Axelby immediately.

There he was, standing drink in hand, idly chatting to a small group of Company officers and ladies.

Fortunately he turned his head in my direction and my eyes shifted from looking ahead to gesturing to an alcove on his right.

Excusing himself from what could have been a group of admirers, he joined me.

"Hello, Jack," he said. "Have to say they've all been singing your praises. Good job you're spoken for. Could have the pick of the ladies here," he added with a wink. "What's to do? You look a little agitated – not like you. Is there a problem?"

"Not sure exactly, sir but thought I'd better see what you think."

"Go on," he said expectantly.

"Well, you see that fellow over there with that group of Company men? I think he could be a Russian spy or some sort of agent. I saw him arrive. He was with a party that walked into the hotel just as we were arriving. Didn't at the time see him face on and had no reason to anyway and so I didn't give him a second glance. It's only just now when he was talking to that group at the other end of the room and happened to turn my way that I caught sight of him."

Major Axelby, having had his senses dulled by the small talk at this reception, suddenly looked very interested and alert, just as he did in the field facing an enemy.

"What makes you think he's a wrong 'un?"

"Sir, you'll know about the sortie into Sevastopol to blow up the Redan before the assault on the town and how Sergei Ivanovich led us into a trap? As we left the beach around the northern shore of the harbour I saw Ivanovich standing at a barrack door?"

"Yes, you shot him as I recall – but is there a connection?"

"I think there is. Although the light at the time was not very good I am sure that this man was standing just to Sergei's left. There wasn't time for another shot and my main target was Sergei anyway. But it's the way he was standing then and the way that that same man was standing just now. I could be mistaken, but I am sure that he was the man standing next to Ivanovich."

"We'll get one of Hodson's Intelligence people to look into it. It's no secret that the Russians are probably bribing sepoys to mutiny. They're good at upsetting folk and stealing their land. They'd certainly gain if we had to quit India. Jack, is there any chance he would know who you are?"

"Don't think so. It was dark. I was shooting into a doorway with the light from the open door behind falling across both their faces. That's if it does turn out to be him. He was after all at the other end of the room just now and I could be mistaken. He would probably know that the Rifle Brigade was in the Crimea and in action around Sevastopol Harbour. But what if any would be the connection between the Crimea and here? And the Brigade does have many riflemen."

"Well, if you say so. I'd be more than inclined to believe your judgement. Best avoid him though – just in case! Anyway I had better get back. Need a drink after all that. I'll be outside at 10.30 and we'll talk more then."

He returned to the little group I had seen him with earlier, while I left the hotel in search of the sergeants' mess of the 93rd. I had heard they were camped in the old cantonment to the south of the town, not too far from our overnight billet.

I made my way back to the hotel just before the arranged time, keeping a wary eye open for the man I suspected was a Russian spy.

On our return Mr Axelby said that he would bring my suspicions to the attention of our battalion colonel. He also thought it would be of great interest to the Governor-General. After all, if the man did turn out to be who I suspected, then he would pose a threat to our continuing attempts at quelling the mutiny.

A few days after our return to our temporary headquarters outside Agra, Major Axelby informed me that according to what our commander had told him, a special watch by Hodson's agents was going to be kept on the activities on the mysterious Russian. Then news reached us that this man seemed to have just vanished.

I thought little more of the matter as events appeared to be moving on apace, though more concerning the 2nd Battalion rather than us in the 3rd. As Nana Sahib was rumoured to be in the area, several companies of their riflemen were sent off to search neighbouring villages. Little trace was found of the rebel leaders, in spite of the men of the 2nd covering many a mile. There were a few clashes with mutineers but fortunately no casualties were suffered by our side as a result of this fighting. Sunstroke, however, still took its toll.

In the meantime we had moved a little nearer to Cawnpore. There, we assisted several other companies of our 3rd Battalion already in the vicinity charged with keeping the road to Lucknow open. That as well as escorting large quantities of stores, including ammunition, in preparation for an attack on that city.

Again there was a rumour that Nana Sahib was leading a force down the banks of the Ganges to help the rebels at Lucknow. Since my time in Jhansi I had done very little and when Major Axelby said that a company under Captain Galbraith was going to investigate the report, I volunteered to go with them.

We left our camp, which was about four miles from Cawnpore, and moved west – feinting to go in the direction of Gwalior before crossing the Grand Trunk Road. Then we turned north-east towards the village of Bela. As was our usual method of advancing anywhere in hostile territory, patrols were sent on ahead. Not too far from us was an escort of cavalry to support us if needed.

The main body of the company moved in staggered

lines across the hot, dry rock-strewn landscape. Sparse, grey-barked trees and bushes sprouted unconvincingly from the thin, parched soil that when the monsoon rains came would turn the waterless land into a claggy, cloying mass that would make walking almost impossible. Dusty roads would become deep, muddy tracks, reducing wheeled traffic to a crawl or a dead stop.

Further off, irrigated by the waters of the River Ganges, I could see a broad swathe of green grasses and rushes. That nearest to us looked bright green in colour while that on the other side of the river looked a faded lime green as it shimmered in the heat haze.

An unescorted caravan would soon pass and the men were directed to keep a special eye on them in case sepoys were using it as cover.

Camels laden with merchandise walked haughtily by, chewing – or so it seemed to me – with that disdainful look as they loudly protested their disgust at being used for such menial work. Then there were elephants, their passengers gently rocking in their square-shaped box seats or houda. Great straps passing under the beast helped keep the goods, princes or whatever else was being carried safely in place. A small figure of a mahout guided this great, grey animal with a touch of his iron-tipped goad. In the procession too were bullock carts variously filled with material or Indians. This was all checked, but the caravan was free of concealed weapons, ammunition or rebels.

Beyond the train we could see a range of hills and perched on one of its ridges was a long disused Company station.

We soon passed another once-grand palace that in its heyday had commanded a ford in the river. India seemed to be the graveyard for countless ruined and abandoned palaces, temples and forts from long-past days of power and splendour. Yet there were still many in use, ornately decorated buildings kept alive by princes loyal to, or tolerated by, the Company. Some had power, others hoped for power depending on the outcome of the mutiny.

As I contemplated the sun-baked terrain in front of me, I was drawn to sights and sounds coming from the mud-hut village that had grown up among the ruins of this once richly decorated palace. Some vestige of its old grandeur remained. Carved columns rose skyward.

As we moved nearer we were once again looking on scenes depicting men and women in the process of natural acts of procreation. How different to the walls and towers of churches across England!

Down at the river's edge women were washing clothes and nearby great cooking pots sat on large fires. Small children splashed excitedly in the water. This was a scene I had already witnessed while marching across India, but it had been repeated many times over the course of centuries and would probably continue for hundreds more. For most of these people and the poor anywhere in the world life was simple, but it could also be violent and short. It probably mattered little who ruled over them, for these people had little or no control over their own destiny.

We found no sign of Nana Sahib but there was rebel activity. They did seem unwilling to engage us, however, and fled before we could inflict any real damage.

"Probably want to keep themselves for confronting us at Lucknow," ventured one of the officers.

We headed towards Sitapur, which was built – like so many forts – alongside a river; this one around 65 miles north of Lucknow. It was a large military station that had fallen to the mutineers back in June last year. Our job now was to dissuade any rebels from marching down the road from Sitapur to Lucknow, but we saw very few sepoys in belligerent mood.

By the beginning of March a troop of Lancers caught up with us with orders for us to return to Lucknow.

While we had been pursuing the 'phantom' Nana Sahib to the north, the 2nd Battalion had also been spending many hots days attempting to catch him to the west of Lucknow.

We all now seemed to be heading back towards that city to join the rest of Sir Colin Campbell's forces, who would soon move in to capture it. As we marched we passed many wagons heavily laden with artillery shells, other ammunition and food.

Both battalions advanced after crossing a bridge of boats over the River Gumti, then moved forward in skirmish order to take up a position to the south and east of the city. After securing our own camp we provided pickets for the main force. The rebels did attempt to disrupt our lines by sending in a large contingent against us but we managed to drive them off without our suffering any loss.

On the 9th March we advanced from our camp at the Dilkusha Palace, which had been re-taken the week previously. Then we moved back over the River Gumti and from there crossed a big, sandy plain. We then turned left and waded across the shallow River Kookrail. It was then on to a position, the Chakar Kothin, in an extended line. This turned out to be a racecourse bandstand. We pushed the enemy before us. While we were doing this a party of the 1st Bengal Fusiliers and a battalion of Sikhs was having a hard time securing a battery of enemy guns. The Sikhs in particular took many casualties from a force of rebels who, though few in number, were well protected by defences they had quickly but effectively thrown up.

On the 11th, after a brief morning parade, riflemen set off in the well-tried skirmishing line clearing trees, orchards and brick and mud buildings. This was not very easy because sepoys lurked at every corner of the narrow streets of the suburbs. We reached a road overlooking an iron bridge. Between there and a stone bridge over the Gumti ferocious fighting took place. The rebels resorted to firing some buildings. A few of their own men were unable to escape and were burned alive.

After securing the area we were ordered to protect a mortar battery from enemy artillery, cavalry and their foot soldiers. That achieved, we resumed our picket duty. At one point we had to drive off a strong force of sepoys attempting to capture the iron bridge and perhaps outflank Sir Colin's main force. During this action I saw once again those tough little men from Nepal, the Goorkhas, also in dark green, as they rushed forward near the Imambara, a large mosque. What a fine body of fighting men they are!

Very soon after this, Sir Colin Campbell ordered the

main attack. Men of the 93rd challenged a very strong rebel force. They managed to chase the enemy out of a hitherto heavily defended house in the middle of the city. From our position we could see the Highlanders and the 4th Punjab Rifles as they surged forward with bayonets fixed. Many of the rebels just fled in total disorder pursued by cavalry, who caught up with and killed many of them.

A Highland officer approached me and said that he had my colonel's permission for me to join him and a small party of the 93rd to rescue a group of European women being held captive in a house in the garden of one of the palaces.

"Seems you have a knack for this sort of thing, Finch," said Lieutenant McTaggart after introducing himself. He was a tall, lean and cheerful looking Scottish officer of no more than 21 summers.

I smiled thinly and handed my rifle to a Highlander.

"I'll be back for this. Look after it," I said. "Lead the way, sir, and let's see what we can do. Is disguise required?" I was relieved when he shook his head.

While the Highlanders protected our flanks and rear, we skirted along a tall garden wall and then dropped silently into a large sunken garden, a charbagh. By now it was dark but we could still make out the shapes of some sepoys idly standing guard outside a small, but still rather grand, house.

"One of the prince's lodges where he entertained ladies, I'm told," whispered the lieutenant.

Although much of the rest of the city by now had fallen, or was about to fall to us, the guards did not appear duly concerned.

"Sir, can I suggest that we slip off to the right and see if we can gain entry to the back of the house? Your lads can then cover the guards and if we're discovered and the shooting starts they can pot the two at the top of the steps."

"Right, let's go," he said after telling a burly sergeant what we were going to do.

We crept past a low wall. The day had been quite hot and the air was moist and full of the scent of evening flowers. The prince had chosen a very good place to 'entertain'.

When we reached the back of the building I was a little dismayed to find it securely shuttered. I forced my sword between the wooden slats and managed to remove several of them without making any noise. The officer during my endeavours stood with his back to me, keeping watch, revolver at the ready. Soon, I had made a hole large enough for us to crawl through.

We found ourselves in a dimly lit kitchen, but as we moved forward the lieutenant collided with a table and sent plates and cups crashing to the floor.

A sepoy, attempting to rub from his eyes the nap he had obviously been taking, lurched in. Lieutenant McTaggart floored him with a blow from the butt of his pistol and caught his rifle before it, too, crashed like the crockery to the floor.

Warier now that we realised others could be lurking nearby, we crept through another room and came to a door with heavy brass fittings. We could just hear muffled European voices from the other side of it. Dropping to my knees, I peered through the keyhole. Around a table sat seven or eight ladies, but at the far end stood an armed sepoy, his weapon cradled in his arms.

I beckoned the officer to move back to the kitchen. We needed a plan and soon.

"Sir, can't exactly tell how many of them there are in the room," I whispered. "Maybe only the one I can see. We know there are two outside, but your sergeant and his men should be able to deal with them. I have an idea that we could try. A bit risky, though, as we don't know how many precisely we are up against."

"That's what they told me. 'Leave it to Finch', they said. 'He'll know what to do'. We'd better try it soon in case someone misses the fellow I knocked out."

"Well, sir, if you think it's worth trying, what I suggest is this. I'll ease the door open as quietly as I can. Once I'm in, I'll rush the sepoy at the opposite end of the room and hopefully take him by surprise. You follow and if there's another by the door you shoot him. That will alert the guards outside, but more importantly will inform your men that we need help. With any luck they'll take care of the two sepoys and if we can persuade the ladies to move quickly we could be away before the rest of the enemy realise what is happening."

"Can't think of anything better," he commented. "Let's get ready."

The lieutenant drew his revolver. I took my sword from its scabbard and we crept back to the door. I slowly turned the handle. It moved and so did we.

I rushed in, my sudden appearance startling the ladies but nowhere near as much as it surprised the sepoy. He had time to look at me but just stood there, perhaps not quite believing what he was seeing. He was too slow in bringing up his weapon either to shoot or to run me through with his bayonet. I lunged at him with my sword and he fell to the floor, dead.

Behind me, there being no other rebel in the room, the Scottish officer had holstered his weapon and was attempting to head off any possibility of hysterics by assuring the women that we were English ... well Scottish in Mr McTaggart's case ... and we were there to take them to safety. It was unlikely that these ladies had not already witnessed much death, destruction and indignity during their captivity. Even so, our sudden dash into the room had come as something of a shock to them.

The lieutenant directed a question at the oldest member of the group in the hope that advancing years had contributed to a calm disposition.

"Apart from this man, the one in the kitchen and the two outside, are there any more mutineers close by?"

"No," she replied. "They do change guard every few hours when they feel like it. So it's possible a new watch may not be too far away. These fiends are billeted just a few hundred yards away. We think, from the odd word here and there, that they are planning to slip away and join the rebels at Gwalior."

The officer said, with some urgency in his voice: "We need to leave. Mr Finch and I will go outside and tackle the two guards."

We moved through another doorway and found the one leading to the outside. We looked cautiously around. Both sepoys lay dead, dealt with silently by the bayonets of the Highlanders.

The officer returned to the ladies and asked them to follow him as quietly as they could manage.

We hoped that our luck would continue and that we would avoid running into any of the sepoys still scattered across parts of the city.

I reasoned that the rebels would not be expecting anyone to break out from the heart of their own camp. They would be expecting an attack to come from the other side of Lucknow and not from where we had just been.

It was quite a difficult return as the ladies were not dressed for nocturnal walking, but we reached the camp of the 93rd without running into any trouble.

They thanked Lieutenant McTaggart and thanked me for rescuing them from who knows what kind of fate.

As I prepared to return to my own camp the Scottish officer turned to me.

"You're every bit as good as I was told."

"No, sir. I think I am just lucky."

"Aye, that may be true but here's wishing that your luck never runs out. Here's my hand and my thanks too."

"Amen to that but thank you, sir," I replied and then turned to find my own battalion's lines.

I was pleased to rest for the whole of the following day.

The talk among the riflemen was that Lucknow would soon be back in its rightful hands and that the task we had come to India for was very nearly done.

One of Captain Galbraith's company asked me how soon I thought our departure would be.

"I think we'll be here a while longer," I said. "There are still too many of their leaders running around free. We need to nail them and only then will the mutiny be over."

On the other hand, events could just as easily drift on, much as they had done in the Crimea.

Lieutenant Thomson added to the conversation.

"There are still a lot of rebels in Gwalior, Jhansi and

elsewhere," he said.

I was quite deflated when I heard him mention Jhansi. Yes, I had found out a few weeks before that she seemed finally about to join the mutiny. The mere mention of the place rather saddened me. What of the Rani? What of us all? We might still face many months of fighting even a guerrilla war. They knew the country better than we did. Nana Sahib had certainly shown us, or rather he hadn't because we had yet to see him, his heels or anything of him, clean or otherwise. Other leaders were also just as capable of using similar tactics. Strike hard and run!

General Rose had been commissioned to prosecute the war west of Lucknow towards Gwalior and Jhansi. That was a task easier said than done. At least now that Lucknow was all but secure, Sir Colin Campbell was free to hunt the enemy wherever he pleased, but it seemed likely that he would want to go and re-capture the whole of Oudh province having all but taken its capital.

I later heard from Major Axelby, who had himself heard it whispered when he had been at Allahabad, that the Governor-General – Lord Canning – had insisted instead that he move against an area that was a hot-bed of mutinous discontent, the Rohilkhand.

A few days after the taking of Lucknow, I was ordered to report to the Commander-in-Chief's headquarters.

As I wandered past the heavily damaged Residency it was difficult not to notice the ill-treatment it had received from besieged and besiegers. Walls, archways, rubble and even bodies were still strewn all around.

I moved through a group of officers and saw the familiar face of Lieutenant McTaggart. In answer to my question of where I might find Sir Colin, he ushered me into a large room. This also showed signs of having been on the wrong end of heavy shelling.

There was the old Peninsular War veteran sitting comfortably behind a large dining table that was strewn with maps and papers. At his left hip was a heavy-looking sword. He wore a dark tunic and well-worn grey trousers. He was the image of what I thought a grandfather or a favourite uncle should look like.

He spoke first.

"Won't beat about the bush, laddie," he said, looking up at me as I stood rigidly to attention.

"Got a job for you. Hear you are quite an expert at this sort of thing. Recommended after your mission to Jhansi a couple of months ago."

His eyes were clear and seemed to sparkle with enthusiasm for all of his sixty and more years.

"You may have heard that General Rose is heading towards Jhansi. Might have managed already to have taken it, had he not been delayed by having to take on and defeat the Rajah of Shahgarh. He is now regrouping to begin besieging Jhansi. You will know, having been around the place, that the fort there is going to be a tough nut to crack."

"Yes, sir," I said.

"He'll likely lose a lot of brave lads in scaling those sheer walls. There's also another problem. We've been out trying to find Nana Sahib and Tatia Tope. If they should turn up with a rebel force behind them, General Rose will be the nut being cracked between them and the fort."

Once more I had that strong feeling that this was leading up to something nasty coming in my direction. In an odd sort of way I did not really mind if I was about to be sent back to Jhansi.

The Commander-in-Chief continued: "We still don't know the whereabouts of the other two leaders but we know where the Rani is. You've met her. Is there still a chance she could be persuaded to keep out of things? It might save a lot of our soldiers' lives. It's a risk for you but we'll give you what help we can."

At this point several senior officers clattered into the room, including my battalion colonel.

"If she remains loyal," he went on, "other lukewarm princes might lose heart and also keep from joining Nana Sahib and Tatia Tope. We are a little desperate to stop this dragging on."

My colonel then spoke.

"We realise, Sergeant-Major Finch, that you have already carried out more than your duty. It's a lot to ask, but as Sir Colin has said, it could save many lives and bring things to a finish. Our thinking is that the Rani must be aware that Lucknow is now in our hands. There's really nowhere for them to go. It's only a matter of time."

"Gentleman," I began, surprised at my boldness, "I am quite prepared to go. I am also curious about the Rani. I found her to be a very courageous woman. I have been hoping all along that she would not join the mutiny."

"Captivated you as well, did she?" laughed a Probyn's Horse officer. "Saw her once, by gad. Striking woman, some might say, a beauty."

"Go with these officers and work out the details. Good luck laddie," said Sir Colin.

We saluted the Commander-in-Chief and soon I was being shown into an ante-room.

My colonel opened the briefing.

"Hope you've still got your disguise to hand. Your beard's fine, Jack. Your skin's fairly dark so it's really just a touch or two here and there. The plan is you'll ride with the 2nd Punjab Cavalry. They'll take you to General Rose's camp outside the fort. That's where the Rani and her army are, so there's no point in going to the palace."

The Probyn's Horse officer suggested he ask General Rose to arrange for some sort of diversion to enable me to slip into the fort, but it would still be no easy task. From only a very brief survey during my earlier visit the walls looked quite formidable, though the sandstone may have weathered over the centuries and as a result could provide a few footholds … if only the sentries above could be kept otherwise occupied.

From the fort's central platform it seemed to consist of a series of heavily fortified rings radiating outwards. The bastions at the corners of the four walls would have artillery and muskets poking through every embrasure. Even a few well-aimed stones would be enough to send me crashing to the rocks below if I was seen.

We went our separate ways after the meeting. I was instructed to meet at the south-western corner of the Dilkusha Palace at 3am the following day.

As my disguise was improving with every wearing of it, I sought out the sergeant who would be checking the pickets and be on duty at that time of the morning. I wanted to make sure that if a suspicious-looking, limping native was hanging around they were not to use him as target practice.

❖

The cavalry turned up at the appointed time and we rode off, slowly at first but as soon as dawn broke we quickened the pace. We rode purposefully towards Cawnpore and on past the village of Orai to the besieged city of Jhansi. I would once again freely admit to not being at my best on horseback, but needs must.

We had made good progress and had not encountered any sepoys on the way, though this was probably as a result of action taken by my Probyn's Horse, the 2nd Punjab escort. Patrols had been sent on ahead to check for rebels and – had it proved necessary – to scatter them.

Hard riding over four days brought us to General Rose's camp. The Probyn's officer said they would remain nearby for a few days for my return. There was, however, disconcerting news that a strong force under Tatia Tope's command was threatening Bundela. This town so far had remained loyal. This new situation posed a threat not just for General Rose but for me. If Tope succeeded in capturing Bundela, it might encourage him to advance on Jhansi. Then with the rebels inflated with success it could prove even more difficult for me to persuade the Rani that to resist was hopeless. A rebel army would, after all, have just won a victory. She might even be persuaded by the rebel leaders to join in an attack on Rose's forces outside of Jhansi.

On arrival at the besieged city I thought it a good idea to remain hidden among the old abandoned buildings that had once been part of a military cantonment below the fort and above the town itself. While I was doing this, my escort would be reporting my arrival to the General.

I looked up at the fort and felt rather daunted by the size and strength of the walls, which rose 25 feet from the natural stone outcrop upon which the fort securely sat. Again I could only marvel at the foresight and skill the original builders of it had shown. Even allowing for the presence of modern artillery and the damage it could cause to walls, there would still be a lot of effort and boldness needed to scale them. Even once there, a hail of musket fire, grape and roundshot would be the reward for those who managed to scramble that far.

As though mocking my efforts to climb its walls, a flag fluttered defiantly from one of those ominous bastions. Directly in front of me lay over 500 feet of largely open ground with just the odd fragment of wall from a long wrecked bungalow still standing. In the confusion of a bombardment and the tension besieged and besiegers would be feeling as they in their different ways engaged in an assault, I might just be lucky enough to gain some footholds on the fort's walls.

Between the British camp and the base of the fort all vegetation had been deliberately cleared save for a few small tamarind trees that would hardly shield a small thin child, let alone a fully grown and equipped soldier or even a scruffy, disguised one. Before any major attack breaches would have to be made in the walls by artillery and engineers would need to place ladders at the rocky base of the structure towering above. All this, no doubt, as defenders poured fire and death down on them in large measure. I turned and looked back towards our camp. There was much activity. Cavalry units prepared to ride off and artillerymen and engineers were completing gunpits ready for the bombardment to begin.

General Rose sent for me and told me that he had instructed a messenger to take a last note to the Rani to make a final plea for her to come out under a flag of truce. This was before I set off. This plea was evidently not accepted, or perhaps the messenger had not managed to deliver the note. Later that day, General Rose suggested I should prepare myself just as the gloom of the evening stole the bright light of the day and at about the same time as his artillery would send the first diversionary salvoes into the fort.

"Time is running out for both of us, Finch," he said. "My scouts have just returned. It looks as though a large force of sepoys is preparing to move against us. A spy has also informed me that Tope is at the head of another large force not too far away from the Betwa River and rather too near Orcha. He may swing south and west and try and catch us in the rear. It's probably too much to hope they are heading for Gwalior rather than here. I'll give you 24 hours. If you're not back by tomorrow night by this time, 8.30, the 30th March, I'll have to assume the Rani is staying put. I may then have to head off and face Tope. Don't want to be caught between him and that monster towering above us there." He pointed up at the fort.

"Right, sir. I understand. I'll go now," I said, as I heard a salvo go screaming overhead in the direction of those formidable walls.

I set off, moving towards the last bit of cover – those old fragments of bungalow. I rested, reassured by fingering Major Axelby's revolver, and then looked up. I could just see mutineers to the right of me on the south wall scurrying along the top then dropping baskets of stones to fill holes in the walls and the two nearest bastions.

"Just like Sevastopol," I muttered, but comforted by the thought of our artillery inflicting damage that might give me some footholds.

Then I launched myself across the remaining hundred or so yards of clear ground until I reached the base of the outcrop. I looked up. Yes! There was a crack running down its length from the base of the wall above. With a little effort I could pull myself up on the broken pieces of stone and then find some gaps in the wall made by artillery fire.

It was hot work but soon I reached the top and peered cautiously over the edge. To my utter astonishment I saw a familiar figure running along the top of the wall, silhouetted against the fire from muskets and cannon discharges. It was the Rani busily engaged in organising the repair of walls almost as quickly as our guns were blowing large lumps of stone out of them.

The repairers, including other women, continued with their task ignoring shells crashing around them. After some minutes she turned and moved down a staircase serving this part of the ramparts and was soon swallowed up by the buildings opposite the entrance to the fort on the other side of the central parade ground.

"That's my way in too," I mumbled and reached down, prodding an empty discarded basket. I filled it from the disturbed stones across the walkway and moved as closely as I could along the wall. I dumped my load into a large depression in the top of the battlement and then moved down the stone steps. I limped around the compound just as another salvo screeched across the void between the British siege lines outside and the wall where seconds before I had dropped my basket of stones. I continued to limp towards the entrance through which the Rani had passed. I drew some comfort from seeing so many sepoys rushing around too busy to notice me. Hopefully I was regarded as just one more sepoy among so many. Quite a lot of them were heading towards the guns, ready to fire back at our lines. Others, armed with rifles and muskets, were getting ready to beat off the expected first wave of assault troops as they climbed ladders. A few sepoys and women continued with repairs.

My one fear was if I was challenged directly. I had picked up a few words of Hindi but was not completely confident I could convince them that I was one of them. If I was really pressed I would hang my head and try and give the impression that either guns had deafened me or had addled my wits. At the same time I would try and keep one hand on my revolver.

I soon found myself in a corridor with rooms off to the left and right. If only this had been the palace I would have had some idea of the layout of that building. But here in the fort I would have to leave it to chance of finding the Rani's apartment.

Then I reached the end of the corridor, turned a corner and rather fell into a room.

"Come in, Sergeant-Major," said a very heavily accented European voice. "We have been expecting you."

Surprised at first, I attempted to back out the way I had come in while reaching inside my tunic for the Adams. But I was pushed firmly forward by one of the sepoys I had noticed had been just in front of me as I had limped down the corridor. A hand other than mine found the revolver and dropped it onto a table by the door. I could also feel the points of two bayonets through the loose, thin Indian cotton tunic I was wearing.

❖

There, seated at a desk and casually waving a pistol in my direction was that elusive Russian. That same one I had pointed out to Major Axelby, but who soon after had disappeared. Now I knew to where! Other men, Indians, sat around all looking rather too pleased with themselves. Again, I felt a familiar cold shudder go down my back. I was trapped. This looked to be the end. I could see no way out.

"We knew you were coming," said the Russian. "The messenger sent by Rose was one of our agents. Told us a lot he had found out about you. You have been a thorn in our side. You and the rest of the British have cost us dearly. No harm in telling you now. This intelligence will die with you. We have been assisting our Indian friends to drive you from this land. In return my countrymen will take over trade and help the country in any way we can. Soon Tatia Tope will be moving up from the River Betwa and will destroy that pathetic little force out there. Then we unite with Gwalior and drive you out of Delhi, Agra and Lucknow. Before many weeks have passed your people will be desperate to escape to Calcutta and take ship. If any remain alive, that is!"

I looked at him, wondering what fate he had in store for me.

"So you work for your government to throw us out of this country?" I asked.

"No, I represent the interests of the Muscovy Orient Trading Company."

"Does the Rani agree with all that you say?" I tried not to sound either disappointed or concerned.

"It does not really matter if she does or not, though she has been badly treated by you British and is likely to give us her full support including her personal bodyguard."

No point in me trying to save myself by saying I really rather admired her and felt that she did have a strong case.

"You are a soldier of the Rifle Brigade, are you not?"

he said, smiling, which meant that I was certainly doomed.

Pride in my regiment meant I could not and would not deny it under any circumstances.

"Yes, 3rd Battalion," I agreed, attempting to stand with a little dignity and trying to ignore the two sepoys still goading me with their bayonets.

"Were you one of a party of men at Sevastopol Harbour when Sergei Ivanovich was murdered by one of your cowardly soldiers?"

"He had betrayed us. He had taken English gold but had led us into a trap. A lot of good men died because of him. So an opportunity presented itself and he was shot."

"He was no spy," countered the Russian. "He was acting under orders. Look at you, rifleman. In disguise. Are you not doing the same?"

"Perhaps, but I have been acting alone and don't betray those I serve with. He did. So he was shot as he stood in a doorway eagerly awaiting news of how many British soldiers had been killed as a result of his actions and betrayal."

"You seem very well informed about my brother's death."

So that was it. That's why they shared some of the same mannerisms. Well I was going to die anyway so I added, as defiantly as I could manage:

"I am, as you put it, 'well informed' because not only was I there on the beach but it was me who shot him."

He didn't seem too surprised by this revelation but merely said: "I thought that might be so. My agents discovered much about you. Both here and in the Crimea. Many of your own men talk with pride about your exploits."

His comment did rather lift my spirits albeit only for a few moments.

Then a figure I recognised appeared at the door. It was the Rani's khidmatgar.

"Her Highness wishes to see you, sahib Ivanovich."

"Very well," answered the Russian sahib.

At that moment, General Rose's artillery began another bombardment that shook the very building we were in. Wall hangings fell to the floor, tables and other objects on them rocked while some dropped and shattered into tiny pieces on the tiled floor below.

The Russian was a little shaken at first (although it may have been irritation at being disturbed by this sudden intervention of the Rani's servant rather than Rose's shells) but he soon recovered his composure as he turned to the two sepoys who were enjoying their prodding of me with their bayonet points.

"Take him to the dungeons," he ordered.

Just as he began to move away he reached across and struck me across the face.

"We shall decide how to deal with you shortly. Perhaps we might have the jullad strike off your head and throw it over the walls into the enemy camp below. Or," he said, laughing, "just blow you away as your people have been doing to many innocent Indians. It would have quite an effect on the British outside if we tie you across the muzzle of a cannon, wheel you out on top of one of the towers, then set it off. That's the only way bits of you are going to get back to your own lines. Or," he said, really savouring the prospect, "just tie a rope around your neck and throw you over the wall and let you dangle for the vultures."

All this was having some effect on me, but I was also feeling a general weariness working over me: fear mixed with the fatigue a man feels when he hasn't touched food or water for too long a time. But I vowed I would certainly not show it and contribute to the Russian's satisfaction. All I could really hope for was the quickest of the deaths he had described with such relish, but with me defiant to the last.

The two sepoys dragged me off using the time it took to go deep into the very bowels of the fort to hit me playfully with the butts of their rifles. We reached a large open space with eight barred doors set into the wall around the edges of this very cold room. Set into the floor in the middle of this gloomy place, which was only lit by flaming torches, were two grilles each the length and width of a man's height. On one side of each grille was a very heavy padlock. With some difficulty, accompanied by a protesting rusty hinge, one of the sepoys managed to lift the grille open. I was pushed forward, prodded by a bayonet and shoved into the void below. The metal of the grille crashed and clanged against its frame as it was dropped back into place.

I was in a dark, dank, evil-smelling hole in the ground. The key was turned once more in the lock. I was quite alone and in the dark as the torches were either extinguished or taken away.

After the beating I had received and my general weariness I struggled to ward off unconsciousness. The thought that the pit might contain certain deadly snakes was perhaps just enough to keep that lapse into oblivion at bay, at least for a while longer.

I managed to sit with my knees tucked under my chin. Then with just my right arm extended and then my left I began to explore my little world. That did not take too long. It proved to be barely as high as I had noticed it to be wide and broad. Across the cold, damp floor were scraps of clothing and in one corner, a heap of bones and a skull. A former occupant who had been forgotten and had probably just starved to death? The walls were cold, bare and damp. I returned to sitting with my knees beneath my chin in a rather vain attempt to keep warm. I tried to focus on the straits I now found myself in. This drew me to conclude that escape was impossible; death merely a matter of time. After some minutes given over to this grim prospect I thought the best thing, the only thing, I could do was to raise my spirits by spending these last hours, days or however long I had to live by thinking back to the love of my life and that first time back from the Crimea when I had met her in that room in Broughton House, a vision of beauty in blue. But this remembering of happier days was turning into self-pity. I resolved to return my thoughts to that dignified end, as befitting a rifleman. I did not want to appear a simpering coward.

Time passed but I had no way of telling just how much. There was one thing that did afford me some satisfaction: every so often, the walls of my little cell trembled as our artillery continued their work. Then it would go silent again and in the pitch black of my surroundings I would strain to hear any sound. All I could really do was to picture in my mind the scene of activity going on beyond the walls of the fort.

Judging by the feeling of hunger and thirst I was experiencing, days must have passed. My only contact with the outside continued to be the shelling. Had I been forgotten? I imagined the Rani scurrying along the walls issuing orders and frantic repairs being carried out.

Then I blinked, eyes straining to adjust as light from a flaming torch began illuminating the space above my prison. It seemed that the dreadful moment had arrived. I was about to meet the jullad, the executioner, for the first and last time.

My eyes smarted as I looked up, but instead of a rough bearded, hateful face I saw the precious countenance of that same person who weeks before I had experienced new pleasures with – the Rani's maidservant. By her side, bent over the iron grille was the khidmatgar who was desperately scraping the padlock with a key. Soon, he managed to raise the grille, reach in and pull me from my confinement.

My limbs were stiff and I could barely move and for some minutes I lay there just gasping for air. Even the large room with its cells was little better than the atmosphere in my dungeon, but at least I was no longer a prisoner in it.

"We must go, sahib. Can you walk or shall I carry you?

I could have wept there and then at this expression of much kindness as well as the concern on the girl's face. If the Rani had joined the rebels then my two rescuers were really my enemies. Yet here they were offering me such sympathy and help.

"No, I think I can manage, but thank you," I said as I stumbled like a drunk. I felt really feeble from lack of food and drink and dazzled by the light from the torch, but the last few minutes had given me an inner strength.

The khidmatgar moved off and beckoned me to follow, while the maidservant stood at my side trying to support me whenever I looked about to collapse, which was often. We moved down passages past rooms until we came to a door. A key was turned and I was pushed gently forward into what looked like a storeroom. The maid (I never did learn her name) cupped a hand under my left elbow and guided me towards a large box or trunk that was to serve me as a chair for my sojourn there. The key was placed in the lock on the inside of the door.

I looked around at my surroundings. Several small oil lamps showed there to be a few more boxes but little else. On one of the other boxes stood a jug. I hoped it contained water. A cloth covered most of a tray. I hoped it concealed food. These hopes were fulfilled. At the top of one of the walls was a narrow, shutterless opening. This would also give a little air and even some more light if I had to remain in this room for any length of time.

"Wait one day," the maid said hesitatingly in a gentle, accented voice. Then she repeated the instruction with the same slow, deliberate tone. English was certainly a foreign tongue and I got the impression that she had made a very big effort to say those words to me. She still looked anxiously at me, with beautiful dark – almost black – eyes. She touched my arm and smiled at me as I made myself as comfortable as possible on the biggest of the boxes. It was as though she was trying to console me and raise my spirits. She certainly had done that and I found her simple gesture of repeating those three words and of gently touching my arm very moving. Such a contrast to my earlier treatment at the hands of the sepoys and what Ivanovich had in store for me.

The khidmatgar, who had been standing at the door checking to see if it was clear of rebels, turned to me.

"Yes, you must stay here for at least one day. Until this time tomorrow. Few people use this part of the fort so you should be safe here. But just in case, here is your revolver."

I gripped the khidmatgar's arm and said: "you are a

very brave man. Please also thank the Rani. She is very courageous and I wish her well. You too," I said, waving my other arm at the two of them, "are both very brave. I thank you both for my life."

As he translated my words, the maidservant smiled, a smile that would remain with me for as long as I lived. Which hopefully, now I had been released from certain danger, would be for a long time thanks to the Rani and her two loyal servants.

Just as the Rani had done all those weeks before, the girl now raised her hands, palms together, head bowed, before moving to the door to keep watch.

The manservant explained what had happened after Ivanovich had sent me off to the dungeon.

"Her Highness heard of your capture and sahib Ivanovich questioning you. I was sent to insist on your release and safe conduct from the fort. He refused. Then the fire from your artillery caused some confusion. He went off to see Her Highness while you were cast into the cell. We were instructed to release you as soon as possible, but the Russian's men were watching our every move. Then sahib Ivanovich left the fort. We believe it was to meet up with Tatia Tope and to attack your General Rose. So we were at last able to find you and hide you here. Many sepoys will still want to harm you.

"So you must stay here. Her Highness told me that the attack on your lines will begin tomorrow and as our soldiers leave you should be able to slip away. Now we must go," he said and with that the two of them moved silently away.

I had been on the point of asking him the maid's name, but was too slow. Even my thanks for what they had done had seemed so inadequate when weighed against the risks they must have taken.

❖

I moved creakily to the door and locked it just as another salvo slammed into the fort. That underground dungeon had shaken with the fall of shells but now I was much nearer and I could both see and feel the walls of my temporary billet quake. This time the noise was almost deafening. It was followed by excited voices and running feet. Then the all-too-familiar sound of grapeshot hitting stone and brick and the screams of men as it hit the less resilient flesh of their bodies.

After eating some bread and cold soup, I gulped down some water then sat back waiting for the time to pass. Being able to hear the action but not do anything and having no real idea of what was happening was frustrating. If I strained my ears in between shell-fire and the crunching of walls as balls landed, I could make out the sounds of bugle calls. Something dramatic, perhaps even decisive, could be about to happen – but I was helpless.

Judging – or hoping – that around 24 hours had passed since my confinement in this far pleasanter little cell then the earth one I had occupied before, I prepared to leave. I reached for the key and very slowly turned it. The rasping, metallic sound it made was probably not as ear-splitting as I imagined. My mind was almost as tangled as my beard, my body aching as I tried deliberately to breathe slowly and steadily to settle my wits. Part of me was on edge but the rest of me was excited at the very thought of escaping from this fort. Before leaving I checked the Adams and then tucked it inside my native tunic. If I ran into trouble I intended taking a few sepoys with me. That defiance had returned and at least I would go down fighting, like a soldier.

I moved out of the storeroom and crept along a corridor, passing the now empty room where I had first been captured. I was retracing my steps but now more boldly, as it occurred to me that if I did run into any rebels they might wonder why one of their number was creeping furtively along one of the corridors. I reached the entrance to this part of the fort.

Through the main doors I could see many figures rushing to and fro. Grapeshot and shells were still pounding the walls. I was focused on the idea of escape and had no time to worry about being hit by one of those shells from my own side. I reached the doorway and looked across the chowk or compound towards the 'pol', the fortified gate that led in and out of the fort. Across to my right I could see that part of the south wall had a large V-shaped gash down most of its height.

In front of me the scene was confused. There were rebels, cavalry, infantry and some horse artillery waiting for the gate to be opened. Horses and men were anxious to go and rush our lines.

Then I saw a sight that stirred my blood. There was the Rani dressed in a red tunic and trousers with a white muslin turban. She could, to a casual observer, easily be mistaken for an ordinary sowar but for the jewels around her neck and those dangling from her wrists. *What a woman*, I thought, *a real leader of her people, albeit on the wrong side.*

Turning to her men, probably numbering around one thousand, she waved her tulwar above her head. The gates of the fort opened and off she rode, leading her followers out and down to attack General Rose below.

I began to follow, carefully picking my way across debris blown from the walls. Here and there were the corpses of men hit by grapeshot or shell splinters.

My disguise was holding up, though after days in that damp dungeon I doubt that my own mother would have recognised me. I reached the Bhanderi Gate, still open after the Rani's departure, but then stopped in my tracks.

Lying with her lifeless eyes staring into eternity was the Rani's maid. Grapeshot or shrapnel had burst open her chest. Folded across her knees was the body of the khidmatgar. From the attitude of his body it looked as though he had been trying to protect her from the artillery storm coming in over the walls. Perhaps they were father and daughter.

Here were two people who had helped save my life. I looked down at them but lingered a little longer, gazing at what had once been a beautiful, lithe young body; but where there had once been firm breasts that I had discovered and enjoyed was now just a bloody mess of muslin, flesh and exposed ribs. I am a soldier used to the cruelty of war but thought, *couldn't she have been spared*

as well as that brave man? Would the earth have stopped
spinning if they had survived and been allowed to grow
old?

❖

I left that sad scene and stumbled on through the gates and down the road towards the town below. The Rani's men had engaged our lines but looked to have been turned away with great loss. A few of the enemy were straggling back dazed and too occupied with thoughts of surviving and of the recent clash to take too much notice of me. Anxious not to be caught between them and our cavalry sent to harass them, I moved to the right and crossed the cleared ground below the fort's walls. My next step was to reach one of the ruined bungalows where I had begun my mission and to catch my breath.

Hearing the clash of hooves on the cobbles of a long deserted and demolished suburb, I looked up to see a Light Dragoon heading in my direction ready to floor me permanently with his raised sword.

"I am a rifleman, trooper!" I shouted. "Please take me to General Rose."

He looked more than a little disappointed, not to mention surprised, when the scruffy figure he was about to kill spoke to him in English, or at least that version of it heard in the meadows, towns and villages of Hampshire. He returned his sword to its scabbard and bade me follow him.

"A little surprised to see you again, Finch," said the general. "They'll soon be calling you 'lucky' Jack Finch, but glad you're back."

"Not as much pleased, relieved and surprised as I am, sir."

In a few minutes I related the events of my excursion into the fort, finishing with, "sorry it was a bit of a failure, sir."

Rose had a reputation for being a good soldier. He had listened patiently as my tale unfolded. The only time he appeared uneasy and when he frowned slightly was when I had mentioned the messenger whose mission had been to bring the Rani to the truce table but how they had been waiting for me instead.

"We've also had a few problems here. My 3,000 men faced about 10,000 rebels up there," he said. "Then we heard that Tatia Tope had crossed the Betwa. I sent the Probyn's Horse you rode in with to look 'em over. They reckon Tope's army was about 20,000 strong. Their vanguard's arrival certainly raised the spirits of the rebels at the fort. Both groups of mutineers had the nerve to light fires and shoot off muskets. Made our chaps here feel a little overawed. Had to act quickly even if it meant taking a bit of a risk. Sent a force to take on the rebels on the 1st April. Sent the cavalry against their flanks while our horse artillery pounded the rest of their column. Their fellows lost the will to continue the fight. Just as well really," he added relief showing on his face, "that they didn't seem, or couldn't be bothered, to check our strength, or rather the lack of it. Had they stood up to us I would be halfway to Calcutta by now.

"Our success reversed the boost that their arrival in the vicinity had given to Jhansi.

"Managed to break the fort's walls. Think they then thought it would be better to attack us first. The Rani was certainly at the head of their cavalry."

"Yes, sir. I saw her set off."

"Caught us a bit by surprise. We were about to assault the walls. We drove them back just before you appeared. She has by all accounts taken refuge in the palace, but even as I speak my men should be searching that building."

"One thing, sir. I'd like to know what happened to that Russian."

"Probably gone on the run with Tatia Tope. Always a chance he's dead, though."

At that moment a messenger arrived with a despatch.

General Rose read the note and turned back to me.

"It confirms she has actually escaped back to the fort," he said. "I have already left a gap in our lines. If she takes the bait, the cavalry are ready to go after her. We have lost enough men so I don't intend forcing her out by storming it."

He seemed to be speaking in quite a sympathetic tone.

I only hoped that she would come to no harm, but also realised there were – many in high places – who wanted her brought to trial. She still had that stigma of a massacre hanging over her. It was also true that all the time she remained at large she was a potential rallying point for rebels.

I was ready to return to my battalion, which was still camped in the cantonment at Lucknow. Just as I prepared to leave on a borrowed horse, a troop of Dragoons arrived. One of them told me that they had chased for around 20 miles and then dispersed a force of Jhansi rebels at a village. The Rani had escaped, having slipped out of the fort as the general had hoped. She was now believed to be heading for the camp at Kalpi of another rebel leader, Rao Sahib. He had been one of the men responsible for much of the anti-British unrest in Bundelkhand.

At least she was still alive, I thought as I climbed into the saddle of a dragoon's horse. General Rose had very decently assigned six troopers to escort me safely back to my battalion.

"You've had enough excitement Finch. The Dragoons will see you back to Lucknow," he said.

Chapter Seven

Soon after arriving back at Lucknow I was told of the entertainment I had missed. A few days before, on the 5th April, a special force – the Camel Corps – had been formed. It consisted of a company each from the Rifle Brigade's 2nd and 3rd Battalions as well as a similar number of Sikhs.

They were introduced to their mounts, each man with an Indian driver to help with their training. Some of the men regretted their volunteering after just a few minutes. But this early encounter did provide much amusement for the rest of the riflemen looking on.

"Was asked to command it. Didn't fancy it. Odd creatures, those camels," commented Major Axelby. "Anyway, Jack, you've arrived just in time. We are taking six companies off to a place called Badshadbagh. Supposed to be a large force of rebels there. May even run into Tatia Tope and a great admirer of yours, a fellow called Ivanovich.

"Oh, the other big news is that the men are going to be issued with a different uniform. More suited to the heat in these parts."

There was quite a delay to our leaving camp as another spy's report put the rebel force about 50 miles in a different direction.

By the beginning of the third week of April we set off in what we hoped would be the pursuit of Tope and other leaders. Would he just melt away again as he had already done on a number of occasions? A covering party of the 7th Hussars followed us a short distance in our rear.

The latest report put Tope and around 30 sepoys in a village just west of Adnul. Lieutenant Buxton and a company of riflemen were detached from our main force to investigate. I went with them as they rushed the seven or eight miles to the area in question. Very soon after arriving, a fire-fight developed. Luckily for us they were only armed with swords and old smoothbore muskets. We quickly overwhelmed them. But Tope had again managed to allude us; that's if he had been there in the first place. He seemed to be very adept at winning the support of the local population who, according to our spies, would hide him from our cavalry and foot patrols. Then, or so it was alleged, he would re-appear somewhere else and with another force attack loyal towns and villages or harass supply lines; all this while avoiding being drawn into a pitched battle. It only served to enhance his reputation and give his followers hope.

We had accounted for around twenty sepoys in yet another of these skirmishes, but only received minor wounds ourselves, musket balls managing to tear our uniforms rather than flesh and bone.

"He's not among the dead," I shouted to an officer of the 7th as he caught up with us at the head of a squadron of his men as we checked the bodies of the dead enemy. Not one of them answered Tope's description of being around 5 feet 7 inches tall, with a low forehead and eyes that gave his whole demeanour a cunning, shifty look.

"He may have reached the cover of those trees over there," said Lieutenant Buxton. "We've checked all the huts in the village. We could advance on an extended line and flush out whatever's in the tope and drive them towards your men on the other side."

Off the cavalry rode at the gallop, while our officer ordered us forward with swords fixed towards the trees.

After 20 minutes the first of the 10 or 12 sepoys broke cover. Like so many other mutineers I had come across, they were no longer wearing their original Company regimental uniform but had reverted to native dress. Others followed and a few threw their weapons away to make their running all the easier.

"Hold your fire!" yelled Mr Buxton as Hussars with swords raised galloped in among them. Soon, 12 rebels lay dead. Once again we checked the corpses whose heads, necks and backs showed deep cuts from the slashing of heavy steel weapons.

But still no Tope.

"Not too surprised really, Jack," said Major Axelby when we caught up with the other five companies. He had walked across to our temporary camp to speak to me while Lieutenant Buxton had gone to report events to the colonel. "I reckon now that Tope, the Rani and the rest of 'em are on the run, they've decided to adopt guerrilla tactics. Must know they can't beat us in a straight fight. But they can make it deuced uncomfortable for us by hitting and then fading away. Good tactics. Hard to deal with. Hit hard, hit often and vanish. Good for their morale, bad for ours. They could be marching up and down this country for years and so could we, eating their dust."

As April drifted on, reports came back to our lines of British success in Bundelkhand. A force under General Whitlock had defeated the Nawab of Banda, but again thousands of rebels had escaped including the Nawab. We received conflicting messages: some said he had reached Kalpi just to the south west of Cawnpore, others that he had taken refuge in temples at Khajuran. If this last one did prove to be true, we were likely to be involved in many miles of forced marches under the hottest of summer suns. Even if we did not engage the enemy sunstroke would lay many good men low.

Major Axelby and Captain Galbraith were instructed to lead a force of three companies, Horse Artillery and a troop of the 7th Hussars in a dash to those temples, while three companies of the 2nd Battalion with cavalry escort were to look for them around Kalpi. Much later we heard that Kalpi

Fort had been abandoned with no sign of any rebels. More rumours placed them around Gwalior. Both battalions were ordered to provide additional companies as well as companies of Punjabi Rifles to protect the roads from the north into Lucknow and from the west into Cawnpore. This they did after defeating a force of mutineers who had suddenly appeared just to the west of Sitapur.

I was with a force under Major Axelby attempting the very arduous forced march towards Banda. We rushed over rough track, crossed a rock-strewn dusty plain, streams and steaming jungle as we covered the 80-odd miles. Our day started just before three o'clock and we marched for about eight hours before taking food and a little water. Then we continued after the hottest part of the day had passed. By seven in the evening we stopped and rested, having marched for many miles during the two or so days it took us.

We crossed the Yamuna River, reached Banda and made contact with General Whitlock's rearguard. The rest of his force was busy moving north-west to Gwalior.

After one day's complete rest we marched south-west to Khajuran, which until a few years before had been overgrown and returned to the jungle.

Our orders were to advance on a broad front, two riflemen deep, while the cavalry covered our flanks. If necessary artillery would pour in fire from behind.

Thirty men under my command were instructed to probe ahead of our line to see if the rebels had dug themselves in. It seemed very quiet, the peace of this holy place broken only by the protesting squawking of birds as we moved forward and disturbed them. Rifle and sword at the ready and senses alert for any rebel activity ahead, we advanced. As we progressed, slowly, cautiously and very deliberately, I felt that same knotting in my stomach. That feeling usually went once if and when we encountered the enemy. By then I would be too busy to be worried.

We passed large statues, figures and temples. During one of our morning parades we had been instructed to treat all holy places, be they mosque or temple, with respect. After all, enough Indian sensitivities had been upset before – and since – the outbreak of mutiny without our adding to them. Holy the area may be, but a greater contrast between this site and our own holy places, churches and cathedrals would be harder to find. Not even the great cathedral at Winchester could compare.

Our small probing party continued to advance. We passed huge stone temples with figures of every kind depicting ordinary tasks, or dancing, or showing the creation and celebration of life in the most basic of ways all around us, sculptured in stone. Huge arches reached above our heads, steps led to inner temples and 20 or more spires looked to pierce the sky.

"Keep alert," I hissed across our skirmish line as eyes looked all around, taking in the antics of the figures instead of concentrating on the possible presence of rather more deadly flesh-and-blood figures.

"You can come back and see what you've been missing after we have swept through here," I added.

This score or more of temples, perhaps as old as Winchester Cathedral, could certainly be used to show a young man all that he needed to know about women and were certainly different to the statues in our own religious buildings, where points of interest seemed only to sprout fig leaves to maintain dignity and spare ladies' blushes.

We reached the end of the buildings and moved into the fringes of jungle. Nothing looked to be disturbed; no birds rising quickly or squawking excitedly other than the ones we had displaced. There were no signs of any rebel activity.

I told rifleman Cooper to return to Major Axelby and say the enemy was not at home.

My musing over what we had just seen – human figures fondling exquisitely shaped breasts, and hands between round smooth thighs – was interrupted by a comment from Hall. There he stood, rifle in the crook of his left arm but with his head almost parallel to the ground as he tried to take in the various attitudes of a group of sculptured lovers.

"Just goes to show!" he exclaimed.

"What?" I asked.

"Why there are so many of 'em in the country if that's what they get up to," he said in what I thought sounded like an envious tone.

"He'll be trying this out on some poor tart," said Wilkinson, pointing to a stone figure with an engorged and impressively large manhood at the ready about to impale a submissive female who wore a smile but little else as she anticipated his entry to her love temple.

Other than the delights of these shrines, our mission had not been a success.

It was decided to rest up for two days and then begin the march back to Lucknow, but not quite with the same urgency that had brought us here.

During the first few days of May we headed north. Our aim was to be at Kalpi by around the 18th of the month.

The plan as Major Axelby described it was to approach the fort there and see if the situation had changed. Had the rebels, after all, decided to garrison it? It was a formidable defensive position built on a huge rock plateau. If the enemy had moved back in, it would be a difficult proposition and we would need reinforcements. Our Horse Artillery had only brought light field pieces for speed of movement, not for laying siege to forts. Shells would just bounce off its walls. Any rebels in the fort would also have the advantage of being able to see an army and its preparations for mounting an attack long before the assault came.

As we moved along the banks of the Damaan towards the River Betwa we were forced to slow down, as we were leaving our supply train too far behind. The delay in catching us up was caused by the reluctance of three elephants and a score of camels to enter the water. It seemed that the crossing place chosen by a scouting party of Hussars for the stubborn animals to bring food and other supplies up to the opposite bank was too sandy. They seemed frightened to go down the bank in case they slipped. Eventually the mahouts managed to persuade those great animals forward. The camels haughtily followed. As the elephants scrambled up the other bank, ears flapping and tails swishing, I looked at the one nearest to me. A small eye, very small considering the animal's bulk, was looking – I thought rather wilfully – at me. What damage it could do to a man if it took against him! I stepped back just in case. Then with a trumpeting and rolling of its head it flicked some of the sand from the dry bank it had just laboured up, across its back. Some of it reached me. I may have imagined it, but the beast looked pleased that I had been sprayed with sand.

After pitching tents, we ate, had tea and rum and turned in ready for the 3am start the following morning.

We were well on the way to where the Rivers Damaan and Betwa met when we heard the sound of gunfire.

Riflemen were ordered forward as a troop of Hussars rode on ahead to our left and right. We had not gone far when one of our skirmishers returned and reported to Major Axelby.

It turned out that General Rose had been in hot pursuit of a large force of rebels who had then divided. They could have been the same group who had left Kalpi and evaded the men of the 2nd Battalion who had found the fort there deserted.

One column of Rose's command was attacked as it picked its way among the rough ground in the ravines on the northern bank of the River Yamuna.

Mutineers had been forced back by artillery and cavalry towards Kalpi. The rest of them were in retreat a little further south to Kunch, not too far from where we were camped.

Among the rebels in retreat was the Rani, who it was believed was heading for Gwalior. There, according to rumours, she would meet up with Tatia Tope and the Newab of Banda.

Rose's latest intelligence was that rebels had not only retreated to Gwalior but on the way had attacked the pro-British Maharajah Scindia and demanded they be given supplies. The Rani was involved in some of this fighting.

On the 3rd June a triumphant rebel army had entered Gwalior. According to one of Rose's spies, Rao Sahib had presented himself with all the trappings of a state royal ceremony. The feeling among our officers was that he might consider himself heir to the Mughal Emperors but no one else east of Gwalior did and he was promised a very short reign.

General Rose wanted to move on and confront the rebels at Gwalior, but fearing this could be just a ploy to draw British forces away from Lucknow and Cawnpore, Major Axelby was ordered to return at our best possible speed. Kalpi would just be bypassed, at least for the time being.

So off we marched again under a merciless sun. The terrain was rough as we passed through the dry gorges of the Yamuna. We reached Cawnpore and the only respite from the heat was when we passed through the sweetly scented shade of ripening mango trees. Even sweeter was the fruit itself.

As we moved on, one of our cavalry scouts reported that there were rebels ahead preparing an ambush. A company was sent off in skirmishing order while the rest of us marched in columns, with Hussars deployed left and right ready to assist the advanced party.

The skirmishers halted just this side of rising ground. Over the brow of the hill were the enemy. The skirmishers' task was to send in covering fire as our main column advanced, the plan being to kill or keep the heads of the enemy artillerymen down as they waited in the ruins of a mud hut village below.

Our two columns – four abreast and with swords fixed – charged down on the enemy as covering fire from our skirmishers whistled past us and into the enemy ranks of gunners and infantry below.

As we rushed down, we fired. There wasn't time or opportunity to reload. They occupied good positions but our sharpshooters had managed to keep enemy heads down. Soon we were among them and involved in fierce hand-to-hand fighting. At one point it looked as though we could push no further forward, but troopers of our 7th Hussars smashed into their flanks and soon flashing steel from them and our swords finally persuaded the enemy to turn and run. They left about 150 of their number dead and dying. We suffered a few casualties but most of ours were less the result of enemy weapons than the result of heatstroke.

Our officers ushered the men to ground that gave partial shade. As much damage had been done to the village, we set up camp among some trees. Then we waited for our baggage train to catch up, though many men barely had the strength to eat their rations, so exhausted were they from the marching, the fighting and the heat.

A day was given over for a much-deserved rest and then it was back to our tents at Lucknow.

It was at about this time that I heard of the death of the Rani.

General Rose had made up his mind to smash the Gwalior and Jhansi rebels in one decisive battle. He had pursued them from Kalpi to a position about four miles east of Gwalior. There, spies had seen the Rani passionately rallying sepoys, riding among them and shouting words of encouragement as her soldiers waited for Rose to attack.

A squadron of cavalry managed to get close to them through a pass that cut across the Gwalior plain in the direction of that huge Gwalior Fort. There it stood perched menacingly above any force willing or desperate enough to take it on. It also served as a main rallying point for all rebels. Had their cause been a united one under a supreme leader based at this fort, things could have proved even harder for Europeans.

I was in the colonel's tent on some task or other when I heard officers discussing the General's campaign.

"If they had been of one mind under one leader, who knows what might have happened. Even the south might have joined the mutiny. As it is the whole thing seems to be crumbling. Ah, Finch. Something that might be of interest to you."

He went on to say how grape and shellfire had begun to fall on the rebels in their entrenched positions.

According to his information, the Rani – with a small

troop of sowar behind her – had moved in to attack an artillery battery. Instead she had ploughed into a troop of Hussars. One trooper drew his sword and as she rode towards him she received a slashing blow from his weapon. She fell into the road, bleeding. The Rani drew a pistol and shot at the trooper. She missed and he shot her dead. At first, she was not recognised for who she really was. After all, she was dressed like a sowar. When the dead and wounded were being checked, her body with its numerous jewels was eventually recognised.

"A lot of people are sorry that she's dead. She made quite an impression on you as well, didn't she, Sergeant-Major?"

"Yes, sir. Shame she was on the wrong side, but she was certainly a brave woman. Might, though, be best for all concerned that it ended this way," I said, but with regret in my voice.

I did feel sorry that she had been killed and as the officer had said, others felt the same. Yet others would be sorry that her being slain in battle meant she had escaped a trial and probable hanging. *At least*, I thought, *she was spared that indignity*. For me she was a beautiful woman. Clever and stubborn but potentially a dangerous opponent. She had also saved my life and part of me still felt, from what I had learned, that she had legitimate grievances. In the end with all the pressures on her she had really little choice other than siding with the rebels; her own people after all.

Her death could certainly have consequences. Either it would reduce the willingness of the mutineers to fight on or, she would become a martyr, a folk heroine. We had Robin Hood, the French had Joan of Arc. Perhaps India now had Rani Lakshmi Bai. If this proved to be the case it might just encourage a more determined and prolonged resistance.

Once again other leaders had managed to escape, including Tatia Tope and Rao Sahib. Somehow they had slipped away from their pursuers and crossed the Chambal River with hundreds of men and a number of guns. This challenged many minds. For how had so many rebels apparently just spirited themselves away? Sepoys, sowars even heavy artillery pieces had escaped ready to fight another day.

❖

While we recovered in camp at Lucknow it began to rain, and rain and rain. On the 8th July, a thunderstorm flooded us out. We were forced to build more substantial quarters, having scavenged material from bungalows wrecked during the sieges. All around, much of the country was flooded and as a result there was little movement.

When we did leave camp several weeks later, accompanied by Hussars and Madras Fusiliers, we marched or slopped our way to Sultanpur on the banks of the River Gumti where for many yards on either side of where the banks should have been, water was ankle deep and thick with foul-smelling, clinging mud. Riflemen were soon drenched to the skin. Wading into dirty, brown river water just had to be done to get anywhere. I decided not to give too much thought to what – apart from the mud – was causing the smell and the discolouration.

We were supposed to be in pursuit of a rebel force, yet as I confided to Major Axelby I thought most of them would be to the west of Gwalior to where Tope had, according to spies, made yet another of his escapes.

"Probably so, Jack," said the major, "but we seem to have a lot of spies and agents telling us different stories. Only good thing about this expedition is that if we are struggling in these conditions then so are they, if they are not too far away. Can't engage an enemy when you are up to your knees in mud."

Then we received definite news from one of our scouts; an hussar had sighted a large force of rebels. He put their strength at around 7,000, mostly infantry, some cavalry and six artillery pieces. The scout had added that the terrain was easier-going to the west. He had only to struggle over the last few miles on his way to us, but around the Grand Trunk Road most of the rains had drained away. Those rebels he had seen were, he thought, moving from around Gwalior and Jhansi and appeared to be heading for Fatehpur. That town was rather closer to

Cawnpore. He also said that they might alternatively swing south and threaten Allahabad as he had also seen a troop of sowar riding across the Yamuna, just below Fatehpur. They could, he had suggested, be a scouting party to see how strong we were at Allahabad.

Major Axelby commented that Allahabad could certainly be the target as there was a strong religious link there, where three rivers met: the Yamuna, Ganges and a mythical one.

"Allahabad would require a very determined force to attack and capture it though," he said. "Maybe they're heading for Jaunpur and then hoping to outflank us by moving up to Lucknow. Or perhaps we think they're being too clever. They may have no single strategy and just go spontaneously, as the mood takes them. If that's the case, we can't always outguess them."

It was decided that we would go and meet a possible attack aimed at Cawnpore and Lucknow. We were then ordered to protect the provincial capital. One company, led by a Lieutenant Green with cavalry escort, was sent off to locate the enemy. Later reports recounted that they had indeed found a large rebel army in a village surrounded by thick jungle. During a scuffle Lieutenant Green received many sabre cuts and other wounds as they moved in on the rebels. Although much fatigued and suffering from a great loss of blood that later would lead to the amputation of his left arm, the lieutenant remained cheerful and became a great inspiration to us all.

Then something not quite so inspirational; once again we heard that Tatia Tope had escaped after fighting a losing battle at Rajgarh.

He was proving a real irritant and again we were sent off to try and find him. This time we headed towards a fort at Ametai overlooking the River Chaibona. After our artillery had pounded the walls for a few hours and created a breach, in went 100 or so fusiliers and riflemen. A few of the defenders put up a fight, but most scattered. The artillery completed the destruction of the walls while we made ready to return to camp.

❖

Two days later, acting on information from spies, two companies from each rifle battalion set off to attack the Rajah of Omethi. He was reported to be south west of Sultanpur. We moved to within several miles of the fort there before being told to stand down as the Rajah had fled, although his men remained in the fort. An hour passed and a messenger from the enemy appeared in our camp to discuss a truce. They would wait at our convenience outside of the fort gates at 12 noon the next day.

A small party – including me – under a white flag was selected to act as a guard to Major Pendlebury of the 2nd Battalion to discuss terms.

As we approached the fort it did appear uneasily quiet. A troop of horse was called up to support us while Sergeant Wilkins from Captain Galbraith's company was ordered to the gate. He stood in front of it, listening, then put his boot to it. One of the gates swung open.

He entered cautiously. He disappeared from view but very soon after appeared on the battlement.

"They've gone," he called down to the rest of us waiting in anticipation below.

We had been tricked.

Our cavalry escort was sent off in pursuit, more out of spite for the deception than with any hope of capturing them.

While they galloped away we returned to our camp not feeling too pleased about wasting our time and energy, not to mention the tingle of nerves felt before engaging the enemy. They could, after all, have been waiting to fire at us. As it was, it was good that we did not have to suffer any casualties.

This kind of activity, of us going to check information provided by spies and returning without having made any contact with any large force of rebels, continued through the months that followed and well into November.

On the 22nd of that month we left Lucknow. This task involving half of the battalion was to intercept another leader, Beni Madhas, with a reportedly large force.

Nothing. This was now becoming an all-too-monotonous routine. Our company returned to camp but days later we were out again, heading for Omrhia Fort. To reach it we had moved through thick jungle rather than across roads that often gave rebels notice of our approach. This time we found them and drove them back. We pursued them and caught up with their force as they sheltered behind the mud walls of a small fort.

Our covering artillery spent the hour or so before nightfall pounding the walls. To save our lives it was decided to leave our attack until an hour after sunrise the next day.

The shells whined over; the walls were smashed but there was no return fire.

Advancing, expecting some sort of response, a small forlorn hope of a half-company of riflemen rushed at a wide breach in one of the walls. Very soon after scrambling across fragments of mud walls, the men reappeared on what remained of the battlements waving their rifles. The mutineers had gone!

During the first week of December we helped demolish the walls completely. On the 6th we were on the march again, this time towards Fatehpur.

I had made several copies of my little map and always took one with me on our marches to plot our progress. Details would be added to my best copy on my return to camp.

A casual observer who studied my best copy and was not used to the wiles of the army might conclude that we spent quite a lot of our time wandering around in circles. Blame not our commanders but the cunning of the guerrilla tactics of our enemy. They were on home ground, often with the connivance of local villages and the wide distribution of spies and agents who could and did give early warning of our approach. They also gave our side false information, which had sent us in the wrong direction on too many occasions.

Just short of Fatehpur our skirmishers came across some rebels. After a brief exchange of fire, the mutineers disappeared.

We camped in a field of tall crops and the next

morning set off for Jaunpur. Here, a little to the north, was another of those well-appointed forts overlooking the River Gumti. It, too, was deserted as were several more we encountered.

Did this mean that the mutiny would soon be over?

On the 10th and 11th we marched along the Faizabad Road covering 30 miles and reached the town on the 14th, camping just below its empty fort.

The next day we crossed the River Gogla using a bridge of boats. Then we forded another river, only to be slowed down once more by the elephants and the baggage train refusing to cross that bridge over the river. A shallow part of the Gogla was found and the beasts finally splashed to the other side.

Then it was on to Gonda and a camp among ruined bungalows.

This was all proving rather fruitless. Our quarry was supposed to be Tatia Tope. He was still involved in a guerrilla war and we were still proving to be just his shadow.

News arrived reporting him to be hiding in the Alwar Hills to the north of Jaipur. If this turned out to be accurate, I for one begrudgingly admired the rapidity of his movements. Others admired the tactics too, but it was felt that apart from being an itch in our flanks he was gaining nothing. A pitched battle would settle it once and for all, but his wandering and our having to follow was tiring not just his people but us as well. Some felt that keeping us wondering and wandering must surely mean that at some point his luck must run out.

Three companies of the 3rd Battalion and three of Fusiliers were sent off with a strong force of Hussars and Lancers to investigate.

We made camp at Zalapur on the Banda River. Just as I was completing my day's rations and was drinking tea with a generous amount of rum, Major Axelby and a captain (an intelligence officer attached to Hodson's Horse) reached my tent.

Here we go again, I thought as I got to my feet and saluted.

"Got a little job for you, Finch," said Captain McVitie.

"Want you to go with a couple of chaps, all suitably disguised of course, and check the lie of the land in Jaipur."

I had kept my beard, now a little bushier than ever before and had folded my sepoy tunic, dhoti and pyjamas in my bedroll just in case.

"If Tatia Tope is around the Alwar Hills and decides to defend the area just to the north of the city, we could have a real fight on our hands," he continued. "The place is full of temples and palaces. Jaipur is protected by narrow valleys, rocky ground and dense, tree-covered hills. Easy for them to hold. Difficult for us to move cavalry around and for infantry, even the Rifle Brigade, it would prove a hard, costly slog. It should be pro-British but Tope is nothing if not persuasive and loyalties may have changed."

"So what should I do?" I asked.

"Have a look around the city. See what the local people think. Your two companions will have the language. Then make your way above the city, north. Two fortresses protect the northern approaches to the city. Those two forts, the Nahar Garh and Jaigarh, overlook Jaipur and there is a third formidable building, the Amber Fort. This was once the capital of the old kings who ruled these parts. This one has massive walls and like some of the other forts you may have come across in India is built around a hilltop.

"We hope Tope is not planning to stay. That's if he's there in the first place. If he is, then it may all depend on the mood of the people. If he can convince them to join him we shall face a big problem. I'll be leading a troop of horse there so anything you do find out can then be brought back to the main force and Major Axelby."

With that the captain left while Major Axelby lingered for a while and I was pleased to discuss the mission with him.

"Your two companions will join you in about an hour's time," he said. "Here's my Adams and I've borrowed this tulwar from one of the Irregulars. Look, we're nearly done in India. For Heaven's sake take care, Jack. See you in five or six days time."

Two men joined me, both Pathans from the north. It was as well that the mutiny had attracted all kinds of men and not just sepoys from the Bengal Presidency. The three of us could now more easily pass for rebels or 'ordinary' Indians; the sort that made identifying who was loyal and who was not very difficult during our progress across central India. If Jaipur was still loyal we would merge in with the townsfolk. If it was changing sides then we should still be able to move around. I hoped!

We set off slowly before dawn with barely enough light to see our way as we attempted the shortest route to Jaipur.

The city was a fine sight with a huge palace at its centre. This was a seven-storey building displaying all kinds of richly decorated scenes surrounded by large, ornamental gardens. My two companions left me at the entrance of the southern end of the palace and made their way towards a very ornate gatehouse. I could just see enough of it to be impressed by the two life-sized elephants carved in marble. I then turned away and walked down narrow streets where craftsmen busied themselves at a wide range of tasks. All kinds of sounds, smells – some good, many not so – and colours assaulted my senses. It seemed here at least the city was carrying out its business as usual.

Two hours later I was joined by the two Pathans, neither of whom had seen or heard of any rebel activity.

We moved to a quiet, deserted courtyard and consumed chipattis and cold tea.

The plan now was to move towards the forts. This would be no easy task: they were well-placed and it took the rest of the day before we reached the first of them, the Nahar Garh. It looked grim in the fading light; this 'Tiger Fort' would be a very difficult prospect if it had to be stormed.

We turned in for the night in a grove of small trees, taking it in turns to keep watch.

After a cold breakfast, a repeat of our cold supper, we moved towards the fort and were both surprised and relieved when we found it was unoccupied.

The next day the Jaigarh, or 'Victory Fort', was reached. It was a fine piece of construction with a very tall tower that commanded an incredible view in every direction. This fort did turn out to be garrisoned but not by rebel sepoys.

One of the Pathans said that he would go to the fort and see if there was news of Tatia Tope. He returned several hours later. His enquiries concerning the progress or otherwise of rebels had not been well received: he had even been accused of being a mutineer himself. They remained loyal, not wishing to bring down British wrath on their heads. Their prince, the Maharajah of Jaipur, had kept out of the rebellion when it first started and wished to remain loyal to the inevitable winners (in his view at least), the British. Amber Fort was also held by people loyal to the Maharajah.

But still no news of Tatia Tope's whereabouts.

I decided that one of the Pathans must return and locate our column while we moved into the Alwar Hills to see if we could find any trace of our elusive quarry.

In due time we were wandering around the hills, but still could find no trace of Tope. Villagers eking out a scant living in those same hills had said, in exchange for a handful of rupees, that a large force of sepoys with guns had passed through on their way to Sikar.

We hurried away and found Major Axelby's contingent. It had been joined by a larger force that had set off with all haste from Agra in mid-January to intercept Tope, who was strongly rumoured to be back-tracking towards Lucknow to the east and not to the west of the Alwar Hills. We did manage to defeat Tope in a skirmish, but once again he slipped away.

Slowly we plodded back towards Lucknow where I was glad to exchange my disguise for my Rifle Brigade issue. From there, the rest of our battalion had been busy responding to rumours of a rebel presence around Gonda but without making any contact with them.

Then on the 12th February we were ordered to Agra; this time the whole battalion. I had been there before, as had some of the other men. On previous occasions their camp had been some distance from the city, while I had gone directly to the Residency without taking in the sights.

This time we were all to be quartered in Agra itself. This was good, for the city was well placed on the Grand Trunk Road and the banks of the River Yamuna.

For the enthusiast of buildings, Agra is a treasure trove. Even the forts and mausoleums – let alone the many palaces and gardens – display wealth and ostentation, a grandeur that would put many an English estate and even St Paul's Cathedral in London in the shade.

Agra Fort, built of red sandstone, offered a formidable sight. Shaped like a crescent on the west bank of the river, it once boasted a moat as well.

We entered through a magnificent gate, the Amor Singh, at the southern end of the fort. Our colonel must have been interested in our taking in the sights before we reached our barracks that were situated to the north of the fort.

We marched into an area called the Jahangiri Mahal. This contained halls, courtyards and even dungeons. It had once been the harem. The men as we passed by, on being told that it was no longer in such use, sounded very disappointed that there were no exotic and mysterious eastern ladies home at the time.

Agra seemed to be full of other palaces and temples; some ruined, others in use.

We passed the Khas Mahal, a marble hall with curved roofs; then passed the grape garden, the Anguri Bagh with its lilyponds. Then on to the royal baths, the Mussaman Burj – a two-storeyed, eight sided tower.

Then there were the mosques: the Gem Mosque, the Mina Mosque, Jewel, Nagina and the Pearl, the Moti Mosque or Musjid.

Everywhere, sandstone reflected the sun's rays and caused us to blink in the bright light of the day. It was also proving quite overwhelming for the men. Many of them had started life in slums. During our time in India we had passed lots of these kinds of buildings but this was the first time we had seen so many of them up close and without the likely presence of rebels.

Another grand building came into view. It had a tall,

slender minaret set at each of the palace's four corners. A row of neatly tended bushes framed a long, rectangular shaped pool, the 'Lotus Pool', where water reflected the arches, galleries and central dome of that magnificent tomb. There was a mixture of colours, marbles, slates and sandstone used as decoration.

For Lieutenant Mackeson this must have seemed like a holiday from our more grimmer activities. Almost every time we stopped, out would come pencil and sketchbook.

"Who built it and what's it for, sir?" asked rifleman Bennett of Captain Galbraith's company, breaking the silence as we gazed in some awe at the structure in front of us.

The officer answered.

"The building's called the Taj Mahal. It was built by a mughal emperor in memory of his dead wife."

"If my old woman thinks she's getting one of them, she's got another think coming," commented Leighton. "She can make do with a nice wooden box like the rest of us. Though," he added, grinning broadly, "I'll supply the nails and even hammer them in."

This was a welcome moment of humour that changed the rather intense mood as we marvelled at that symbol to a man's lost love. I wondered what George Williams would have said about the splendour in front of us. For another few moments I thought back to my own love and pictured her sitting in the room where I had first seen her.

Our billets did not quite match up to the sights we had seen, but were certainly an improvement on the tents and other quarters we had been experiencing recently.

There were many distractions for the men in the narrow streets of the old part of the city, from those brothels in the oldest and most neglected quarters to the nautch about to be held regularly in one of the palaces, and the bazaars where goods of every kind were on sale ... and then there was that strange attraction of the snake-charmers.

There were still duties and patrols to carry out: the mutiny was not yet over.

I had been curious about some of the amusements and distractions on offer and had wandered down to one of the squares where a barefoot, turban-headed native played his pipe or pungi made from some sort of gourd. From a wicker basket a cobra uncoiled itself. Very deftly he grasped the vile serpent under its head that had puffed up, I supposed to menace its prey. It had certainly done that to me when I had confronted one. Then he returned it to its basket and replaced the lid. Small coins, annas, were thrown into a cup. Then he prepared for his next performance.

I accepted the risks of soldiering and had come across various snakes in India and loathed them. At home snake-catchers did, as far as I was concerned, a great service by destroying our own brand of vipers. But snake-charming here seemed a very odd, certainly dangerous and unpredictable occupation.

On another occasion I had been invited to attend a Mehfil as a sign of goodwill towards a local prince. This was an evening of traditional singing, dancing and the recital of poetry. It was certainly an experience.

Then there was the nautch: a diversion very popular among soldiers. Well, among all men. I had heard about the delights of this particularly revealing dance. Now, it seemed, a minor prince who was so grateful for being saved from the excesses of the mutineers was inviting all soldiers to his newly acquired palace, the Jahangiri Mahal. There he put on a show employing a professional troupe of dancing girls. It was strongly rumoured that he had used bribery not only to acquire this palace but to obtain a special licence to offer such a diversion.

When we had first marched through the palace grounds the men had been disappointed to learn that the harem no longer existed. There was much anticipation when it was discovered that although there were no beautiful veiled wives of a former ruler, there was instead a collection of very nubile young dancers.

They certainly put on a show in every sense. There was no crevice, crease, curve, mound, hair or any other part of a dancer's body that was not turning, bouncing, gyrating or showing itself.

There had been attempts by the civilian authorities to do away completely with this particular kind of dancing; it had almost disappeared thanks to the actions of various churchmen. Efforts during the early part of the mutiny to ban the dance completely were made because it was believed that sepoys would infiltrate such gatherings and listen out for talk from loose tongues. Somehow the army had been persuaded that no such spying would take place, as only loyal soldiers would be invited, though military commanders had not gone out of their way to encourage the activities of a dance troupe either.

These dancers wore the flimsiest of transparent material; a choli, a kind of bodice. As their wrists and hands made symbolic gestures called 'mudra', and their arms and legs moved perfectly in time with each other, they created the most alluring, enticing, provocative and arousing spectacle. Even the sap in the limpest of men would rise. Each dancer wore little cymbals on the tips of her fingers, and little bells or chungro on her wrists and ankles. In her navel was a ruby and the hair on her head was worn up and criss-crossed with strings of tiny pearls. A golden token separated her eyebrows and each girl wore a nose-ring. As they danced, they sang. According to what I had been told, each dance they performed acted out a story, usually linked to the activities of one goddess or another. I could only hazard a guess at the story being told. To accompany their singing, a small band provided music. There were six musicians, although at times it did sound as though they were fighting each other rather than harmonising. One of the servants had described the instruments to me. There was the one-stringed ektar, the two-stringed dotar; the tanpura with four strings, and a two-headed drum, the damaru; another drum, the chendra, was played with sticks. The whole ear-splitting sound was completed by the sundari, a double-reeded wind instrument.

It all sounded very shrill to our European ears, so unlike the sound of our own music; either the kind countryfolk in my own village might play or the sort of orchestra that had played during those special evenings at Durford Hall. Not that music and singing was what the audience in the palace had come for. I also noticed that some of the men seemed more than a little drunk. After a while I realised that the refreshment freely supplied by the palace's servants was bhang – a spicy, milky drink flavoured with a local opiate.

Looking at the dancers it seemed as though the sculptures on the many temples had come to life ... though we were spared the male contribution.

There was little doubt that the performance inspired at least some of our young riflemen to seek appropriate fulfilment in the narrow streets and gali, the alleyways of the old city.

Indians, while appreciating beauty be it in stone or flesh and blood, did not seem as moved by such attractions as Europeans. Just a different way of life, I supposed.

Four or five days had passed before three companies were sent out again in pursuit of rebels. There were still reports of their movement between the Alwar Hills and Sikar to the west of our station and to the east between Bareilly and Shahjahanpur.

Again it was said to be Tatia Tope who was causing our officers to act. We did manage to kill or disperse small bands of rebels, but nothing was seen of him. Towards the end of March, we heard that he might well be hiding in dense jungle. This was not so good, as an army could hide in such cover; a man could be standing three feet away and not be seen. We made some effort to sweep through, but all we achieved was to disturb a variety of animals from small monkeys to a very angry tiger. This large cat did not enjoy being chased from its hiding place, attacked one of our men and was shot dead.

Then stations across India received a very welcome message. Tope had been captured; betrayed by one of his own men. Two weeks after this, on the 18th April, he was hanged for his involvement in the mutiny, especially for the murder of many innocent women and children.

We continued to go out on small patrols. This was fast becoming a meaningless task. There were, it was true, still a few dissidents in the villages as we moved through them, but the real fight had gone out of them. By June of '59 it was generally agreed that the mutiny was over. This was good news particularly as the temperature was rising and was well over the 100 degree mark. Too hot, too humid, that even officers were suggesting that to be involved in such fruitless marches in pursuit of phantom rebel leaders was a waste of time.

Chapter Eight

It was official.

At a special parade on Friday the 8th July, peace was officially declared.

As we had discovered during our regular patrols, there were still rumblings of discontent among the local inhabitants and we were instructed to remain vigilant. Any unrest was coming not so much from mutineers but more from the badmash, those criminals who had been released or had escaped from prison while the authorities were busily distracted elsewhere. Thieving, rape and murder had marked their contribution to the revolt. Mayhem had been their driving force rather than a desire to kick the Company out of India. Now they had nothing to lose: there was no amnesty for them and they knew that if they were caught they faced the hangman's rope.

It was also time to begin the long process of repairing the damage done. Some aspects of this were easier to do than others. Residencies, bungalows and all manner of other buildings, as well as roads and bridges, could be restored. These were easy to see. Less obvious was the loss of face. Many Indians had been caught up in the mutiny; many just wanted to return to what had been their life before the outbreak had begun. Now they feared being singled out by loyal troops. Scores of villages had been destroyed to redress real or imagined wrongs on both sides. How to reward loyal sepoys? How to prevent a repeat of the mess that had started things off in the first place?

We assisted in a few bridge repairs but our real job was now done. It was time to think about going.

Major Robert Axelby had been offered a colonelcy in the regiment, but decided it was time to resign his commission and return home. He had served his country and the Rifle Brigade with honour: it was time he went home to claim his birthright – that estate in Wiltshire. His father had been infirm for years and to all intents and purposes the estate had been his son's for some time. His father had then died during Robert's service in India.

Major Axelby spoke at length to me before leaving, first to Calcutta and then by steamer to England.

"It's time to go, Jack," he said. "I'll miss it, though leafy Wiltshire won't quite compare with the Cape, Crimea or Agra, but I've not seen my wife and children for ages. Don't think it will be easy though. I'll miss the companionship, what we've achieved. I'll even miss you, Jack. It's been a privilege to serve with you.

"What about you? You've done more than enough and should go home to Nell."

"Yes, I'm thinking of going too," I said. "Feels strange. Now we've helped bring peace back, for some reason I feel down. I've waited for two years for this moment but …" and I felt my voice trailing off, "… can't really explain it. But sir, I feel very fortunate in having served in the Brigade alongside you. Thank you for all you have done for me."

"Well, now we have both congratulated and thanked each other, let's go home," he said. "Don't look for an excuse to hang around. Go! Just think back to that day in Winchester when you had to say goodbye to her. I think everything has been a bit of a shock for you. Even the weeks at sea didn't really allow time to give all that you had learned a chance to be put in some sort of order. Then we went straight into action and you've been involved in some lively and dangerous missions. You also met Edward and William and that can't have been easy. You're a good man – an honest man, Jack Fortune. Don't feel any guilt. What you are getting when you get home is well deserved.

And I don't know if this is a secret or not but I hear that the colonel's putting you up for an award for your selfless duty. Live for those who lost their lives. Don't they call it karma in these parts? You have done well and good fortune is now yours."

"It still gives me a strange feeling," I said. "So much has happened – you're quite right about that, sir."

"Yes, Jack, but you – we – have survived. That's the main thing," he said. Then he added, "I'll call at Broughton House and say you are leaving India and hope to be home before Christmas."

He stood up, shook hands and left, turning back to say: "don't let yourself down, Jack. Think of Nell. I'll catch up with you some time next year. Counting on an invitation to the nuptials!"

There had been times – of course there had been times – when lying on my charpoy at night all that I could think of was Nell and getting back to her. In many ways the thought of her, the feeling of her body next to mine and of a tender kiss, had sustained me. Now all that was in reach. Well, after a few months of sea travel at least. My only real reservation was would she still feel the same about me? A nagging worry was that after my return from the Crimea I had only temporarily filled the gap left by James' death. My time away, out of sight, had perhaps healed that need.

I had done as her mother and Lady Fortune had suggested: I had attended to army business for over the year they had mentioned. That extra time had not been of my choosing but that of circumstance; of the persistence of the rebels in avoiding capture.

I sat in my quarters thinking back over the events of the last two years or so.

From that first meeting … Winchester … then India. My spying missions … meeting the Rani of Jhansi … the Rani's maidservant … and the many clashes with rebels.

"Yes," I concluded aloud, "lucky Jack. Just as General Rose had said."

I was indeed a lucky man.

I took Nell's locket from where I had kept it safely hidden and gazed lovingly at it while I opened the hunter and touched the lock of her hair. Yes, I loved and wanted her. That night of loveless passion back in Jhansi Palace, the friezes of procreation, the dancing girls, all were fuelling my need and desire for Nell Broughton. Letters from her, though always late to catch up with battalion movements, had still confirmed her feelings for me.

Around the time one of her letters had caught up with me, I had just returned from that first time in Jhansi.

Included in the many pages of beautifully written news of life around Broughton House was a photograph of Nell sitting bolt upright in a chair, but beautiful – in that room where I had first seen her on that hot summer's day three years ago. There she was in the little picture, hands clasped in her lap but her face illuminated – or so it seemed to me – by the gentlest and sweetest of smiles.

As well as assurances of love and of counting the days until we were together again, she always wrote of walks she had taken to that spot by the pond, to my parents' cottage. This last piece of news created a special scene in my head and brought a smile to my lips. I pictured my mother bobbing and curtseying as the woman I loved dropped in. Of my father rising painfully as his bones complained at his attempts at straightening up in the presence of a lady. Years of hard work, of knowing his place, would have made this a natural response. Then he would have fixed her with his tired gaze, the almost perpetual frown on his face softening as she charmed them both. As I looked at the hair and then the photograph and re-read this and other letters, I knew that Robert Axelby was right. I must go home!

I had also written, but only in general terms, about India and certainly nothing about the dangers or of a more intimate encounter. All this after confirming my love and saying that I too was counting the days. Now those days had run out.

The very next morning following Major Axelby's

departure I went to see the commanding officer of the 3rd Battalion.

"Been wondering when this day would come. Major Axelby said to expect it very soon. Know why you are here."

"Yes, sir. It is time to move on. I have been a rifleman for almost ten years. In here," I said, pointing to my head then to my heart, "a rifleman I shall always be."

"You'll be a great loss to us all, Sergeant-Major. Many thought you'd do very well as an officer. But I hear you have great expectations. Your record in the Brigade has been excellent. I am particularly aware of the efforts you have made not just in leading men against the sepoys, but when you have risked your life in the very heart of the enemy's camp. The Governor-General is also aware of your contribution and has informed their Lordships in London and particularly Her Majesty. It was an honour to add my endorsement, but every officer in the battalion had also done the same. You have our respect and thanks.

"There will of course be a medal, but that hardly seems adequate. But go, Sergeant-Major and good luck to you."

"Thank you, sir," I managed to say, "but I have had much help. Major Axelby, Captain Galbraith, James Fortune and so many others. As I said earlier, I am at heart a rifleman. Anything I may have achieved is because of that."

I saluted. The colonel leaned across the simple table that served him as a desk and firmly shook my hand.

Very mixed emotions accompanied me as I left his office. I felt overwhelmed by his words and for a moment doubt that I was doing the right thing briefly flickered in my head. I still had to go, but it was very satisfying to know that I had the respect of so many in the battalion – I did feel that I had earned it!

All that was left to do was to say a few farewells and pack my belongings. The 'goodbyes' could be a difficult task even for a soldier like me. I had certainly changed since the days as a new recruit of doing drill and learning to be a rifleman. I had seen so much: too much death and misery.

The rest of the battalion would be staying on in India

and then off one day to who knows where? Perhaps another war. I had been lucky and as I said my goodbyes I wished them luck too.

Then it was off to make arrangements for my passage from India.

There was a constant stream of traffic from the station of Agra to Lucknow and Cawnpore, then by bullock cart, even elephant, train and river steamer to take ship from Calcutta. I hoped to avoid a third rounding of the Cape by sailing from Calcutta to the Red Sea. From there it would be overland to Alexandria and on across the Mediterranean. This route would greatly reduce the total journey time by four or more weeks, compared to that of going round the Cape of Good Hope.

The first part of my return home passed very well; no storms, no heavy seas to contend with. This was due in part to the fact that the voyage between Calcutta and Suez was a regular service provided by the Peninsular and Oriental Steam Navigation Company, the only delays being necessary ones for the taking on board of coal at Trincomalee in Ceylon and Aden at the mouth of the Red Sea.

I fell into conversation with a Company administrator about events in India during the recent mutiny and the prospect of returning home.

This was only his second long leave in about twenty years. The last time home he had married, taken his new wife to his station at Calcutta and now with their three surviving children they were on their way to England. He had obviously received broad details of events at Delhi, Cawnpore and Lucknow, but showed much interest when I told him about some of our exploits pursuing rebels over hundreds of miles of rivers, jungle, in and out of villages, forts and palaces including Jhansi. Some details of that adventure I left out!

I supposed that, as he was a Company man, he would be a little reluctant to agree that some of the troubles had been the fault of the Honourable East India Company. He was of the opinion, however, that talk around Government House in Calcutta more than hinted that the British Government might soon have to take over the Company's role in India as the only way of ensuring that such disruption might be avoided in the future.

We reached Suez and prepared to travel to Alexandria for a Peninsular steamship to take us home.

Ahead we could see a shimmering desert haze as we drew nearer to the dock. My travelling companion warned me of the 'trek', as we called a long slog overland in South Africa, to come before we reached our Mediterranean point of departure. He confided that we would be hauled by horse-drawn wagons across the desert. The last time he had done that journey he had been amused to see a string of 'ships of the desert' as he called them – camels – carrying coal to fill the bunkers of a growing number of steamships. These beasts, he said, moved with that odd gait that I had seen on so many occasions while criss-crossing India.

Then he said it would be by Arab dhow for a time on the River Nile and at long last the Mahmoudieh Canal from Cairo to Alexandria.

Happily, though, things had changed. The Peninsular and Oriental, the 'P and O', had taken over the service between the two. This new route cut out much journey time and swept away the uncomfortable wagon ride and the need to change between such conveyances and water-borne transport.

As we waited to board a train for Alexandria we noticed a small group of what we soon discovered were French bankers and engineers passing nearby. They were waving their arms and pointing at a large map and generally looking very excited, which the French always seem able to do for very little apparent reason. It seemed, when we enquired, that plans were continuing with the idea of building a canal to allow ships to sail from the

Mediterranean to the Red Sea and on into the Indian Ocean. I was very surprised at this, but we were assured that the first shovel-loads had already been dug. For Britain there were obvious advantages to such an endeavour: a quicker route to protect our interests in India. I wished the project well. Anything to avoid having to sail around the Cape and those extra weeks, depending on the weather, that it could take. Not that I planned to ever do that voyage again.

In due time we boarded the train and after a few days in Alexandria boarded the 'P and O' vessel for the final leg of the journey. After a gentle cruise across the Mediterranean and a coaling stop at Gibraltar, I finally reached Portsmouth on Thursday the 17th November.

I took a train to Southampton and then onto Winchester, arriving at seven o'clock that same evening. During the time I had been travelling on the trains, I had thought to go on directly to Broughton House and Nell. After some deep pondering I decided duty still required that I attended to Rifle Brigade matters first. It would also have been difficult, I concluded, to have gone to the House and then force myself to return to Winchester.

I walked up the familiar drive from the barrack station to the commanding officer's office. He wasn't there but I was advised to report the following morning. In the meantime I thought to look in various barracks and the sergeants' mess. My reception there was most agreeable, for I found men of my old battalion – the 1st – in residence and news of the Brigade's involvement in India seemed well known and much admired and respected.

Since I had last seen them they had gone from Glasgow to Newcastle then on to Portsmouth, where they occupied various barracks within that town including Clarence Barracks where we had been billeted before sailing to the Crimea. Now they waited for new orders to Aldershot and then it was off to Dublin. There was some envy that for them the last few years had seen nothing like the activities of the 2nd and the 3rd Battalions in India.

Stories were shared and much beer and rum drunk as old comradeships were renewed before I fell into my temporary billet at one o'clock in the morning.

Chapter Nine

Old habits do die hard: I was up with the lark and after breakfast walked quickly to the commanding officer's office, the same one Major Axelby had used before our departure for Aldershot in 1857.

After the usual formalities and pleasantries were observed, I was outside the barracks – still in my best uniform – by 9.30am. I carried two large valises, the one crammed with a variety of souvenirs such as carved elephants, tigers and even a king cobra and the like for my family and a few sketches of forts, palaces and that magnificent building, the Taj Mahal at Agra, given to me by Lieutenant Mackeson. Also carefully wrapped was a fine necklace for Nell, presented to me by a very courageous woman. The other valise contained some of my possessions including the locket. And somewhere between Winchester and the steamship was a trunk with the rest of my worldly goods as well as more souvenirs.

I wandered down the steep hill of the high street through the archway that had formed part of the old city's defences and on towards the stables near the Cathedral, where on previous occasions I had hired carriages. Today, it was a phaeton with driver and a pair of greys.

Off we set for Broughton House by way of the river. The driver pulled up and I jumped down and walked the few steps to my favourite spot, that same section I had tried to describe to Edward all those months ago. I took a special gold coin – a makul – from my pocket. It was of quite high value but that did not matter. I had been keeping it for this very moment.

In some ways I was surprising myself by this and by the way I had been feeling recently. Previously, perhaps before India, I would have agreed with many of my acquaintances who would not generally have regarded me as possessing an especially sentimental disposition. It was a possibility, though, that involvement in three bloody wars, what seemed the sadly inevitable waste of good men, the massacre of innocents, the torture and maiming of so many and my own occasional discomfort, that years in the army had contributed to a shift in my character. This and my survival and change in fortune were certainly giving me reason to view the world differently. Above all there was Nell!

There was, regrettably, always likely to be death, destruction, disorder and despair but there was also beauty and selflessness. Perhaps my being spared was part of some great Universal Plan. I did not know, but as I thought back over all that had happened I suddenly felt overwhelmed and humble.

I fell to my knees, hands clasped tightly together, so much so that I could feel the edges of the coin cutting into my palm. Then for a few seconds I just sobbed uncontrollably.

A voice broke into the tide of emotion that was engulfing me.

"You all right, sir?" called the driver.

After a little hesitation during which time I attempted to calm myself, I answered:

"Yes," I said in a fairly tremulous voice. "Thank you."

My composure almost fully restored I stood up, considering myself lucky to be able to take in the living scene spread out before me and beyond: the mainly leafless trees of the first frosts of the late autumn in the air and the clear, sparkling water framed by grassy banks and those oh-so-familiar bushes just above. Topping this whole natural view, like one of those huge temple domes in India, were fluffy grey-white clouds and the steel blue of the sky. A prospect, however, that was so unlike those broad sweeps of mountain ranges of the sub-continent with its parched plains and almost impenetrable jungles. What a contrast to the green, gently rolling hills of Hampshire.

I threw my coin into the water. Then, raising my right arm in solemn salute, I called:

"For you Edward, William and George," but with a distinct lump in my throat.

Vowing to keep my promise to seek out George Williams' family in Whitechapel, I turned and walked back to the phaeton.

"On to Broughton House, driver, if you please," I said and settled back, if a little apprehensively, to enjoy the view that I had not gazed on for over two years. But the best view, the one I longed for, was still to come. This was not the river, fields and trees but another natural beauty. I ached with anticipation, tempered with a little nervousness for my first sight of Nell.

In due course the driver pulled up at those formidable, familiar gates. I stepped down.

"Go on to Lower Durford and call at the Finch cottage," I said. "Tell them that I shall see them very soon and then you return to Winchester. My thanks to you."

By this time a familiar figure stood hastily buttoning his waistcoat with one hand while undoing with some difficulty the lock of the small gate with the other.

The phaeton driver busied himself turning the carriage ready to journey on to my parents' dwelling.

"Is that you, sir?" the gatekeeper asked, squinting at me with narrowed eyelids. "Do you want the main gate opened up for you to drive down to the house, sir?"

"No, thank you. I'll walk."

I just wanted to hear that oddly comforting, crunching sound as I set off down the drive just as I had done three years before. I was amused to see a small figure set off running in the direction of the house, having appeared from the lodge's backdoor. I soon dismissed this from my mind as I had a more pressing meeting in prospect.

Soon I reached the point of the drive where it becomes a circle, allowing carriages to drop their passengers and to turn back down the drive. The gardens and fountains thus encompassed looked just as neat, though lacking the colour of spring and summer. The late autumn day was still bright but much cooler than on my first visit. I certainly did not need to splash around to cool myself off, as I had wanted to do at that time. I was, however, feeling very warm – but that was fired by the expectancy of embraces to come rather than the late season's sun.

I looked up. There she was, standing alone at the top of the staircase. Lifting her skirts slightly, she moved quickly but carefully down the stairs while I moved from rifleman's pace to a run.

We met at the bottom step. She flung her arms around my neck. I hugged her, lifting her off her feet. Our lips met passionately. Two years of longing melting away. Moments of near ecstasy passed before we could speak.

"Oh, my darling, Jack," she gasped. "You've returned to me safe and sound, after all we have read about the dangers you have faced. Robert Axelby called about a month ago to say you were well and hoped to be back before Christmas. He spoke so well of you. How brave you have been in Hindustan! He is so proud of you. We are all so proud of you. Now here you are in my arms. I can hardly believe it. Do tell me that you are here for good."

"I am never going to leave you, darling Nell. You will marry me, won't you, Nell?"

"Yes, my darling – and mother will be as good as her word and will love and support us. You made a big impression on her and she has been at pains to tell her friends what a man you are. My man!" she added, with pride in her voice.

We turned and slowly walked up the steps arm in arm. Servants and family members looked on from the windows of Broughton House. At every step, we paused to kiss. I looked at those beautiful eyes as warmth and love swept over me.

The sights, sounds, smells and dangers of India would never be totally forgotten, but in the sweet embrace of Nell, they would fade.